Books by Sharon Kimbra Walsh

Single Titles

For the Love of a Marine
A Fallen Hero
Ambush of Love

Ambush of Love

ISBN # 978-1-78686-045-3

©Copyright Sharon Kimbra Walsh 2016

Cover Art by Posh Gosh ©Copyright 2016

Interior text design by Claire Siemaszkiewicz

Totally Bound Publishing

Published in 2016 by Totally Bound Publishing, Newland House, The Point, Weaver Road, Lincoln, LN6 3QN, United Kingdom.

AMBUSH OF LOVE

SHARON KIMBRA WALSH

Dedication

To my Mum and Sister,
To Peter — always there and always patient — with love,
To my editor, Jamie Rose, who has the patience of a saint.
Thank you all.

Dear Heart, Why him?
Unknown

Chapter One

Scorched by the searing sun, the arid, parched land stretched for miles in all directions. Stunted, prickly thorn bushes grew randomly, eking out a poor existence, roots buried deep beneath the seared landscape, always searching for moisture to sustain life.

Twisted, spindly trees struggled pathetically to survive on the desolate, barren land, their branches stripped of all but the hardiest of leaves, even those curled into withering parodies of life in an attempt to hide away from the unsympathetic sunlight.

Approximately two kilometers away, a range of tall mountains—cleaved asunder here and there with deep crevices and fissures—thrust serrated summits toward a sky of washed-out blue, a vast canopy of emptiness without even the smallest wisp of moisture-bearing cloud in evidence. Jagged profiles wreathed in thin vaporous mists, the craggy, rocky slopes were dotted with threadlike waterfalls, the tumbling flows sparkling in the rays from the glaring, bloated sun.

Clouds of dust—disturbed by the patrol—hung motionless in the still, hot air, minute particles finding their way through the fine seals of ballistic combat helmets into eyes and mouths and inside combats, chafing skin raw. The air was hot and dry, so much so that if inhaled, it leached all moisture from lips and dried up saliva in mouths.

The tall British army officer paced slowly along what passed for a road—a poorly maintained track full of deep ruts and potholes—his stride relaxed and methodical, primarily to remain focused on his immediate surroundings but also to conserve energy.

He rolled his shoulders in an attempt to ease the weight of his bergen. Alert for signs of snipers or IEDs, his keen eyes ceaselessly roamed about him, his modified SA80A2 with its underslung grenade launcher, SUSAT sight and common weapon sight tracking every movement.

Lieutenant Nick Ryan—aka LT or 'the Old Man', thirty-two years of age—was starting to feel tired and thirsty and his feet hurt. His body armor with its hard and soft plates—configured for additional freedom of movement for this specific mission—felt as though it had doubled in weight, his pack as if it were filled with blocks of cement. His combat shirt and T-shirt beneath were soaked with sweat.

He was eager—as he assumed the rest of his men were also—to get back to the FOB, the forward operating base—for a mission debrief, shower and scran. At this stage of the mission, however, his sole aim was to get Bravo Recon Section through the next few clicks alive and in one piece.

He had learned the hard way—through the lack of focus and mistakes of others—that one moment's loss of concentration could result in someone being hurt or even killed. He therefore pushed all thoughts of future comforts to the back of his mind—a feat that had served him well on past deployments—and stepped away from his position as point man at the head of the patrol.

Turning to face the line of men behind him, he noticed that while they still maintained a ragged formation, their movements were lethargic, with shoulders slumped and feet stumbling through the fine dust and sand. He realized that concentration within the section was beginning to flag, a dangerous situation while in an area teeming with insurgents.

Nick spoke a password into the confines of his helmet then waited for the voice-activated heads up display, commonly called HUD, to stream onto the inside of his tinted full-face shield. After a few moments, flickering green lines resolved themselves into schematics of route maps and combat situation reports—sitreps. He uttered a different password and the displays faded, leaving behind their PSMs data that kept him updated on their physiological status.

He studied the readouts sent directly to his personal central information system from the medical sensors embedded in the thin lining of his men's desert, multi-terrain pattern combats. They showed the body temperatures, heart rates, hydration and stress levels of each man and he found himself smiling with amusement.

Individual biomedical data showed the slightly decreased heart rates and respiration of almost every member of Bravo Recon. It appeared that his men were dozing on their feet, as if they were out for an afternoon stroll through a park at home instead of the inhospitable climes of Afghanistan.

Deactivating the PSMs, he said, "Comms," which triggered his communications system and abruptly said, "Come on, lads. We're nearly home."

His voice entered the communications network of his section and from there into each individual helmet. His mouth twitched again with amusement as at least half of his men's heads jerked up, their bodies reacting with surprise at the sound of his voice.

"Two more clicks and you can have your downtime. I know this heat is a bastard. You're all knackered and probably thirsty, and you want to get back to the FOB. This is the time when your concentration will start to lapse and you could lose focus. If that happens, make no mistake, you *will* get your backsides kicked.

"The *mujis* will have us bagged and tagged by now and they *will* have intel on us. More than that, they'll know how long we've been out and that we're tired and, therefore, easy pickings. You all need to stay alert and concentrate. You are at your most vulnerable right now because being nearly back at base. You're only focusing on that. Right now, you need to keep eyes on at all times, no matter how crap you're all feeling."

Nick's intention had been to shake Bravo Recon from

their heat-induced torpors, and he hoped that his words had made the appropriate impact. He was satisfied when they straightened their shoulders, their pace quickened and they lifted their SA80A2s a little higher, the action offered as a warning to any hostiles who might be observing them.

He returned to his position as point man and checked the immediate area. He quickly noticed two Afghan men approximately twenty meters away, puttering slowly along on dilapidated motorcycles. They were keeping pace with the section, watching them through binoculars, their worn-out engines sounding muted in the still air.

Nick felt a rush of adrenaline and quickly lifted his right arm out to the side in the direction of the intruders, raising two fingers. Activating his comms, he ordered, "Eyes right, Bravo Recon. Two dickers at twenty meters."

Lifting his weapon, he aimed it at the Afghan men. Keeping his keen gaze on them, he heard the faint noise of rifles lifted in unison behind him and he raised a hand in an attempt to stop someone's twitchy finger from increasing its pressure on a trigger, thereby causing an international incident.

"Wait out," he ordered calmly.

The Afghanistan men, seeming to realize that *they* were now objects of interest, immediately turned their motorcycles about and sped off in the opposite direction.

Nick waited until the bikes were some distance away before lowering his hand, then his weapon. He kept his gaze on the fleeing men, quickly disappearing into a shimmering heat-haze. His irritation quickly turned to anger as he supposed that intel regarding the number of men in his patrol, amount of firepower and weapon type was probably speeding on its way to enemy commanders.

Christ! Bloody bastards!

"Move out." Raising his right hand, he gestured for the patrol to move on, aware that Bravo Recon Section might be on the receiving end of an ambush before reaching the safety of the FOB.

Corporal Jessie McAllister—twenty-four years of age—stared out of the open side door of the army Wildcat Mk2 helicopter. Squinting in the harsh sunlight, she watched the shadow of the helo flashing across the parched landscape beneath her, and her spirits sank even further.

"Holy shit!" she exclaimed and heaved a sigh of resignation. She glanced quickly over her shoulder at the other passenger to see if he had heard her unladylike expletive, but as he had done the whole trip, the soldier continued to ignore her. Feeling as though she wanted to poke her tongue out at him for his ignorance, Jessie turned back to her study of the countryside spread out below her.

Oh, perfect. My home for the next six months is going to be Hell.

Prior to her deployment, her parents—military veterans in their own right—had given her the benefit of their vast knowledge, regaling her with stories of their experiences in country—both good and bad. The reality, however, was beyond her wildest nightmares. Her impression of her new country—Kunar Province in the Korengal Valley—had deteriorated from resigned acceptance to dislike, the further she had traveled from Base Kandahar.

From what she had seen so far, most of Afghanistan consisted of flat beige and ochre-crackled earth, dotted with sparse, stunted vegetation, broken up by irrigation ditches and dry, shallow *wabis*. No sign of human habitation broke the empty monotony of the landscape, not even the mud and brick ruins of a compound or a single animal racing to find shelter from the inhospitable conditions. The tableland looked unforgiving, lonely and abandoned.

Since her arrival in country, Jessie's spirits had plummeted lower at every turn, until at last she'd begun to question the choices she had made over the last year, decisions that she now considered she'd made rather hastily.

Since she'd been a child, she had wanted to emulate her

parents and join the military. She'd opted for the Marine Corps and had passed the tough basic and advanced medical training with ease. Now that she was here on her first overseas deployment, she found herself wondering why she had done it, constantly asking herself what she was doing on the front line instead of being safe at home with a nice boring nine-to-five job.

If the men and women with whom she had spoken had told the truth, it was a man's world in Afghanistan, and women should have no part in it. *That* particular label hadn't changed much over the years. With major advances in technology and a reorganization of the US armed forces, there still appeared to be a lingering ingrained sexist attitude toward females.

The US military seemed to want to keep women in desk jobs, forgotten about and therefore *out of trouble*. Much to Jessie's annoyance, it appeared that according to general opinion, women — even though they had proven themselves on par with men — appeared to remain the weaker and lesser-skilled sex.

In relation to herself, a tiny cog in the US military machinery — for some unknown and completely illogical reason — had decided to attach her to a British unit. Why the British army needed a US Marine medic she had no idea, but she had accepted the new orders with resignation and equanimity.

Her one failing grace was that she had inherited her father's stubbornness, a fact that her mother had brought up to her on a number of occasions. So with this ammunition, she was determined to prove to herself, to the men of her new world and to the authorities, that they were wrong and that she — as a woman and an individual — was perfectly capable of fulfilling a combat role.

As much as she tried to convince herself that acceptance meant nothing to her, Jessie was conscious of a feeling of apprehension about her imminent arrival at her new home. The thought of what her new section's reaction to her presence might be had created a nauseating coil of dread in the pit of her stomach. Her nerves swooped and jived like a plague of agitated butterflies, and she felt a little sick.

She swiped at a droplet of sweat that had trickled from beneath her helmet. Even with the side door of the Wildcat pushed all the way open and a wind howling around the interior, the heat was almost unbearable. Dressed in full battle gear, including the new lightweight PPE, her personal protective equipment, it felt as though the blood in her veins was quickly heating to the boiling point.

Her helmet with its nine-millimeter thick mandible guard and HUD face shield—configured and contoured to fit the shape of her skull and the sides of her face—constricted her head like a metal band. Perspiration coated her face and long strands of wayward hair, having managed to creep from beneath the confines of the helmet, flew about her face, clinging to her cheeks and finding their way into her eyes and mouth.

Clamping her weapon between her knees to prevent it from slipping from her grasp and flying out into the slipstream, Jessie straightened in her seat and ran gloved hands across her face, attempting to free the latticework of hair entwined across her nose and mouth.

God, I'm so tired.

With twenty hours of flying time behind her, combined with the energy-sapping heat, she felt as though she could sleep for a week. Top of her list, however, when she finally arrived at the FOB, was a shower. She had her doubts, though, that she would find anything remotely like one in existence. She had a sinking feeling that she would inevitably end up having to share ablutions with the men, causing embarrassment for all concerned.

Jessie sighed and gave up trying to tuck her wayward hair out of the way. She turned to stare out of the door once more, this time raising her head to look up at the blue sky. She wondered if some form of epiphany would suddenly strike her from the heavens, enlightening her as to how she could extricate herself from the mess in which she now found herself.

Instead, the harsh brightness almost blinded her. Her eyes watered and burned, and she cursed herself for not having the foresight to lower her face shield, just another mistake to add to her steadily lengthening list.

Lowering her gaze, she waited for her vision to clear, then stared in the direction they were flying. Through a rippling heat-haze, she made out the first signs of civilization in the shape of a compound located at the base of the mountains. The helicopter had started to make a smooth descent in that direction and, as they neared it, Jessie supposed this was to be her final destination.

She could make out a large, rectangular base surrounded by what she estimated to be four-meter high walls of cream-colored Hesco. Anyone trying to scale the heights would find it impossible to negotiate the smooth angle and achieve a breach. High steel gates broke up the straight lines of one wall, while security towers covered in khaki-colored camouflage netting loomed strategically at the base's four corners.

It had to be FOB Elabat in all its glory.

She heard the rotor blades slow as the Wildcat continued its rapid descent. With the sound of the moaning wind diminishing inside the fuselage, she slung the strap of her SA80A2 over her shoulder, reached for her pack and kit bag to prepare for the landing and braced her booted feet against the ridged metal floor.

They appeared to be approaching an area of flat land some meters distant from the FOB, and Jessie edged closer to the open door, dragging her bulky kit with her. Poking her head out, she kept an eye on their approach for any sign of insurgents popping their heads up to observe the actions of the helicopter.

She was also able to gauge the security of her new home. Bordering the FOB on three sides were piles of spindly, half-dead thorn bushes, felled trees and large piles of boulders with a ten-meter deep no-man's land between the vegetative barrier and the base walls. It meant that an insurgent attempting to get close to the base would have to cross it in full view of two of the security towers, and she felt a modicum of reassurance in that.

The helicopter landed smoothly and delicately with barely a bump. After getting to her feet, Jessie crouched slightly then jumped down to the hard, dusty ground. Clouds of dust – stirred up by the rotor blades – immediately engulfed her head and body, and she coughed and spluttered.

Waving a hand in front of her face, she tried to protect her eyes from the stinging particles. Belatedly, she lowered her face shield, grabbed her pack and bag and took a few stumbling steps backward, ducking beneath the slowly spinning blades. The soldier passenger – still acting as though she did not exist – leaped down to take up a security position alongside the helicopter, keeping a watchful eye on their surroundings.

Undecided as to what to do next, Jessie looked around. The co-pilot joined her and, as she glanced at him, she saw that he was staring at her with a wide grin on his face. Reaching around her into the Wildcat's interior, he grabbed for a large khaki sack just inside the door and, as he did so, his body – intentionally or otherwise – brushed against hers. He winked and jerked his head sideways.

"Well, come on then, darlin'. You hang around out here and you'll get your pretty backside shot," he shouted.

Jessie heard the note of contempt in his voice – as if she had broken some important cardinal rule. Hot and tired, she glared at him, biting back words of retort. As if dismissing her as being of no consequence, the co-pilot turned his back and jogged away, holding the heavy sack as though it weighed nothing, his weapon held casually at his side.

Feeling slightly defeated, Jessie started to follow him. As she came out from beneath the shadow thrown by the helicopter, the searing heat instantly beat down onto her head and body, enveloping her in what felt like a stifling blanket. Her heavy pack swung violently from one shoulder, the kit bag seemed maliciously intent on tripping her up and the SA80A2 pounded her back like a wild thing. Her breath hissed harshly through gritted teeth, sweat trickled down her face and her lungs felt tight and burned from the hot air.

She guessed the distance to the base to be no more than one hundred meters or so from the landing zone, however, after only accomplishing half the distance, it felt as though she had completed a ten-kilometer exercise run, carrying full equipment. A sudden anxious thought that she might well pass out from heat exhaustion before reaching the heavy gates crossed her mind. She quickly quashed the notion, noticing that one of the gates was already open in anticipation of their arrival. Two soldiers stood on either side of it with weapons raised.

Reaching the base, the co-pilot entered and, with relief, Jessie prepared to follow. It was at this point that her legs — weak with fatigue and the excess weight she carried — suddenly buckled and she tripped, stumbled and almost fell flat on her face.

Struggling to regain her footing and what little composure she had left, she heard a derisory chuckle from one of the soldiers on security duty, felt a hard hand on her back and a shove almost aided her in completing her tumble to the ground.

Chapter Two

Remaining on her feet with an effort, Jessie spun around. She was shocked and angry, her face burning with heat—and not all of it from the sun. She was ready to let the man who had pushed her receive the scathing edge of her tongue.

The heavy gate—with a discordant screech of hinges—closed, and the soldier who had assisted with her ungainly entrance turned to face her. He grinned cheekily as he said, "You can't hang around out there, babe. It's not a garden party."

Taking note of the defiant expression on the man's face—almost as though he was goading her—Jessie temporarily forgot where she was and stepped forward, her ready temper rearing to her defense.

Lifting her face shield, she glanced briefly at the rank stitched to the front of the soldier's body armor and, thrusting her face close to his, murmured angrily, "It's *Corporal* McAllister to you, Lance Corporal. *Not* babe."

Enunciating each word slowly and carefully in a tone low enough so only he could hear, she continued with as much venom as she could muster. "Listen to me carefully, you fucking moron. If you *ever* do that again, I'll make it my personal goal to make sure that you speak in a falsetto for the rest of your ratty little life."

Jessie glared at him, an intense feeling of satisfaction flowing through her when she saw the soldier's face flush red and his smug, deprecatory smile slowly dissolve. With a final disdainful snort—dismissing him contemptuously—she spun on her heel, grabbed her pack and bag, then strode away from the gate with as much dignity as possible. She gritted her teeth as she heard an amused-sounding laugh from behind her.

Well, I handled that well, didn't I?

Beginning to feel increasingly discouraged, Jessie mused that what had just happened had been a really bad start.

Oh well, time to move on.

Determined to dismiss the incident, she walked a few meters inside the FOB, stopped and stared about her. Approximately half the size of a football field, her new home was larger than she had anticipated but still smaller than other bases on which she had served.

To her left, on a wooden platform covered with interlocking anti-slip flooring, was a square sand-colored tent with two smaller tents at one end, all draped with netting of the same color. Someone had chalked a large black cross with the words *Medical Center* beneath it, with an arrow pointing in the direction of a tent flap.

Jessie grimaced, her usual sense of humor soured by the events of the day. "Really?" she asked herself.

She was used to training and working in large military hospitals, and the single tent looked barely big enough to contain the equipment and supplies she would need to carry out her duties safely and successfully.

To her right were a number of other long tents, two of which resembled accommodation tents, and others that she could not begin to assign a use to. Behind her, parked in a line, were two huge Oshkosh M-ATVs — all-terrain vehicles similar in design to MRAPs that were designed to withstand IED attacks, along with two multi-purpose transport carriers. All the vehicles were painted in the same bland desert camouflage as everything else within the FOB.

Jessie knew that two recon sections, forming a platoon, were deployed at FOB Elabat as part of the ISAF, the International Security Assistance Force, under Operation Herrick, her own Bravo Recon and Charlie Recon.

Operating completely independently of each other, each

section had a commanding officer and a section leader, and each carried out their own missions. A platoon leader and his entourage had command of the entire FOB. The base, therefore, should have been bustling and noisy but, for the moment, it appeared she was completely alone.

She had not expected a fanfare of trumpets or a drum roll on her arrival, but she *had* thought that someone would have had the courtesy to meet her, even if it was just to show her where to go and what to do.

Jessie's irritation levels rose another notch on the 'I'm getting ready to blow' scale as she realized that it appeared she was not worth the effort and that she was only there to treat minor wounds and make sure that the men did not succumb to injuries sustained under hostile conditions.

Dropping her equipment to the ground, she lowered her mandible guard so it rested beneath her chin then she removed her helmet, tucking it beneath one arm. Groaning with relief as the weight left her head, she relished the warm breeze that stirred the damp strands of her hair and began to dry the perspiration on her face.

She continued to gaze around, her eyes eventually coming to rest on a canopied and netted enclosure with a number of mismatched, rickety metal tables and benches in evidence. Beyond them was a small kitchen, obviously the chow area.

Jessie noticed somebody lying full length on one of the benches and, feeling relieved that here at least was someone who might be able to help her get squared away, she hesitantly made her way toward him. As she drew closer, she saw it was a bare-chested man in shorts with a white cloth draped across his face. Completely unaware of her presence, he remained relaxed, with arms folded across his chest and legs crossed at the ankles. Jessie felt a brief surge of concern when she noticed a bandage on his right foot stained with a reddish-yellow fluid, usually a sign of infection.

The man did not stir as she reached his side and she stood staring down at him, waiting impatiently for some form of acknowledgement. When a soft snore escaped from beneath the white cloth, she finally realized that he was asleep.

Feeling flustered, Jessie placed a hand gently on the man's bare arm and shook him. The soft snores promptly ceased, a breath hitched, then the small rumbling noises continued.

She shook his arm again, roughly this time. The sleeper's response was a violent jerk, the cloth fell away from his face and the man stared up at her, still half-asleep and clearly dazed. Almost in the next instant, his eyes widened comically and he uttered a yell then promptly rolled off the bench onto the ground.

Surprised at his sudden movement, Jessie stepped hastily backward, trying hard to stop herself from bursting into laughter at the man's comedic actions. All sense of amusement promptly left her however when he glared at her.

"What the fuck?" he exclaimed. Looking around then back up at her, he groaned. "Oh, fuck me, a bleedin' bloody bird. God help us."

Jessie stiffened at the insulting remark. A combination of weariness and the beginnings of a headache, along with it being the third time she had been on the receiving end of a rude comment about being a woman, was causing her to very quickly lose the will to be civil.

"What the *hell* did you say?"

She watched as the man struggled to his feet, wincing as he unwittingly put weight onto his injured foot. He slumped down onto the bench and leaned down to rub his leg.

"You heard what I said. You're not deaf as well as dumb, are you? Bloody Yank," the man snapped, with annoyance in his voice.

Her jaws starting to ache as she clenched her teeth with aggravation, Jessie replied as politely as she could, "No, this *Yank* is *not* dumb. It just seems like a heck of a stupid comment to make, not to mention rude, about someone you don't know."

"Yeah, yeah, I get it. You're offended. Tough shit."

The man went silent for a moment then raised his head. Pronouncing each word slowly, as though Jessie was a child or might not understand English, he said, "We were expecting a male medic. It should be fucking interesting when the lads get back, not to mention LT's reaction."

Jessie heard him chuckle to himself as if he found the whole situation extremely amusing.

"You've *gotta* be kidding me. Christ, you're pathetic," she said, trying to quell her rising temper. "Where is everyone, anyway?"

"Out on patrol," was the brief reply. "That's sort of what we do around here."

Taking a deep breath, Jessie gazed down at the man's bandaged limb and, in an attempt to divert a confrontation, asked in a conciliatory manner, "Do you want me to take a look at that foot? It looks infected."

The man raised his head and shook it vigorously. "Not a fucking chance. It's fine as it is."

"Oh, suit yourself," Jessie snapped, finally losing her inner battle to remain civil. "Come and see me when your foot gets gangrene and rots off."

Knowing that she had responded childishly to the verbal assault but still seething, she turned on her heel and strode to where she had left her equipment. Utterly disgusted about the treatment she had just received, she collected her kit and headed toward the medical tent, stomping her dust-covered boots on the ground. She wished whole-heartedly that she was out of this place and back among normal, civilized people.

Stepping up onto the platform, she walked the short distance to the entrance and, pushing aside the flap, went inside. She discovered netting impeding her way, swore vehemently, struggled through it, then came to an abrupt stop.

"This…is it?" she asked herself, gazing around.

She found herself in a space approximately four meters long by six meters wide with two large vinyl windows, facing out onto the center of the FOB. Dust motes spun and danced in the rays of the sun streaming through them. Two portable microclimate cooling units hanging from the ceiling were humming softly and cooled air faintly wafted through now and again, disturbing the sluggish atmosphere holding sway inside.

An examination table held pride of place in the center, covered with a strip of white protective paper. Attached to and lining the walls were a number of medical storage bags, each containing supplies and small equipment in vinyl pouches.

A large container of water rested on a long aluminum table, together with a small stack of clear drawers containing dressings, syringes and other first-aid paraphernalia. Lying open on the floor beneath the examination table was a large medical pack, an item she would eventually have to spend some time inventorying, as it was a primary piece of equipment and something she would be required to take with her whenever she left the FOB.

To her amazement, the medical tent *was* surprisingly well-stocked and perfectly adequate to deal with minor injuries a casualty. Jessie wondered, however, what would happen if a situation ever arose where she had more than one patient. From what she could see, there was only a single examination table, no beds and certainly no sign of any chairs. She wondered where she could obtain more furniture and decided that she would need to approach Bravo Recon Section's commanding officer once she had settled in.

To her right was a smaller tent flap, also with mesh net covering it. It appeared to lead through to one of the smaller tents, so after dropping her bags to the floor, she made her way toward it, boot soles squeaking as she went. Pushing her way through, she found herself in what was obviously going to be her personal sleeping quarters.

It was a small area with a vinyl window looking out onto the tents opposite, and it contained an old-fashioned camp bed, bedside locker and head-high racks of plastic shelving lining one wall. Harsh sunlight streamed in, even though someone had hung up a grimy blind — obviously with a view to ensuring her privacy — which she found slightly heartwarming.

A single pillow rested neatly on a folded sleeping bag and army blanket, the bed pack stacked regimentally at the head of the cot. Even though she could feel a faint draft from the portable microclimate cooling unit hanging from the ceiling, she was relieved to discover an ancient portable fan, together with a chemlamp, beside the bed. This was an added bonus to the single strip light hanging alongside the cooling system. With the exception of these two homely items, the space was sterile and purely functional in nature.

Jessie could see the outline of a smaller flap and, moving toward it, pulled it back. Peering in, she discovered a shower tent, together with a chemical toilet. This time, her relief was enormous. At least something was finally going right. Any future embarrassing experiences at sharing ablutions with the men had been negated by the presence of the shoddy little shower tent.

She sighed again and turned to go back into the main tent. Passing the examination table, she picked up a clipboard with sheets of paper attached to it and saw that they were standard field medical forms.

A medic needed to fill in one of the forms each time someone was injured, wounded or killed in action. This was a vitally important procedure, as the information would be readily available to the hospital receiving the medevacked casualty.

The top form had been completed and held information about an injury that had occurred to one of the men the previous day. Jessie read it with interest. She discovered that the details related to someone who had cut their foot and, as she read on, she realized that the injury had been to the man who had greeted her in such a rude manner on her arrival. She noted the treatment given, glanced through the rest of the forms and, finding that they were blank, placed the clipboard back on the examination table.

Feeling a little lost, she paused for a moment in the center of the tent. The heat was almost palpable and wrapped its vaporous arms around her, suffocating her. A surge of homesickness that made her want to cry.

Cripes! I so miss home.

Tears burned her eyes, but she blinked them back vigorously, determined that she would not cry. She gazed one last time at her surroundings, then wearily picked up her bags and went back to her quarters, throwing both items and helmet on the bed.

Eager to get out of her equipment, she pulled the release pins beneath both arms of her body armor, allowing it to part down the sides, and she quickly pulled it up and over her head, throwing it to join the other items on the bed. She released pins at each of her elbows and knees and her limb protectors dropped to the floor. Her body instantly began to cool, and she plucked her combat shirt away from her damp skin, blowing air out between pursed lips.

Noting a set of portable power sockets hanging on the wall above the bed and desperate to relieve the heat, she plugged in the fan. Placing it on the bedside locker, she turned it on full blast. Immediately, cold, rejuvenating air started to stir the sluggish atmosphere, and she stood with her face inches from the whirling blades, enjoying the chilly flow.

With her senses partially energized, Jessie turned to the task of unzipping the various pouches and pockets of her backpack. She spent the next ten minutes placing neatly folded T-shirts, shorts and underwear on the racks provided and setting out her toiletries and her faithful iPod with its charger and speakers. Finally, she carefully extracted three photographs from an outside pocket of her kit bag and, after placing it and the now empty pack on the floor, then kicking them out of sight beneath the low bed, she sat down to study them.

The first photograph was of her in uniform, taken with her parents just a few weeks before her deployment. Her father, tall and fit at fifty-seven with her own dark blond hair and cobalt-blue eyes, looked both proud and sad at the same time. Her mother, still looking beautiful at forty-eight, was smiling her wonderful smile, short, curly hair gleaming, eyes glowing.

Jessie knew that she had the best parents a girl could ever have. She and her kid brother had grown up in a house that had always been full of love and laughter, as clichéd as that might sound. Her mom and dad had always allowed her and her brother Jake to make their own choices with the firm condition, however, that they first sat down together as a family to discuss it.

On informing them that she was joining the US Marines, they had accepted the decision, knowing that it had been her obsession since childhood, but she had recognized in them the natural concern of loving parents. She had received all the support that she could have ever wanted, though, and she loved them for it.

The photograph prompted her to wonder where Jake was. He had decided to join the Marine Corps at twenty and he was already in Afghanistan, his deployment occurring a few months before hers. She had received one letter from him where he was stationed at Camp Bastion—her original and more favored place of deployment—but she had not heard from him since.

The second photograph she turned to *was* that of her brother, and she smiled to herself. Jake and she could have passed for twins, as he had the same blond hair as she, as well as the deep blue eyes inherited from their father. They both had a smattering of freckles across their noses and identical dimples located on the right cheek. Hoping that he was safe, she turned to the third and final picture. This time the smile faltered on her lips.

Chapter Three

The picture was of a Marine in full dress uniform. Tall and well-built with dark brown hair, he was grinning at the camera as though life were a joke and he the only joker in it.

"Mark," Jessie whispered, feeling a lump form in her throat.

She ran a fingertip down the length of the photograph. Sergeant Mark McAllister had been killed in action in Afghanistan six months after they had been married. Even a year after his death, the pain she felt at his loss still lingered, always hovering just below the surface.

She missed him. He had possessed the ability to make her laugh, even when she was at her lowest ebb. Although he had been overseas for most of it, their short marriage had been happy, and his death had left her feeling bereft and empty.

Jessie sat in the silent tent, staring at the photograph. Putting a hand inside her combat shirt, she withdrew a silver chain from which hung her dog tags and her wedding ring. Fingering the white-gold circle — warm from lying next to her skin — she rose to her feet and propped the three photographs upright on the bedside locker so that they rested against the side of the tent. She suddenly felt incredibly tired and she lay down on the bed, gazing up at the blank ceiling, idly playing with the ring.

This was not what she had envisioned the next few months of her life to be. On arriving at Base Kandahar with a layover of some four hours before transport could be provided to fly her to Camp Bastion, she had been given new orders that a CTM, a combat trauma medic, was needed at an FOB way out in hostile territory. She would be replacing a battle fatality and her first thought at the change of orders was that she was actually filling a dead man's or woman's boots.

Jessie was now miles from civilization, in what was supposed to be one of the most dangerous insurgent-populated areas of Afghanistan, treated like a contagious disease by at least one member of her new section and feeling a deep sense of loneliness.

Closing her eyes, she went back over the conversation with the injured man, trying to figure out why he had reacted so badly toward her. She had done nothing to antagonize him. Well, all right… Perhaps she had retaliated a little too robustly, but he had deserved it.

Her thoughts meandered on, then began to scatter with weary confusion. Her mind suddenly gave in to fatigue, and she slept.

* * * *

Jessie awoke abruptly some time later. Unsure of where she was and wondering what had woken her, she heard the sound of voices outside the medical tent and realized — with a resurgence of butterflies in her stomach — that Bravo Recon Section must have returned from their patrol. She could hear the scrape of boots on gritty ground and coarse laughter, the type that could only come from a group of adrenaline-fueled men.

She sat bolt upright, panicked, then swung her legs over the side of the cot. Standing up, she hastily smoothed hair back from her face and tucked in her combat shirt, attempting to make herself look presentable. The prospect of facing a group of irascible and contemptuous males filled her with nervous tension, and she hesitated before making her way to the tent entrance. She stopped before exiting, biting her lip.

After a few seconds, finally realizing that she could not

procrastinate any longer, she gathered what remained of her courage and was about to pull back the flap when a voice – recognizable as coming from the man who she had met earlier – sounded from not more than a few meters away from her.

"Oi, lads. Our new medic arrived while you were all away enjoying yourselves."

Jessie noted that the statement incurred little response until the voice concluded in a tone that sounded as though it was about to impart top secret information, "He is a *she* and…a bleedin' Yank!"

There was silence lasting a number of seconds following this announcement before groans and swearing erupted, and Jessie's heart sank.

So, this is how it's going to be.

Jessie wished that she could escape somewhere, even if it was off the base and into the inhospitable land of Afghanistan. She'd rather do that than have to put up with facing her antagonistic and unfriendly section members.

"You must have had a wet dream, Dingle," spoke a new voice, one that sounded husky, upper class and a little amused.

Jessie was startled when a warm tingle trailed up and down her spine, and she felt her pulses quicken a little at the sound of it.

A voice can do that to me? Yeah, right. Whoa, girl. Just rein it in.

The next voice came from the injured man. "LT, sir, I can promise you on my honor –" What sounded like derisive-sounding snorts came from the other men, but the first voice continued on stoically. "This was *not* a wet dream. I was lying down thinking profound thoughts –"

Another round of derogatory comments interrupted the speaker's attempt to impart his information.

"You are so full of shit, pal."

"You are one fucked up grunt."

But the familiar voice continued. "Wait up, you arseholes.

Let me finish, will you?"

The noise diminished slowly, allowing the man to go on. "If you sods will let me…as I was *trying* to say…I was lying down thinking profound thoughts, and she woke me up. Sorry…interrupted my thought processes. She asked me where you bunch of tits were and if I wanted her to look at my foot. I told her no fucking way."

There was more laughter, and, listening intently from inside the tent, Jessie started to grow angry.

This is ridiculous.

"So, what does this bird look like then?" asked another voice.

"Well, not that I looked seriously hard, you understand, but she is a bit of a knock-out — drop-dead gorgeous, actually."

"Did you do the honorable thing and show her around, Dingle?" the cultured voice asked.

"Like fuck I did, LT, sir. After we spoke for a bit — politely like, you understand — she stormed off into the medical tent. A bit high maintenance, I think."

Furious and having heard enough, Jessie swept back both the netting and flap and hurried out onto the platform. Stopping dead and planting her hands on her hips, she surveyed the eight men arranged in a half circle in front of her, all of whom were clad in full combat gear, body armor and carrying weapons. They were resting easy in front of a tall soldier standing with his back to her.

She glared at them, waiting for them to notice her presence. One by one, their attention turned to her, the noise petering out into silence, their gazes seeming to pin her where she stood. Before she could voice her anger and disapproval at their comments, loud wolf whistles and catcalls accompanied by a number of crude comments rent the air.

At the noise, the tall man slowly turned and, despite finding herself very uncomfortable at being on display under the gaze of eight pairs of eyes in faces that held expressions ranging from interest to contempt, Jessie was alarmed to discover herself facing a far more dangerous challenge to her wellbeing.

The officer was still wearing a sand-colored, pixel-camouflaged helmet with visor raised and mandible guard lowered, revealing a clear view of his features. He had the darkest brown eyes she had ever seen set in a tan, good-looking face. Dark stubble adorned his chin and jaw line and the descriptive word *rakish* popped into her mind.

Jessie felt taken aback at her instant reaction to him. That chocolate-brown gaze was staring at her with such intensity that she felt as though they were penetrating her clothing right through to her skin.

Without warning, nerves suddenly quivered all over her body, causing sensations she had never experienced before. Her pulse rate accelerated and she had a confused sense of her emotions turning cartwheels.

Wha…? This is Lieutenant Nick Ryan? Oh, God damn it!

She watched as Lieutenant Ryan folded his arms and looked her up and down. "Well, Dingle," he announced slowly. "She's certainly a female. I'll give you that."

As raucous laughter greeted his words, on the heels of the feelings he had instigated in her, Jessie felt an intense dislike for the man. It was as if he was trying to ridicule her in front of the others and with her usual fiery temper, she was about to give vent to her anger, forgetting that this might bring down a variety of repercussions on her head, when the Lieutenant asked, "All squared away, Corporal?" Jessie noticed that he had lowered his head slightly and was studying her from beneath the rim of his helmet. The shadow thrown onto his eyes made them appear almost black, and a frown had drawn his eyebrows into a dark line.

Nick Ryan couldn't take his eyes off Bravo Recon's new CTM. He found himself a little shocked at the fact that he now had a female in his charge and, therefore, under his care. He had never had a female under his command in all three of his tours in country, and he couldn't make up his mind how he felt about it.

His priority request for a medic had been expedited, so on receiving her file that day and reading the unusually brief bio—which had not mentioned whether he was a she or *vice versa*—he had thought no more about it. It had never crossed his mind in the slightest that the male he had been expecting could be a she. Even though Dingle had mentioned that their new medic was female, he had thought that the young soldier was being his usual joking self.

Of more importance to him was the fact that her presence appeared to have caused a mixed reaction among his section. They had never worked alongside a female before, and she was indeed a *looker*, as Dingle had described. Where the impressionable men under his command were concerned, it was going to be like bees after honey. However, what made him feel more uneasy was his own reaction to her.

Tall and slim but curvy, she had hair as tawny as a lion's mane streaked with golden highlights. Her eyes were a deep cobalt-blue, fringed with long dark curling eyelashes, in stark contrast to the blonde of her hair and the tan skin of her face.

Nick admitted—reluctantly—that she was enough to turn any man's head, including his own. Although he was appreciative of her looks, he felt uncomfortable at how instantly attracted to her he was.

Furthermore, his first impression of her was that she might prove to be a handful. There was a look in her eyes that seemed to show she was tempted to retaliate at some of the comments the men had made, and she wouldn't hold back.

Without taking his eyes off her, determined to nip any trouble in the bud, he said, "Right, you lot. You can stand down. Go and get some scran."

There was murmured appreciation at the order and, with the scuffle of boots, the men moved away, ridding themselves of their body armor and helmets and chatting loudly as they went.

Nick continued to stare at his new medic in silence. He noticed that she had tilted her chin in a stubborn and challenging manner, and it provoked him.

"You never answered my question, McAllister," he said. "I asked if you were all squared away. Do you think it beneath you to reply to a question from your commanding officer?"

Nick wondered why he felt the need to put this woman in her place. He assumed it was because he wanted to make her fully aware that he would not tolerate any disrespect toward himself or the army. He firmly believed that orders were there to be obeyed without question, and he was not about to let a feisty, obstinate woman disrupt his section. At least, those were the reasons he gave himself.

The woman stiffened her shoulders and her chin seemed to jut out even farther.

"I *am* all squared away, sir," she eventually replied, her tone barely civil. "And I was thinking about your question."

Nick found her American accent not only attractive but also sensual. He didn't like the direction his thoughts were taking, so he pushed them from his mind and saw that a frown marred her forehead. He suspected that she was royally pissed at him and everyone else in sight, but he found himself reluctantly admiring her spirit.

"Well, that's very good, Corporal. There's hope for you yet. Go and get some scran. We leave on patrol first thing tomorrow morning at 0500 hours. You missed the earlier mission briefing, but I'll repeat it tomorrow morning. Try not to be late."

As the words left his mouth, Nick realized he was baiting the newest member of his section, and he mentally berated himself. Unable to retract the remark, he turned to join his men but came to a stop as he heard, quite clearly from behind him, a muttered, "I'll pass. Thank you, sir. I wouldn't want to cramp any of the section's style by my *female* presence."

She had uttered the word female as if it were a derogatory term and, when he swung back to reprimand her, she was staring at him with a baleful look in her blue eyes.

Nick remained where he was for a moment, bemused at the fact that his rank had not prevented her from standing up to him. He suddenly found his mouth twitching with amusement and, letting her comment slide, he turned away and strode to the DFAC to join his weary but boisterously voluble men.

An arrogant…rude…conceited…egotistical…so far up his own backside jackass!

Having exhausted her mental repertoire of 'polite' insults on behalf of her commanding officer, Jessie stood glaring at him as he walked away. She felt an intense dislike — the feeling way out of proportion to the situation — for the handsome Lieutenant Ryan.

She found herself having to make a conscious effort to swallow the insubordinate responses that were hovering on the tip of her tongue. Turning away, she strode into the medical tent, all the while feeling that if she had been alone, she would have thrown an almighty fit.

What the hell? How dare they treat me like this?

Jessie clenched her fists with aggravation and suppressed anger and walked hurriedly to where the medical pack lay on the floor. Picking it up, she slammed it down onto the examination table.

Hoping it would calm her down, she meticulously began to check each of its pouches, concentrating on counting the contents, hunting through the supplies where she thought she needed extra and making sure that everything was in date. Each item she took from storage to place in the pack she checked off from a list hanging from a hook by a piece of string.

It took her some twenty minutes to complete the task but, finally satisfied and indeed much calmer, she set the rucksack back down on the floor, ready for the patrol the next day. After checking that she had her own basic field medical equipment in various pouches on the front of her body armor, she turned on the chemlamp and sat down on her cot, suddenly at a loose end.

Feeling glum, she leaned forward and, balancing her elbows on her thighs, rested her chin in her hands. Staring at the blank wall of her tent, she listened to the male voices and coarse-sounding hilarity outside and suddenly she felt terribly lonely. It sounded as though they were having a laugh, and she wished that she could go and join them.

Glancing at her wristwatch, she saw that it was only 1900 hours, far too early to settle down for the night. She was hungry and thirsty but was reluctant to venture outside to join the others. They had made it abundantly clear that they wanted no part of her and were not prepared to make her feel welcome or help her to settle in. She had taken enough insults to last her a lifetime and she wasn't about to subject herself to anymore.

Jessie was never one to back down from a personal problem. If she felt something was unfair or knew she was in the right, she stood her ground and never allowed anything to get her down. She always kept smiling, no matter how she felt, but, right at that moment, she was tired and miserable, and this was one of the rare occasions when she had no fight left in her. She tried to cheer herself up with the thought that tomorrow was another day and with a good night's sleep, she would feel a great deal better than she did now.

She jumped slightly when there was a soft slap on the outside of the tent and its flap, together with the netting, was pulled back to reveal the soldier Dingle. He stood in the opening, craning his neck at an angle and peering toward where she was sitting in her sleeping quarters.

Chapter Four

Jessie was startled at his surprise appearance and immediately wary, expecting further derogatory comments. Remaining seated, she straightened up, staring back at the soldier, who she saw had a sheepish expression on his face.

"What do you want?" she asked in an unfriendly tone.

"My foot," Dingle announced, as if the two words could explain everything.

Although it was somewhat unkind, Jessie wanted to make him feel as embarrassed and uncomfortable as she had felt earlier. She shrugged, pretending she didn't understand what he was referring to.

"Your foot?" she echoed, hoping that the expression on her face was one of confusion.

She watched Dingle look away and heard him sigh. His face flushed bright red and he said at last, "LT ordered me to come and get my foot checked out."

Jessie remained quiet—enjoying the man's obvious discomfort—then she stood up and went toward the examination table.

Dingle stayed where he was, partially inside the tent, obviously reluctant to enter, so she turned and said impatiently, "Well, come on in then. Contrary to what you dickheads seem to believe, I don't bite."

Turning her back on the apparently nervous man, Jessie went to the supply table, collected a plastic bowl and, after filling it with water, added a few drops of antiseptic solution. Carrying out a brief search, she found an antibiotic spray, together with all the supplies she would need to dress the wound, and she placed everything on the examination table. She finally pulled on a pair of gloves and folded her arms, waiting and watching as the soldier approached, reluctantly dragging his feet. He stopped directly in front of her when he couldn't move any farther forward.

Jessie continued to stare at him in exasperation until finally she ordered impatiently, "Oh, God damn it! Will you sit up on that?" and she pointed at the examination table. She knew she sounded irritated and abrupt but she had no intention of changing her tone of voice.

Dingle jumped awkwardly up onto the table, kicking off one of his shower sandals once he was comfortable. Silently, Jessie gently lifted the injured foot and began to unwind the grimy bandage.

"I did it a couple of days ago—" Dingle stammered, tentatively beginning to explain the background to his injury.

Jessie cut him off abruptly. "I know how you did it and when you did it," she responded coolly. "Strangely enough, I have actually learned to read. I saw the medical form completed by your previous medic."

She finished unwinding the bandage and threw it in the waste receptacle behind her. She noticed immediately that the dressing beneath had adhered to the wound and attempting to remove it would almost certainly cause a great deal of pain and probably inflict additional injury. As much as she still felt annoyed with this man, she didn't have the heart to cause him further discomfort, even if her insulted feelings were urging her to do so.

"The dressing has dried to the wound," she explained briefly. "If I try to remove it, it will probably hurt like hell." She glanced up at him and smiled.

Dingle winced and looked anxious. "Er...you won't do that, will you?" he asked nervously.

Jessie continued to remain silent—staring at him—hoping that she had managed to produce a thoughtful expression on her face as if she was turning over the options in her mind that his question had raised.

Resentment and a lack of forgiveness however, were not part of her true nature, particularly when it came to a patient. She could not keep up with her unfeeling and uncaring attitude any longer and she finally smiled at him more naturally.

"No, I won't," she replied, her tone slightly warmer. "I'm a medic, not a sadist sad-masochist. I'm going to have to soak the dressing with an antiseptic solution so that it becomes unstuck. You'll have to grin and bear it. Is that okay?"

Jessie saw a relieved look cross the young soldier's face, and he nodded in agreement. She proceeded to soak a small bundle of cotton wool in the solution in the bowl and, without wringing out the sodden ball, trickled the water onto the dressing. She heard Dingle's hiss of pain, glanced up and saw that he had clenched his teeth.

After long minutes of soaking the stained dressing, Jessie picked up plastic tweezers and began to gently lever up the corners. The gauze finally came free, and she was able to see a nasty, deep gash just beginning to heal but with small suppurating areas around the edges.

Engrossed in her task, she gently began to bathe the wound until the crusty edges were clean and it looked a great deal healthier. Once this particular task was completed, she dried the gash with fresh gauze then, looking up, said, "There's a slight infection in it, but don't worry. Your foot isn't about to drop off. I'm going to spray it with antibiotic and dress it. It's not ready for the air to get to it, and we need to prevent the infection from getting any worse."

She tried not to smile when she noticed a greenish tinge to the soldier's face. She liberally sprayed the wound with antibiotic, reached for the clean bandage then proceeded to redress the foot, eventually fastening the end of the bandage down with an elasticized gripper.

"There you go," she said, carefully lowering the injured limb.

Stepping back, she glanced at Dingle to see a fleeting

expression of respect cross his face.

Flexing his foot experimentally, he nodded, "Feels good. Thanks, Mac."

Jessie tensed at the unexpected abbreviation of her surname, wondering for a moment if this was the start of more insults. About to make a retort, she hesitated, realizing that the nickname might be an olive branch. Perhaps she had been overreacting, been too sensitive and defensive over each remark made at her expense since her arrival.

"You'll need to come back and see me tomorrow to have it re-dressed," she said instead, ignoring the friendly overture. She was still not entirely sure that he was trying to make amends for their earlier confrontation.

"Is there a chance of getting out on patrol tomorrow?" Dingle asked, his voice hopeful.

Jessie shook her head. "Not a chance. Heat build-up in your boots will make your feet sweat, and that will only cause the infection to get worse. Another twenty-four hours should be okay. I'll need to speak to the Lieutenant to give him my report. I'm sorry, Dingle."

Jumping down from the examination table and finding his discarded sandal, Dingle shrugged. "No fucking problem," he said. "Thanks again, Mac." Giving her a quick wink, he walked with a slight limp to the entrance to the tent.

Watching him go, Jessie reached up to take the hairpins from her hair. Releasing her mane from its plait, she fluffed it up then ran her fingers through it, feeling it flow luxuriously around her shoulders and down her back.

She noticed Dingle stop and turn back, as if struck by a sudden thought. She felt bemused when he remained silent—staring at her—his mouth opening and shutting, mimicking that of a stranded fish.

She was about to ask him if there was anything wrong when his face turned bright red and he cleared his throat.

"Look, Mac. About earlier on…"

Jessie raised a hand to quiet him. "Forget it, Dingle. There's no need to apologize. Let's just put it down to getting off on the wrong foot, okay?"

"Who the fuck said I was going to apologize? You're being pretty presumptuous," Dingle exclaimed then laughed. "Okay, yeah, I was. Look, I'm really sorry. You must have thought I was a complete dick. Why don't you come outside and meet the lads. I bet you could do with some scran and a drink."

Jessie shook her head, intending to decline the invitation, then hesitated. She *was* hungry and thirsty and it was far too early to go to bed. Even though she was tired, if she went to sleep now she would probably end up waking halfway through the night.

"Are you sure?" she asked nervously. "I don't want any more crap from anyone, Dingle."

"All that shit earlier was just dick waving and showing off," Dingle explained. "The lads are well known for making arses of themselves. I being the exception, of course."

Jessie nodded and laughed. "Oh, of course," she agreed.

She realized that if she was going to integrate herself into the section, this might be the only opportunity she would have to do so. If she didn't take it, then her time here was going to be miserable.

Eventually nodding in agreement, she asked, "One thing before we go. Can you *please* tell me what the hell 'scran' is?"

She saw a perplexed expression cross Dingle's face then he grinned. "Oh, yeah, you're a Yank. You wouldn't know… It means food."

"Oh…right…yeah. Of course that's what it means. Why didn't I think of that?"

Shaking her head, she joined Dingle and followed him outside, involuntarily stiffening her shoulders in preparation for a further onslaught of insulting comments.

Nick Ryan sat with his back against a table, elbows resting on the edge, legs stretched out in front of him. He loved this time of day the most, with a lowering sun casting a blaze of gold and orange across the sky and the temperature dropping. The smell of frying bacon, together with the odor of coffee wafting up from the urn, teased his senses and he closed his eyes briefly, allowing himself to relax.

"Wonder where 'ole Dingle is?" Yeti mused. Built like the alleged monster of legend with elaborate tattoos up the full length of both arms and one in the shape of a cobweb covering the top of his shaven head, he slurped loudly as he drank from a plastic thermo cup.

"Getting his leg over?" responded Lug Nut, a tall, skinny member of the section who sported a crew cut, shaped flat on top like an anvil with an elaborate tattoo encircling his neck, taking the form of a twisting pattern like that of a corkscrew.

His comment elicited coarse-sounding grunts from the other men.

"Or she's cut off his foot...or maybe something else," Mungo went on. With angelic features and a slim, graceful body, his physical appearance belied the image that his nickname might conjure up in a person's mind.

"She looked like she wouldn't think twice about cutting someone's balls off, let alone poor Dingle's foot," added Yeti.

"All right, lads. Enough of the remarks about our new medic," Nick said lazily — eyes still closed — too relaxed to do more than issue a half-hearted order. "Let's give the lady a chance. We should not forget that she's going to be pulling our said balls out of the fire whenever it's required."

"For fuck sake, LT," Shrek announced. His pudgy face, incongruous on top of a muscular, stocky body, held a baffled expression. "She ain't no lady."

"That's enough," snapped JR, the section leader, a tall, good-looking man who glared at the lance corporal with displeasure.

"Fuck me backward!"

The sudden murmured exclamation came from Yeti, who grasped Lug Nut's arm, arresting that man's voluble speech on the pros and cons of Dingle getting his leg over with the new medic.

"You're not my type, Yeti, me old mate. But thanks for the offer though," Shrek answered, then he also fell silent.

Opening his eyes and turning to survey the men to see what was going on, Nick saw them glancing at Yeti — some smirking — to assess his reaction to Shrek's comment. Completely ignoring the remark, Yeti continued to stare in the direction of the medical tent. The section followed his gaze and silence fell over them all with the exception of a murmured, "Wow," from lean and hairy Wolf, whose eyes almost bugged out of their sockets.

Nick, frowning at the unnatural quiet, followed the men's gaze with his own in an attempt to find out what the distraction was. He found himself staring directly at the new medic as she accompanied Dingle toward them, and he felt as though something had slammed into his chest. His heart stuttered before racing on, and his stomach began to tie itself in slow, tingling knots.

He had never experienced such intense sensations at the sight of a woman before, and it set up an instant stubborn denial that it was *this* woman that was the cause of him feeling them now.

He couldn't help but notice that she had released her hair from its confines. The mass now hung around her shoulders and down her back, the descending sun's rays gleaming on the golden strands. She was smiling at something Dingle was saying and the brilliant smile completely transformed her tan face from pretty to beautiful.

With a sinking feeling, Nick had the sudden notion that the arrival of Jessie McAllister in their midst was going to create more personal inconvenience for him then he had ever had to deal with in his life before. She was trouble with a capital T.

As Jessie reached the men, she glanced warily at them and smiled shyly, feeling ill at ease.

"Uhhhh."

She heard a strange grunt come from one of the soldiers, who then coughed and said to Dingle, "Still got your foot then, mate?"

Turning toward Jessie, Dingle winked, then surveying the gawking men said loudly, "This is Mac, lads. Be nice. She's all right."

"Mac?" Lieutenant Ryan queried in a strained voice.

"Well, LT, sir. McAllister is too big a fucking mouthful to say all the time, so it's Mac."

Feeling a little warmed by Dingle's support, Jessie turned to glance at the Lieutenant, only to find that once again he was staring at her with the same unfathomable look in his eyes that he had shown earlier.

He'd removed his helmet, and she had a clear view of dark brown wavy hair—a little longer than a conventional military haircut—and a tan, aristocratic face with full lips and a square, firm chin.

Something stirred in her stomach, a faint trembling that careened outward to pulses all over her body and sent them racing. Aware that she was feeling a little too much interest in her commanding officer, she cleared her throat nervously and began, "Sir..."

Her voice trailed off into silence as feeling uncharacteristically flustered and tongue-tied in his presence, Jessie found it difficult to speak to him about Dingle's injury. The man was making things difficult for her by remaining silent, with no sign of a welcoming smile on his face. He appeared to be waiting for her to say something more.

Watching his face, she saw him raise an eyebrow. "Spit it out...*Mac*," he said at last.

He made her nickname sound like an insult, and Jessie felt a surge of annoyance. The dislike—now mixed up with other questionable emotions—was growing stronger.

She held the man's gaze with her own, trying to dismiss the sizzling sensation that was tracing up and down her spine. She swallowed, then said as quickly as she could, "I've examined Dingle's foot. I think it's slightly infected, so with all due respect, Lieutenant, in my opinion he remains unfit for duty. Twenty-four hours should see him fit, but I'll need to see the injury before I can sign off on it."

Jessie finished her report, certain that the words spilling from her mouth at breakneck speed had probably sounded completely garbled. She glanced around at the men, noting that one or two were staring at her with their mouths agape, while another was glaring at her as though he disliked her intensely. Her face flushing at being the focal point of their attention, she turned back to Lieutenant Ryan, waiting for him to respond.

Nick stayed silent. He couldn't have answered her at that moment, even if he had wanted to. He felt mesmerized by the woman's beautiful blue eyes and, as his gaze moved downward, her full lips. Finally realizing that he must look moonstruck, he nodded. "Very well, McAllister," and saw the medic's nervous expression change to one of relief.

Turning to Dingle he said, "There you go. You have my permission to skive off for another twenty-four hours. By the way, if you say 'LT, sir,' one more time, I'll make your life a living hell—a bloody good deal worse than the *mujis* ever will, anyway. You are definitely pissing me off."

"Yes, thank you, LT, s…" Dingle responded. "That's awfully good of you…LT. I'll take everything you've said onboard. Now, who's for more bacon sarnies?"

As the other men responded eagerly to the offer, Nick quickly got to his feet. He needed to get as far away from Jessie McAllister as possible, the farther the better. Despite his strenuous denials, her presence was having an extraordinary effect on him. The stirrings of the powerful attraction he had felt for her at their initial meeting was becoming stronger, despite it only being the first day of her deployment.

Unfortunately, he did need to speak to her. He gave every

new arrival into his section a private induction speech in which he outlined the dos and don'ts of life on an FOB, making sure that they understood what their role was to be. He was filled with reluctance at the thought of talking to *her*, wished that he could by-pass it just once, but the rule that he had made for himself forbade him to ignore his duty.

"I will love and leave you, lads," he announced. He hesitated, then added as an afterthought, "I need to get some work done for tomorrow. I bid you goodnight. McAllister, you're with me." With that final remark, he turned and strode away to his tent.

Chapter Five

Here we go, probably a lecture and more belittling remarks, the usual crap.

Jessie reluctantly made her way to the lieutenant's tent, her boots almost dragging in the dust like a child who knows that they are in for a roasting. On eventually reaching his accommodation, she hesitated briefly, took a deep breath and, drawing aside the flap, went in.

She found Lieutenant Ryan already seated on a camp chair behind a rickety metal table, its top littered with papers and maps. He was leaning on its surface with his arms folded as though waiting for her, and there was an impatient look on his face.

Jessie spared a brief glance around, taking in the neat and tidy interior, sparsely furnished with a camp bed and cabinet with a uniform hung neatly on hooks. She jumped slightly, her attention snagged by a cough and, feeling her cheeks burn slightly, she turned back to the lieutenant.

"When you've finished making an inspection of my tent…" he began, leaning back in his chair and picking up a pencil, twisting and turning it between his fingers.

Jessie felt herself stiffen. "Sorry, sir," she responded.

"I suppose you've become aware by now that we were expecting a male replacement," Nick stated without hesitation.

"Lieutenant?" Jessie wondered if she had heard him correctly.

Is that the only reason I'm here? Just so that he can remind me that I'm a female?

"Your arrival here has created quite a bit of upheaval

among Bravo Recon Section," Nick continued. "I will not have the men distracted from their duties or situations of a personal nature creating problems. This area of Afghanistan is notorious for its insurgent activity, therefore, exceedingly dangerous. I need to keep my men—and yourself, of course—alive and safe while you are in my charge. I take it you know the regulations about fraternization among men and women and relationships of any kind while you are in country?"

Jessie glared at Lieutenant Ryan, trying to make sense of his words and the warning that he seemed intent on giving her.

"Sir? Are you telling me to...stay away from the men?" She was so angry that she could barely speak.

Lieutenant Ryan continued to stare at her in silence.

When there was no response, Jessie continued, her tone cold, "With all due respect, Lieutenant. As hard as it may be for you to grasp, I'm here to do a job, the same as the rest of you. I have no intention of causing any...problems. I can assure you, as well, that my being female does not make me any less capable of doing my job."

"Well, McAllister, I'll just have to take you at your word, won't I? Until I find out to the contrary, of course. At the first sign of any conflict between you and the men, I'll have you shipped out. Do I make myself clear?"

Jessie felt an angry retort surface on her lips. *Who in the hell does he think he is? The man definitely has a thorn up his ass and a massive problem with women – or just with me.* Biting her lip, she swallowed then cleared her throat. "You've made it perfectly clear, Lieutenant," she snapped.

"That's all for now. You can go."

"Yes, sir," Jessie said through gritted teeth.

She about-turned smartly and almost ran to exit the tent. Lieutenant Ryan's voice brought her to an abrupt halt.

"There's one more thing, Corporal."

Jessie turned, feeling her blood boil. "Yes, sir?" she said slowly, her jaws aching from the strain of clenching her teeth.

"When you're in uniform, have your hair confined."

Repressing a growl of fury, Jessie said as evenly as she could, "Yes, sir," spun around, and hurried through the netting. If it had been a door, she would have slammed it behind her as hard as she could. As it was, her dignity and impressive exit went completely out of the window when she almost got herself tangled in the tent flap before she managed to extricate herself then storm off.

Once Jessie McAllister had left, Nick groaned. He turned on his chemlamp and for a few minutes sat staring at the wall. He couldn't dismiss the image of the woman standing at attention before his desk, her blue eyes dark with emotion, her cheeks flushed with anger. Tantalizing thoughts of how her body might feel beneath his hands and how her rich mane of hair might feel silky when he clenched his fingers in it made him stir restlessly in his chair.

He thought back over the brief meeting with her. He hadn't said all that he should have — her presence had assaulted his senses, causing most of his normally voluble speech to dry up — and his tone had been abrupt and unwelcoming. Her body language and the angry inflection in her voice had shown her reaction to his insinuations, which had almost bordered on being insulting.

Nick rested a booted ankle across a knee and leaned back in his chair, clasping his hands behind his head. He *did not* like the way his emotions — as heady and intoxicating as they were — were responding to Jessie McAllister.

He had never allowed himself to become involved with a woman during his army career. Nick had always been a soldier first and a man interested in women second. He believed that the personal feelings that arose during relationships could interfere with his commitment to the army and, furthermore, with his role as an officer.

He had successfully erected a barrier around any emotion regarding the opposite sex and, so far, he had been extremely successful at keeping himself free of entanglements. This woman arriving in their midst had all but demolished his guard in a few short hours, and he was nervous at the sudden ambush on his control.

While Nick knew that he *did* feel an unusually intense attraction for her, he also knew that it was going to go nowhere. Having the hots for someone caused distraction, loss of focus and created too many hazards for those he commanded, let alone being totally against regulations. She was also a lower rank, and anything between them would be extremely detrimental to both their careers.

He needed to re-focus completely on his role as an army officer, and any diversion from this would be contravening his own ethics. He felt frustrated and irritated that he was going to have to make an effort to keep his distance from her. It was going to be difficult, but it would be better for them both.

On reaching what he considered to be the final decision on the matter, Nick picked up some notes that he had been working on relating to Bravo Recon Section's early morning patrol the following day and, in a few moments, he was deep in his work.

* * * *

Once outside Lieutenant Ryan's tent, Jessie slowed her pace and tried to calm down. She was stunned at what had just transpired. That she had just been on the receiving end of a verbal warning about causing trouble among her new section was something that she had never experienced before, and she seethed with anger and bewilderment.

She knew what Lieutenant Ryan had been insinuating and, while she could perhaps understand his reasoning, she was furious that he had inferred it had been her intention to spend the time during her deployment flirting with the men and causing trouble. Lieutenant Ryan did not know her and he had no right to judge her based on the simple fact that she was a woman.

Jessie made her way disconsolately in the direction of the mess area, feeling a little cheered at the friendly greetings that came her way as she found herself a seat.

After about ten minutes, she grew aware that the men's conversation had become a little wooden and contrived. Her presence in their midst had inhibited the way they had been interacting with each other, and they were attempting to speak politely and struggling to curb their profanities. After hearing their constant slip-ups, the abrupt halting of their conversations and frequent apologies, she suddenly slammed a hand on the table.

"God damn it, you guys! Give it a rest, will you? You are seriously irritating me. Your use of 'fuck' is not going to make me blush or get me to request a transfer out of here. My ears are not going to fall off and neither will I faint. Does that help you out?"

There was a surprised silence. Jessie noticed all of the men staring at her with shocked amusement, then all of them laughed, accepting her comment. For the rest of the time she spent with them, the atmosphere was far more relaxed, and she enjoyed a hot cup of coffee and a mushy but very good bacon sandwich cooked by Dingle. However, by 2100 hours, she was flagging. She was so tired that she could barely keep her eyes open, and eventually she yawned and stood up.

"Sorry, guys," she announced. "I need to get to my pit. I'm absolutely beat. I'll see you at 0500 hours for patrol."

"Need some tucking in?" Shrek asked, Jessie noticing that he winked slyly at Lug Nut. "I'm very good at it. Honest."

She laughed. "No doubt you are, Shrek, but I think I'll pass, thank you. I'm a big girl now. Goodnight, you bunch of morons."

Turning, she left the laughing men and strode off to the medical tent and sleeping quarters. Once inside, she sighed, relieved and happier now that it appeared she was winning over her new section.

Two matters preyed on her mind however — that of Lieutenant Ryan's unreasonable attitude toward her and the fact that she was starting to find him so attractive, even after the barbed comments he had made.

In complete contrast to the attraction was an intense dislike of his arrogance and what she perceived as his self-importance. With these mixed feelings, she was confused at the seesawing of her emotions, hating to admit that he had a smile to die for and his well-spoken voice sent erotic trickles of feeling up and down her spine. His dark gaze, whenever it met hers, made her want to melt.

Jessie couldn't get the thought of Nick Ryan out of her head, and it was beginning to truly annoy her. She needed to get a grip, because she was only in Afghanistan to do a job. She had to forget that he was a very attractive man and focus on the fact that he was her commanding officer and out of bounds. Period.

Another factor and one of primary importance was that she still loved her husband. She had to deal with whatever aberrant feelings she was developing for Lieutenant Ryan quickly and harshly — lock them away somewhere in the back of her mind and forget about them.

After drawing the blinds at the window of her sleeping quarters, Jessie quickly got undressed then into her nightwear. Climbing tiredly into her sleeping bag, she turned off the chemlamp, set the alarm on her wristwatch for 0400 hours then closed her eyes.

With the exception of the murmur of men's voices from some location nearby, a heavy blanket of silence hung over the FOB. She couldn't believe how quiet it was. You could have heard a pin drop. She sent a mental goodnight to her brother, wherever he was, and to her parents, then before many more minutes had passed, she was deeply asleep.

Chapter Six

The alarm on Jessie's watch sounded its muted ring, and she sat bolt upright in bed. It was so dark that she could barely see a hand in front of her face, and the FOB was silent. It was obvious that no one else was up, and it meant that if she showered and dressed quickly enough, she could have her breakfast in peace.

Untangling her legs from her sleeping bag, she swung them over the edge of the bed then stood up. Groping around in the blackness, she eventually found the chemlamp and turned it on.

Dim white light bathed her sleeping quarters, pushing back the shadows and bringing a little warmth to her surroundings. For a brief moment, the warm rays brought on an intense pang of homesickness. However, this was a new day, a fresh start, and she quashed the feeling, determined to make the best of her situation.

As she hunted for her shower kit and towel, Jessie thought back to Lieutenant Ryan's brief but sharp talk with her the previous day. She felt the familiar burn of anger at his unfair accusation and quickly dismissed his memory from her mind. She finally discovered the items she required and, picking up the chemlamp, she hurried through to the shower tent.

She used the toilet, wrinkling her nose at the chemical smell that seeped from it, then she stood the chemlamp on the toilet lid. Hastily taking off her nightwear, she stepped into the shower and turned it on.

She immediately let out a squeal when cold spray drenched her sleep-warm body. In an effort to dodge the chilly droplets, she ducked and dived about the confined space until at last the water began to heat up and eventually became warm enough for her to be able to bathe, albeit vigorously and in a rush.

Once finished, she toweled herself dry, then quickly went back to her quarters, depositing the chemlamp back on the locker. She spent a few minutes drying her hair, plaiting it then looping it and pinning it so it lay flat against her skull—the only style that would enable her to wear her helmet comfortably.

In ten minutes, she was dressed in full combat gear. With her helmet tucked beneath her arm, she picked up her medical pack and weapon, and she was ready to venture outside to find herself some breakfast.

Exiting her tent onto the platform, she glanced about. It was still dark. Dim red lights glowed in each security tower and at the gates, but apart from the two-man security team on duty there, the FOB was deserted and silent. Looking across toward Lieutenant Ryan's tent, she noticed a light from a chemlamp shining inside and saw movement through a crack in the flap. She wondered how long he had been up and hoped that he wouldn't appear to ruin her breakfast.

She continued on her way to the mess area, where a single strip light hung haphazardly from the canopy, shining dimly over an industrial-sized urn. Setting down her pack and weapon, she placed her helmet on a table then went to the container. Discovering it was empty, she noticed an enormous kettle beside it, already full of water, and after finding a plug and socket, she did what was necessary to get it boiling.

Five minutes later, she was reclining on a bench with her back resting against a table, legs stretched out in front of her, eating toast and drinking hot, sweet tea. For the first time in twenty-four hours, she was almost able to relax, and she felt a little less apprehensive about the patrol that morning.

She was nervous about it — she had to be honest with herself — but knew that she was perfectly capable of doing her job, despite Lieutenant Ryan's remarks to the contrary. She had high pass marks from her training to prove it, but now she needed to pull it all together in a combat situation, and that might prove to be a different matter.

Jessie continued to munch on her toast, taking sips of the hot drink and relishing the soft breeze playing with the wispy tendrils of her hair and the moments of peace.

Dawn was breaking and the light was now a deep navy blue. The sun was rising in a golden glow, tendrils of red, orange and yellow flaring across the sky, scattering the trillions of stars into the firmament. The smell of cold, damp sand with a faint underlying odor of oil stung her nostrils. It was so much cooler at this time of the day — the sun still depleted of its power, and the heat that would increase later not yet in evidence.

Jessie glanced at her watch. With thirty minutes to go before the start of the patrol, she closed her eyes, trying to quench the nervous tension building in her stomach.

She heard noises coming from one of the accommodation tents and realized that her peace and tranquility was about to be shattered. Sure enough, Bravo Recon Section came streaming from their tent, jostling and shoving each other like a small herd of young buffalo.

"Morning, you guys," Jessie greeted, opening her eyes and smiling at the line of men as they lumbered toward her.

"Morning, Mac," came a chorus of replies. They threw their equipment haphazardly onto benches and tables as the rabble descended on the kettle to make hot drinks and prepare the breakfast of their choice.

"Please tell me that you lot have taken showers?" Jessie asked, almost certain she knew the answer.

"Showers?" Shrek answered, glancing at her and pretending confusion over the word. He sniffed loudly beneath one armpit. "Oh. You think I need one? Anyway, what the feck is a shower?"

Jessie laughed. "You load of swass and swalls," she exclaimed. "What would your moms say?"

Dingle glanced in her direction. "Okkaaayyy," he said slowly. "Pardon us for being fucking dumb but...swass and swalls?"

Jessie laughed. "Sweaty asses and balls," she replied innocently and drank a mouthful of her tea.

Dingle inclined his head in her direction, as though offering praise at her one-upmanship, then went back to ferociously spooning cereal into his mouth from the bowl he held lopsidedly in his hand.

"You can be mum, Mac," Mungo piped up, his mouth full of toast. "Well, you can be my mum, anyway."

"Fuck, Mungo," Shrek huffed. "You're a bit slow on the uptake, pal. We discussed and closed that subject hours ago."

Jessie laughed out loud, enjoying the teasing and banter. "Very funny, but I don't think so. My MOS does not involve cleaning your asses and most definitely not your balls. What would my parents say?"

"Gosh, really?" Lug Nut interposed. "I am mortified. That is such a rotten shame. Are you absolutely fucking positive that you won't be disobeying an order? You do know that it's a court martial offense for you to refuse to carry out those important responsibilities?"

He glanced sideways at Jessie, who saw the teasing expression on his face. "I really will have to write to the US Marine Corps' top brass to get that clarified. Perhaps I could get your orders changed."

"You're a bloody moon chicken, Lug Nut," Dingle announced, staring at his friend. "I'm getting fucking worried about you, mate."

"Fuck you," Lug Nut responded amiably.

"Ha, funny, ha," Jessie replied. "Try it, Lug Nut. You might find a grenade up your ass the next time you bend over for someone."

Lieutenant Ryan's voice interrupted the outburst of

laughter. "Morning, you lot. You're in full voice this morning. I take it by your boundless energy that everyone is ready for our early morning jaunt?"

"Yup, LT."

"Fucking A, LT."

"Righto, LT."

Jessie tried to keep a straight face as she listened to the chorus of unenthusiastic answers that came from the men who then returned to the task of hastily demolishing their breakfasts.

Quickly turning back to her cooling tea to avoid looking at the Lieutenant, she sipped at it. As he neared them, though, despite her best efforts, she found her eyes drawn to him as if he were a magnet and she iron filings. Her heart began to pound with a nervous, skittish excitement.

Dressed in full combat gear, carrying his pack in one hand and weapon in the other, he moved with a careless grace for such a tall man. There was an alert expression on his face, and he held himself in a relaxed but confident manner.

Jessie knew that these were the traits of a good officer and soldier, and she felt her dislike of him replaced with a warm surge of emotion. Her face flushed with heat as he drew closer but he only glanced at her briefly before turning away without acknowledging her presence.

She felt a bitter disappointment and was surprisingly hurt at his dismissal. She turned quickly back to her drink, still confused as to what she had done to this man to make him dislike her so much. It was obvious that he did not want a woman under his command and this annoyed her. It was virtually unheard of for a commanding officer to have such a discriminatory view of women.

Nick ordered, "All right. Get your battle rattle on and form up."

He thrust his arms through the webbing of his pack before putting on his helmet, and he strode to the center of the FOB. Once there, he folded his arms and waited patiently for the men to put down their drinks and grab their equipment. They jogged to form up in a line facing him, putting helmets on carelessly, some fighting to thrust their arms through bergen webbing and others still munching half-eaten pieces of toast.

Jessie quickly donned her helmet, pounding the top of it to seat it firmly on her head. She thrust her arms through the webbing of her medical pack, made sure the release pins were working on both her body armor and the pack, so that she could drop it all in an emergency, then she picked up her weapon. She followed the men, found her position in line and stood at ease.

Lieutenant Ryan glanced at her and without a trace of a smile on his face said, "You made it then, Mac."

Uncertain as to his meaning, but suspecting that it was some kind of a demeaning comment, Jessie frowned then glared at him, wishing that she could smack his handsome face.

"Yes, Lieutenant, I did," she eventually answered, satisfied when she heard that her voice sounded clipped and cool. "Sorry to disappoint you."

She bit her tongue, instantly regretting the insubordinate response that had involuntarily sprung from her lips. She heard hisses coming from the closest members of her section as they waited for recriminations to come from their commanding officer.

"Fuckin' hell, Mac," whispered Dingle from where he was standing beside her. "Can you get any stupider?"

Nick held Jessie's gaze for a few more seconds, on the verge of giving her a rebuke for her response to him. He then berated himself for antagonizing her and, without making any further comment, he turned and began pacing up and down in front of them.

"You bunch are a load of gagglefucks. What did I do to deserve you lot?" Nick gazed at the section lined up in front of him. "Come on, Bravo Recon. Get your kit on straight, your helmets properly on your heads and...finish your breakfasts on the double."

Shaking his head, he waited until the men had finished getting themselves straightened out, then began his briefing.

"All right, pay attention. In a few minutes, we'll load our weapons and form up at the gates. I know we've already had a mission briefing, but for the benefit of our new medic here, we'll go over it again.

"Our mission objective is to patrol a couple of clicks into the mountains and carry out a recce. An EOD Team cleared out most of the IEDs and mines a short while ago, but insurgents have been in the area recently, so if the *mujis* run true to form, we might come across more of them.

"There will be two primary things you will need to watch out for...snipers and IEDs. You should know this already, but for the benefit of those who have an aptitude for being dipsticks, watch out for disturbed dirt, piles of debris in the middle of our route and wires buried in rubbish and soil. People hanging around, pacing the patrol, acting suspiciously, could be there to set off IEDs by remote control.

"If the route is clear of IEDs, then snipers might be present. You need to keep eyes on at all times, both visual and on your HUDs. If you don't, you could get yourself and the rest of the section killed. Keep focused and concentrate. If you see any movement, any suspicious activity, report it without delay. Do not think that if you are wrong it might make you look like a dick. I'd rather each of you be a live dick then a dead one.

"A Watchkeeper drone has carried out a sweep of the area and data suggests that the route and surrounding location appears to be clean of *mujis*. Don't hold your breath on that, because intel may change. Is everybody absolutely clear on what I've just said? Anyone have any questions?"

Bravo Recon glanced at each other and shook their heads. Nick noticed that most of them looked a little uneasy.

"You *will* all get back here in one piece if you pay attention and *do not* lose focus. Now, load your weapons with one magazine of thirty rounds. Go!"

The section scattered toward a small area of sandbags to the right of the gates, and Nick followed them. He waited a short distance away, observing to make sure that no one made a mistake and blew off their own limbs or somebody else's. He noticed Jessie join them, withdraw a loaded magazine from a pouch on her body armor and skillfully slot it into her rifle. As she and each member completed the task, they hurried to form up once again in a line facing the gates, one behind the other.

Satisfied, he strode past his section and took up position as point man. A gate opened — screeching in protest — just wide enough to allow a single body to pass through and two soldiers darted outside to carry out a security check of the surrounding area.

Having taken part in more missions than he could count, Nick still found himself caught on the hop each time they ventured outside the wire. He could never figure out how the *mujis* could obtain so much intel about both foot and mounted patrols. Even though times, routes and routines varied from mission to mission, dickers still could be seen loitering along planned routes, noting their comings and goings, collating evidence, then relaying it back to their commanders.

Allowing the security team to carry out a swift recon, Nick activated his HUD, erased all other data except for an enhanced green map of the surrounding area, then studied the readout carefully. The central information system programmed into his helmet updated itself at regular intervals with information from Command and the Watchkeeper drones that patrolled overhead. He could now see that the terrain about the FOB had no pulsating red dots, showing the hidden locations of any Taliban.

He still relied on his own physical senses in combination with the HUD and although he couldn't fault the state-of-the-art technology that the British military used, it made him feel acutely uneasy if he failed to use his own eyes and gut instincts when out on any patrol.

Having satisfied himself that Bravo Recon was in the clear for the time being, he shrugged his weapon from his shoulder and stepped outside the gate. Stopping, he automatically directed his gaze toward the landscape ahead of him, his eyes quickly taking in each rocky outcrop and stunted bush where an insurgent might hide.

Once his surveillance was complete, he raised his hand, activated his comms and said, "Shields down. On me. Move!"

Gripping his weapon in his hands, holding it across his chest with one finger resting lightly on the safety catch above the trigger, Nick stepped to one side and watched as Bravo Recon obediently filed past, each member lowering their face shield, scrawls of green imaging immediately dancing over one half as they activated their individual HUDs. He waited for the tail-end Charlie to exit the gates, then hurried to the front of the patrol.

Chapter Seven

Jessie—hands shaking nervously—followed behind Lug Nut. She activated her own HUD, bringing up a map of their route, a green line tracing its way across the small schematic on the left side of her face shield, and she immediately noted that the area appeared clear.

Despite the fear, her military training began to take over. Her eyes automatically began to sweep the landscape in forty-five degree sections and up the mountain slopes to her right, ensuring that she never kept to a set pattern of observation, her body following the direction of her eyes.

The section moved slowly across the landing zone and turned right onto a well-worn stony path. It meandered its way between a crumbling rock wall and debris-filled ditch on the left and thorny scrub bushes on the right. The only sounds were the scrape of boots on the uneven ground, the muted clink of equipment and wind blowing through the dry, brittle branches of the bushes.

Jessie settled into a slow methodical rhythm, her eyes constantly searching the area around her. She concentrated her gaze mainly on the upper slopes of the nearest mountain.

She had never been able to fully rely on the accuracy of her HUD. She preferred to back up computer data with her own observations. Most Homo sapiens had a primal sixth sense that alerted the psyche to danger. Machine or computer could never replace human gut instinct.

There were never any guarantees that the enemy would show up on the digital schematics. For all she knew, the Taliban could have invented something that could successfully blanket their body heat and electronic images, preventing the signals from getting through to the drones, then to individual central information systems.

She was therefore aware that a sniper *could* be hiding among the rocks or vegetation and would have the distinct advantage of being in an elevated position and able to pull an ambush on them before they became aware of it.

As time passed and the patrol progressed, instead of becoming calmer, Jessie found that she was breathing far too fast and she had to force herself to take deep breaths, letting them out slowly.

The morning became warmer, with dust kicked up by their boots and — unfettered by what little dew the night had spawned — rising into the air. Instead of settling back down to the ground quickly as most dust did, it hung in fine, shimmering clouds — living up to its nickname of moon dust — where it clung to combats and exposed skin.

Jessie tried to moisten her lips with her tongue but found her mouth dry. Her eyes, even protected by her face shield, felt gritty and irritated, the arid, hot air leaching the moisture from them. Her pack weighed heavily on her back and sweat trickled down her spine.

As she turned in one of her slow three-hundred and sixty-degree circles, she noticed Shrek behind her.

"How are you doing, Mac?" he asked, his voice sounding inside her helmet.

"It's fucking hot," Jessie complained, hearing a disgruntled tone in her voice. She finished her circle to face front again.

"Tell me about it," Shrek returned.

An hour passed with nothing to disturb the silence until Nick Ryan's voice came over the comms in the helmets.

"All on this net…take five. Get yourselves hydrated."

With some relief, Bravo Recon crouched down at the edge of the path, all raising their face shields and retrieving water bottles to take long drinks of water that had already become warm from the heat of the sun.

Jessie raised her visor and took a mouthful from her own bottle of water. She swished it around her mouth, spat it out then drank her fill. She glanced at Lug Nut, who had turned to glance at her, grinning.

"What?" she asked.

"Very ladylike," he announced.

"*I* never said I was any lady," Jessie rejoined, wiping perspiration from the part of her face not covered by her helmet. She glanced around at their surroundings. "How can I be a lady in this goddamned place?"

"I hear you," Lug Nut responded.

"Okay, on your feet. Let's get going," Lieutenant Ryan ordered. "And please show some enthusiasm. My grandmother has more energy than you lot," he added, as uttering loud grunts and groans, the section stashed their water bottles and clambered to their feet.

The patrol moved off once more and after ten minutes, Nick spoke again. "All on this net… Okay, eyes on, lads," he announced. "We're about to reach a tricky place. The path starts to climb and it narrows. It also bends quite a bit, so the front of the section will not be visible at all times. There's a possibility of trouble. Stay focused and stay *quiet*."

Grasping her weapon tightly, Jessie swallowed. Fear tightened her throat and her hands trembled slightly. Her legs felt like they were made of lead. She hoped that if the time came, she could conduct herself as well, if not better, than expected of her. This first patrol was a chance to prove and establish herself as the section's medic and perhaps to even gain a few smarty points from Lieutenant Ryan.

As the Lieutenant had warned in the briefing, tall, gnarled bushes began to close in on them. The path grew steeper and more twisting and winding. The sun rose higher in the sky and it grew hotter, the dust thicker and more irritating. The higher they climbed, the more twists and turns appeared, and it was becoming more and more difficult to keep the front half of the patrol in sight.

Approaching a particularly sharp bend with the four front members of the section having already disappeared around it, Jessie glanced to her right up the side of the mountain and saw a small, bright flash. Her heart stuttered slightly with surprise and consternation, and she frowned. Holding her breath, she screwed up her eyes, the better to see through the tint of her face shield.

Moving slowly, she watched, unsure of what she had seen, then — as she was about ready to give up hope of confirming the anomaly — the flash came again. Quickly, she brought up the schematic of their route and ran her eyes across the green shimmering outlines. It took only a few seconds before she noticed the single, small red pulsating dot of the enemy in the exact location she had seen the brief flash.

There was someone there who shouldn't be.

Triggering her comms to use on the open network, she said as calmly as she could, "Lieutenant. I see something at two o'clock, one hundred meters up the mountain by the tall lone tree. It looks like sunlight striking off something. Confirmed one — repeat, one — single target on my HUD."

As the other members of Bravo Recon received the transmission, they immediately turned to the right. As they did so, there was the sound of a single gunshot. Terrifying in its suddenness, it reverberated around the mountains, the sound slowly disintegrating and fading into vague echoes.

Jessie immediately dropped to one knee. Various shouts and questions erupted as the section attempted to figure out what was going on and from what direction the shot had come. She turned around and shouted over her shoulder to the kneeling men in the rear, "Is everyone okay?"

When voices answered her in the affirmative, she turned to face front again. She froze with fright when she heard over her comms the words, "Medic. Man down. We need the medic up here!"

For a brief second Jessie hesitated then swore loudly.

Get your ass moving, girl.

Slinging the strap of her weapon over one shoulder, she dropped to her knees and began to crawl forward along the hard ground toward the bend in the path.

"What's the situation?" she asked into her comms, trying to keep her voice steady. Fear bloomed in her stomach at what she might find around the bend.

"LT is hit," was the unexpected response, one that sent Jessie's heart plummeting to join the fear in the depths of her stomach.

"Fuck!" she exclaimed, her voice trembling slightly.

Desperate to get to the injured officer, she crawled faster along the rock-strewn ground, stones and small pebbles digging into her knees and scraping at her fingers. As she moved, she called up her PSMs, scanned through each name until she reached Lieutenant Ryan's and quickly deciphered what she was seeing — rapid pulse, heartbeat and respiration and lowered blood pressure, all symptoms of mild shock.

"I want everyone eyes-on up that slope. Stay alert," she heard JR order, then the scrape of boots on the ground as everyone moved to obey.

Jessie finally rounded the bend in the path and, with a sharp stab of horror, saw Nick Ryan slumped on his side on the ground — the unbelievable sight of his helmet lying beside him — unmoving. JR was crouched beside him, scanning the land, the butt of his weapon balanced on his left thigh.

She scrambled the last few meters in a crouch, pulling her pack's release pins as she went. As it fell to the ground, she dragged it along beside her until she reached the downed man.

"Sir, can you hear me? Can you speak to me?" she asked loudly, shaking Nick's arm gently in an attempt to obtain a response from him.

When he did not respond, she asked again louder, "Lieutenant, can you hear me? You need to say something, even if it's not very nice."

Lifting her visor, she pulled off her combat gloves and dug deep into the pouch on the front of her body armor for her nitrile ones. As she pulled them on, Nick rewarded her by emitting a loud groan and a curse.

"Fuck!" he exclaimed. "I hear you, Mac. I'm not fucking deaf."

Hearing his voice slurred with pain, Jessie tried to keep her voice steady as she replied, "That's good to know, Lieutenant. Now, why don't you explain to me what happened and why your helmet is lying on the ground when it should be safely on your head?" She saw that he was attempting to sit upright and added quickly, "Lie still for me, sir."

Ignoring her, Nick continued to struggle to get himself upright. He failed significantly at the first attempt, then finally succeeded but swayed alarmingly, groaned, then hung his head.

"Stubborn and pig-headed," Jessie murmured beneath her breath, watching him.

"Oh, my fucking head!" Nick moaned.

"What happened, Lieutenant? Do you hurt anywhere else?" Jessie asked. "Did you hit your head when you went down?"

Having asked the questions, she quickly and efficiently carried out a basic body assessment, running her hands up and down his arms and legs in an attempt to find other hidden injuries. She found none.

"Have you any other injuries, sir?" she asked insistently. "I need to know what happened."

"I was idiot enough to remove my helmet, Mac, and I was shot. And no, I don't have any other fucking injuries," Nick answered impatiently. "Does that answer your questions?"

"Yeah, Lieutenant, it does, and, may I say, said with your usual impeccable manners. Can you look at me?" Jessie stated, putting a hand on either side of his face and gently raising his head.

On examination, she saw that he was very pale. Blood covered the right side of his face and dripped steadily down onto his body armor. Catching sight of the wound, she inspected it closely, gently probing its edges. Nick winced at the manipulation but remained silent.

It was obvious that a bullet had grazed him but, even so, Jessie found herself heaving an internal sigh of relief. There was a long, deep furrow across his right temple and it probably hurt like hell, but she knew that at a different angle and an inch lower, it would have gone through his eye and entered his brain, most likely killing him. It was a relief that the *mujis* were notoriously bad shots, but the thought that things could have been so much worse made her feel sick and, for a split second, she struggled to maintain her composure and professionalism as a medic.

"Looks like you ran into a bullet," she said softly. "Bit of a dumb thing taking off your helmet…with all due respect, Lieutenant."

"It looks that way, Mac, and, yes, I have to agree it *was* a dumb fucking thing to remove my helmet. Now, can we *please* skip the preaching part of your treatment and move on?"

In obvious pain, Nick grimaced at her, his dark brown eyes holding hers, the expression in them hard.

Feeling flustered, Jessie asked hastily, "Any other injuries, sir? Did you hit your head when you went down?"

"We've already been through that, Mac," Nick answered, sounding thoroughly disgruntled. "So, for the second and final time, no, I did not hit my head, and I'm fine. Bit of a headache though."

"I'll bet, sir. I need to check your eyes, then I'll see to the wound."

Comparing the size of his pupils, Jessie tried to suppress the traitorous thoughts that were popping into her head as she carried out the examination.

His eyes are so dark they're almost black, and he has the longest lashes… Enough, girl! What in the hell are you thinking? Get a grip. Here I am on a combat patrol in a potentially hostile situation, dealing with this man – my commanding officer even – and all I can think about… Oh no, I'm not going there.

Jessie gave herself a mental shake. Hastily she said, "Your pupils look okay, sir."

Quickly skimming his PMS data, she noted that none of the readouts had deteriorated significantly. "Your PMS says that everything is within normal parameters, so I guess you'll live."

She turned to her pack and quickly removing a packet of sterile swabs, ripped open the sealed wrapping with her teeth, then she said quietly, "Close your eyes for me."

She began to wipe the blood from his right eye, the side of his face and finally the deep furrow on his temple. She did it as gently as she could, but it obviously hurt, as every now and again he uttered a small hissing sound.

"Sorry, sir," she said softly each time he winced.

Irritation evident in his voice Nick snapped, "For God's sake, Mac. Stop saying you're bloody sorry. You're driving me mad."

"Sorry, sir," Jessie said automatically and, again, her voice locked in her throat as his gaze roamed over her face. She felt the color bloom in her cheeks and quickly averted her own gaze and sprayed antibiotic on the wound. She placed a dressing on it, followed by a protective outer one, then sat back on her heels.

"There you go, Lieutenant. How do you feel?"

Putting a gloved hand gently to the dressing, Nick shook his head. "How do you think I feel?" he replied, his tone a little sharp.

"A little grumpy, sir? You probably have a hell of a headache as well, and you might be feeling a little bit green, which is *why* we need to get you back to the FOB."

"No bloody way." Nick raised his head sharply, winced, and closed his eyes briefly. "We'll be finishing this mission if it kills me."

"You might be lucky in that," Jessie replied, removing her bloodstained gloves. "Sir, you can't go on with this patrol in the state you're in. You're bleeding like a stuck pig. You also feel like crap, and you're only going to feel a lot worse unless you rest. The bullet graze won't kill you, but the heat might."

"While I appreciate your concern and will take your eloquent and apt description of my demise under advisement, the answer is still no. I will *not* go back to the FOB without completing this patrol. I'm fine."

Jessie could see that the Lieutenant was glaring at her with a stubborn expression on his face, but she was not about to back down.

"As much as I respect your point of view, Lieutenant, I have to disagree. While you are the officer in command of the section and therefore make the decisions regarding the tactics and safety of its members, I, as medic, make the ones regarding the men's medical safety and I say that we need to get you back to the FOB for further treatment. Don't be obstinate, sir."

With that last remark, she turned to JR, who had maintained his silence throughout the interaction. She raised her eyebrows, seeking his assistance in deciding the matter.

"I make her right on this one, LT," JR said, supporting her. "With you injured, the patrol is one man down anyway."

"That settles it then," Jessie said feeling smug. "Come on, sir. I'll help you up."

Nick continued to glare at her as though he had every intention of arguing until he got his own way, but suddenly he capitulated. He sighed and held out an arm. Straightening to a stoop to avoid becoming a target for the sniper, Jessie grabbed his wrist with both hands and pulled him to his feet, whereupon she had to grab the back of his body armor to stop him from toppling forward.

"Whoa," she said.

She retained her hold on him to keep him steady and was about to retrieve his helmet when Nick suddenly bent over and vomited on the ground. Jessie turned to JR and raised her eyebrows again.

Nick straightened, wiping his mouth. "Sorry about that,"

he said, then turning his head gingerly asked, "Anybody sight that sniper yet?"

"Lieutenant, please let JR do the job of Section Leader that you gave him. I'm sure he's perfectly capable of getting us back to the FOB in one piece and keeping us out of trouble," Jessie announced.

Nick turned to her and said, "You are one bossy and irritating female. Did you know that, Mac?"

"Yeah, I've been told that before. Thanks for confirming it, Lieutenant," Jessie replied. "Are you ready to move out now?"

Nick Ryan nodded, groaned, then retched dryly. "Shit," he moaned miserably.

JR advised the rest of the men of the new objective, then added, "Keep your eyes peeled for that sniper and be extra vigilant. Keep your HUDs online. We don't know how many of them are out there. LT is on his feet but compromised."

Jessie picked up Nick's helmet, nearly forgotten in the turmoil, then handed it to him, saying softly, "Here you go, Lieutenant."

Nick turned and took it from her. "Thanks, Mac," he said in a grim voice before carefully forcing it onto his head, wincing as the front of it pressed down onto the bullet graze.

JR moved to take point as the section turned back along its route to the FOB. Jessie adjusted her pace to that of the Lieutenant, frequently checking his PMS data and watching him keenly for any signs that his condition was deteriorating. Occasionally he staggered slightly but each time she reached out to help him, he straightened, gritted his teeth and kept going.

Jessie found her dislike of the man fading, and this new facet of her attraction for him filled her with a sense of panic. She reminded herself that he was opinionated, conceited and rude. On the other hand, she admired his stamina and his determination. He was certainly a tough man, and she found these additional traits to be just as charismatic.

Chapter Eight

Due to the patrol having to adjust their pace to that of Nick Ryan, the return journey took twice as long. By the time the section reached the base, the temperature had increased dramatically and the men were wilting.

As the welcoming sight of the Hesco walls came into sight, Jessie found herself having to hold the Lieutenant's arm more frequently to guide his footsteps, her concern increasing as he became more and more unsteady on his feet.

The gates of the FOB were open in preparation for their arrival and Bravo Recon filed through. The men groaned with relief and, quickly dropping their packs and releasing their body armor and limb protectors, reached for their water bottles. Ordering them to get food and relax, JR dismissed them before disappearing into the operations tent to debrief the platoon commanding officer on what had happened.

Jessie removed her helmet and started to lead Nick toward the medical tent. He suddenly baulked and dug in his boots.

"Where am I going?" he asked, swaying, his words slurred.

"I'm taking you to the medical tent, Lieutenant. I need to give you further treatment," Jessie answered, sighing. She folded her arms and prepared herself for another battle of wills with the stubborn man.

"No," Nick answered. "You can treat me just as well in my own tent."

"Negative, sir," Jessie answered firmly. "Twenty-four-hour observation for a head wound. Besides, what would the neighbors think, a woman in your tent?"

Nick paused, then uttered a small chuckle of amusement, wincing as he did so. "Okay, you win, Mac, but only because I'm too knackered to fight."

Jessie led him up onto the platform and into the tent. Dumping her medical pack and weapon on the floor, she guided him toward the examination table. While he sat up on it, she hurried to her sleeping quarters, released her protective equipment, threw her helmet onto the bed, and grabbed for her pillow. She went back through to where he was sitting with his head bowed and, placing the pillow at the head of the table, said gently, "Let's get you out of your kit, sir."

Cocking an eyebrow slightly, Nick murmured, "Really, Mac? Now that's an offer I can't refuse, although right at this moment I'll need to take a rain check on it if you don't mind."

Jessie found herself blushing, something she hardly *ever* did. His teasing sent her stomach fluttering with the familiar butterflies, but she smiled reluctantly at his humor in the face of his obvious discomfort. Slipping his weapon from his shoulder, she walked to stand it against a canvas wall then returned to pull the pins of his body armor. Lifting it gently over his head, she dropped everything on the floor.

"I'm going to give you some strong analgesics, sir. They'll make you feel kinda drowsy, so you should sleep. I need to take your vitals every thirty minutes, but I'll try not to disturb you," she said, trying to make her tone sound businesslike.

Without waiting for an answer, she went to the storage unit and withdrew a bottle of pills. Shaking two into the palm of her hand, she poured water into a small plastic cup, then took them back to the pale-faced man.

Handing them to him, she said, "Here you go," then she watched as he threw them into his mouth, following them up with a swallow of water.

Handing the cup back to her, Nick said, "Thanks."

Jessie nodded and said, "Lie down, and I'll get you a blanket."

As Nick lay back on the table and rested his aching head on the pillow, he immediately smelled a faint perfume. Even though it hurt, he turned his head slightly and took a deep breath. His senses swam.

Closing his eyes, he breathed in deeply until distracted by a combat casualty blanket thrown over him. He turned his head back and opened his eyes. He saw her standing over him with a clipboard in her hand, and he raised his eyebrows.

"I need to fill out a medical form," Jessie explained. "Then I'll take some vital signs."

Nick nodded, closing his eyes again. He wanted to sink down into the pillow and immerse himself in the delicate fragrance that was drifting up to surround his head like an invisible cloud.

He felt fingertips on his wrist and flinched as a sensation — like an electric shock — ran up his arm. He felt bereft as the pressure left his skin but relished the feeling when her cool gentle touch returned to the bullet graze on his temple. He opened his eyes again and saw her making notations on a clipboard.

"Will I live?" he asked in a solemn tone.

He saw her glance at him, her eyes wide like those of a rabbit caught in the headlights of a car. She coughed, swallowed and in a voice that sounded slightly husky to him answered, "Well...Lieutenant, your pulse is slightly rapid but the wound has stopped bleeding and looks clean. So, yes, you'll live. Now go to sleep."

Nick closed his eyes obediently, but his thoughts about the woman standing so close to him wouldn't allow him to sleep.

You need to sort this out, Nick Ryan, old chap. Remember regulations and your ethics. Fuck, I feel like I'm fighting a losing battle.

Jessie remained standing by the side of the examination table looking down at the man lying there. It appeared that the medication was working because he seemed relaxed and finally asleep.

She briefly closed her eyes, trying to calm nerves that suddenly felt jittery. Opening them, she found herself studying his face. She eagerly took in the full, sensuous lips and the dark stubble on his firm chin and jaw line. Instead of making him appear untidy, it only served to make him look more attractive. His dark eyebrows were slashes on his pale face and his hair was wavy and swept back from his forehead. One wayward curl had flopped forward to rest like a question mark between his eyebrows. The completely unconventional military style was unruly and sexy, and she felt an irresistible urge to run her hands through it, to feel its springiness and thickness.

Jessie hesitated, wondering if he was actually asleep. Biting her bottom lip, she fought the urge to touch him. She knew that if she did, she would not be able to go back from making that first move.

For what seemed like a long time, she stood motionless, thoughts erratic until the desire proved too strong. Unable to stop herself, she leaned forward and gently brushed the wave of hair off his forehead.

At her touch, Nick's eyes flew open and he stared at her intently, perfectly alert and not asleep as she had thought. Jessie was mortified and her cheeks grew hot with embarrassment. Tongue-tied, she waited for a reprimand, but instead he remained silent, his gaze locking with hers, then his eyelids slowly closed again.

She waited a few minutes, then rested the back of her wrist on his forehead, as if to test for a fever. He did not move at her touch, and she confirmed that this time he was indeed asleep. She checked his pulse again, noted its rate on the medical form and finally allowed the tension to seep from her body. He was stable, his good-looking face pale but peaceful. He was finally out of it.

Focusing fiercely on trivial tasks, Jessie went about replenishing the medical pack and tidying up the tent. She had no intention of dwelling on what she had done. She picked up her combat equipment then went through to her sleeping quarters to stow everything neatly before returning to her patient.

She checked on Nick again, finally realizing—with a sense of defeat—that she had fallen to calling him by his first name. Finding that he hadn't moved, she wandered aimlessly about the tent. Her stomach was clenching nervously with reaction to the events that had taken place on the patrol and with what had happened to the man lying comatose on the table.

Although he was safe and his wound minor, she felt a little unnerved with what had happened to him. She acknowledged that even after such a short space of time, the pain that he had suffered had affected her deeply. The idea that the outcome could have been so horribly different wouldn't bear thinking about.

Out on patrol she had wanted to react to what had happened to him on a purely personal level instead of that of a CTM. It was a situation she had promised herself she would never allow to happen. Yet here she was, struggling to keep the upper hand with common sense and logic but fighting an internal battle against a serious attraction for an officer—her *commanding officer*—and a man she barely knew.

What in the hell am I thinking?

Her musings brought on a flare of panic, and she berated herself silently.

The thoughts persisted however, nagging and taunting her with their persuasiveness. She did not want to feel this attraction for any man, let alone one she barely knew, and she felt an immense guilt and a betrayal of Mark and his memory.

There came a slap on the outside of the tent and she raised her head, startled. The flap and mesh net were pulled back to reveal the austere face of Major Hayward, the platoon commanding officer. As he strode into the medical tent, Jessie came to attention.

"Stand easy, Corporal," he announced and joined her at the examination table. He studied the comatose form of his lieutenant.

"How is Lieutenant Ryan?" he asked.

Relaxing slightly, Jessie swallowed. "He's stable, sir. His head wound is relatively minor and all his vital signs are normal. I've given him some strong analgesic, and he should be on his feet in about twelve hours."

Major Hayward nodded. "Will he be fit for patrol tomorrow night?" he asked.

"Yes, sir. I would think so, barring any complications, of course."

"Very well, Corporal. Carry on...and good job."

With that, the major turned on his heel and left, the flap falling with a crackling sound behind him.

Realizing that she had been holding her breath, Jessie let it out and sagged against the examination table. Glancing down at Nick, she straightened the casualty blanket, checked his pulse, then glanced up again as there was another slap from outside and Dingle revealed himself in the opening.

Smiling at him, Jessie put a finger to her lips and said softly, "Come in."

Dingle entered, grinned briefly at her, then looked down at the sleeping officer. "Me and the lads were wondering what the verdict is on LT?" he asked.

"He's going to be fine," Jessie replied reassuringly. "All he needs is a bit of rest, and he'll be back on his feet in no time."

"Fucking ace," Dingle responded. "The lads will be chuffed. He's a good bloke is LT, one of the best."

"Is everyone else okay?" Jessie asked. "No side effects

from the patrol?"

"Nah, they're all tough fuckers," Dingle answered. "Hopefully I'll be out with their sorry asses on tomorrow's patrol. Listen, I wondered if you wanted some scran and a drink. I know you can't leave here because you have to keep an eyeball on the lieutenant. I can bring you something."

Jessie glanced at the young soldier and offered him a smile. She saw a blush suffuse his face and she tried not to laugh.

"That would be great, Dingle. Thanks. Can you also find me a chair so I can sit down in here?"

Dingle nodded. "I'll be back in five," he said and left, leaving Jessie alone once again.

He returned about ten minutes later, holding a plate of fried sausages, baked beans and toast, with a plastic cup of coffee balanced precariously on the side. He also carried a folded camping chair.

Smelling the hot food, Jessie felt her mouth water. She hadn't realized how hungry she was.

After handing her the plate, Dingle set up the chair beside the examination table then, as a parting remark before he left again, said, "If you need anything else, just shout out."

"Thanks, Dingle, I'll do that," Jessie said sincerely and sat down on the chair to eat.

The hours passed slowly as she kept watch over Nick. He remained in so deep a sleep that he appeared unconscious and didn't move as she religiously took his vital signs and noted them on the medical form.

By 2100 hours, it had begun to get dark inside the tent. Not wanting to disturb his sleep by turning on the strip lighting, Jessie left him alone to go and collect the chemlamp from her sleeping quarters. Bringing it back, she plugged it into a socket and turned it on.

Dingle and Shrek arrived with another drink for her, stayed for a few minutes, then left. She could hear their voices and the others of Bravo Recon outside as they talked and laughed, their banter sounding unusually subdued.

Seated in the camp chair, Jessie eventually dozed. It had been a long day and she was tired, but she had only been asleep for a short time when she was startled awake by movement on the examination table. She was on her feet in an instant, leaning over Nick to find that his eyes were open.

"Hey, Lieutenant," she said softly and the brown gaze fell on her face when he offered her a small smile. "Do you feel like sitting up?"

Nick licked his lips as though they were dry and he nodded.

"You've been lying down for a long time, so you might be a bit dizzy when you first sit up. I'll help you," Jessie said.

Putting a hand on the back of his neck and holding on to his right arm, she gently raised him until he was sitting upright, supporting him when he swayed.

"How do you feel?" she asked, watching him closely.

Nick rubbed his face, then studied Jessie. "A lot better but thirsty," he replied, his voice sounding a little hoarse.

Smiling at him, Jessie said, "No problem. I'll get you a drink of water, then I'll need to check you over again and put a clean dressing on that wound. I can then sign you off. After that, you'll be pleased to know you'll be free to go."

Leaving him where he was, she poured water into a small plastic cup, handed it to him, then fetched dressings and a blood pressure cuff and began to carry out her final checks.

As she rolled up the sleeve of his T-shirt, Jessie glanced at him and saw that he was staring at her intently. "Lieutenant?" she questioned quietly, then cleared her throat nervously when he shook his head.

Trying to concentrate on what she was doing, she read the result from the blood pressure cuff with rather more concentration than was needed, checked his pulse and the reaction of his pupils. She changed the dressing on the wound, completed the medical form, then said, "Right, sir. You're on the mend and free to go. If you get any more headaches or the wound becomes infected, come back to me."

Nick nodded and swung his legs over the side of the table. Silently, he stood up, paused, gripped the edge of the table as though unsteady, then moved away from her to collect his equipment. At the tent entrance, he turned to her.

"Thanks for everything, Mac." There was a small, gentle smile on his face and his eyes were warm.

"You're welcome, Lieutenant," Jessie answered, then he was gone.

She remained staring at the tent flap and uttered a small moan. Her gaze drifted down to the rumpled blanket and torn white paper. Nick Ryan was a dangerous man and way out of her league. She needed to quash the stealthy, wayward feelings that were about to cause untold mischief in her life and which were lodging in a tenacious, relentless way in her heart.

She absentmindedly folded the casualty blanket, put it away, then tore off a fresh strip of white paper to cover the examination table, throwing the used piece away. For the next few minutes, she cleared up the supplies she had used, then stretched and yawned. She was shattered. She needed a shower then bed, in that order. Picking up the chemlamp, she wandered into her sleeping quarters, collected her wash kit, then went into the shower tent.

She took a long, hot shower, washing her hair slowly and thoroughly, feeling herself relax slightly, although her mind remained sluggish with fatigue. Once finished, she dressed in her nightwear then went back to her cot. Lying down on it and pulling the sleeping bag over her, she tried to relax, one arm beneath her head, her mind full of the events of the day.

She remembered how she had felt when she had heard that Nick was hurt and her reaction on seeing him lying on the ground. Her feelings for him were far from professional. Her emotions were pushing and pulling her in different directions and, for the first time in her life, she found herself dwelling obsessively on a man to the detriment of everything else.

She mused on what it would feel like to have his arms around her and have him kiss her. She wondered if he might reciprocate her feelings and the thought sent a thrill of excitement shooting through her. She quickly dismissed the thought.

Why would he feel anything for the likes of me? He probably has a girlfriend or a wife stashed away somewhere.

This thought acted like a dousing of ice-cold water and caused a sharp pang of jealousy in the pit of her stomach.

Balling her fists, Jessie covered her eyes with them as though blocking her vision would erase the unsettling thoughts of Nick from her mind.

She had no idea how to deal with the storm of emotions that seemed to have appeared so quickly and in so short a time. She still remained tied to Mark – had not yet recovered from his death, or so she believed – so having feelings for another man triggered remorse and guilt, which in turn, would not allow her to contemplate having a relationship with anyone else.

Jessie flung herself over onto her side, the cot creaking beneath her weight, and closed her eyes. She was determined to banish all thoughts of Lieutenant Nick Ryan from her mind. She would avoid being alone with him, stay out of his way and talk to him only when necessary.

Satisfied with the weak plan that seemed to offer her a way out of the dilemma that she was plunging into, she managed to drift off to sleep, her last thought being that dismissing her feelings for Nick Ryan was going to prove far more difficult than she anticipated.

* * * *

In his tent, Nick lay fully clothed on his cot, one hand behind his head, legs crossed at the ankles, staring up at the ceiling. The wound on his head ached, and he felt sick and groggy from the painkillers but markedly better than earlier that day.

There was something else bothering him. It was like an itch that he couldn't quite reach to scratch. It needled and irritated him, always there, manifesting itself in a feeling of restiveness and edginess. What ailed him was not as easily treatable as his physical wound had been.

He stared pensively at the white ceiling of his tent. Even with his eyes open, the image uppermost in his mind was that of Jessie McAllister. He remembered the way she had looked at him from under her lashes, the smile that lit up her eyes and her gentle voice as she was treating him earlier that day. He could still feel her soft touch when she had thought him asleep and had brushed the hair off his face.

Nick closed his eyes and felt an ache coiling in his groin. He couldn't remember the last time a woman had turned him on so much and he stirred, feeling uncomfortable.

He wanted to take her in his arms and kiss her until she begged for more. He longed to make her respond to him until he had her moaning with wanting him as he wanted her. He wanted to make love to her, show her the feelings he had for her, but they were on an FOB with no privacy and no time for talking at length about anything of a personal nature.

In agitation, Nick ran a hand through his thick hair, flinching as he accidentally nudged the wound on his temple.

"Fuck!" he exclaimed, partly from frustration at his thoughts and from the stabbing pain that shot through his head.

He sighed and turned on his side, punching his pillow almost angrily.

I've got to nip this whole thing in the bud. I cannot allow my feelings for this woman to get in the way of what I am out here to do, no matter what I feel for her.

Restless, Nick tried to quell his errant feelings and push the thoughts of Jessie from his mind. He needed to sleep but tossed and turned for what seemed a long time, before, exhausted and head aching, he finally drifted off.

Chapter Nine

Nick came out of his tent and saw Jessie. He stopped and folded his arms, watching her worshipping the sun, gorgeous hair cascading around her shoulders, long, tan legs stretched out in front of her, and he couldn't stop the smile from forming on his lips.

During the early hours of that morning, he had finally admitted to himself that he had fallen very heavily for Bravo Recon's medic. It went against everything he believed in where the army was concerned. However, although he had used military protocol in an attempt to find a way out of the emotional tangle he was sinking into, it seemed weak and nonsensical compared to the depth of his feelings for Jessie McAllister. He was on the brink of losing his own personal war with himself.

He glanced at his watch and knew that he needed to get going. He glanced once more in Jessie's direction and hesitated. He was torn. Should he ignore her, try to pretend that she was just another member of his section? Alternatively, should he go and join her for a few minutes, get talking to her, learn something about her? He fought with the urge to deviate from his strict morning routine, then, at last, shaking his head, he went slowly toward her.

Although she had only been on the FOB for a couple of days, Jessie had begun to enjoy the early hours of the morning with the sun just rising, the peace and quiet and the air cool with the newborn day, lacking the searing heat that would come later.

Seated at one of the mess tables, she bit into her usual

slice of toast before taking a large gulp of strong tea from her thermo cup, relishing its heavily sugared taste. She was much happier than she had been. Her section was well on their way to accepting her and it appeared that she had proved herself out on patrol as a medic.

The only thing that kept disturbing her peace of mind was Lieutenant Nick Ryan. She had not slept well the previous night, one of the reasons she was up so early. After tossing and turning and much soul searching, she had promised herself that she would try to avoid him as much as possible, treat him only as her commanding officer, focusing solely on her role as a CTM.

Feeling that she had satisfactorily put the matter of Nick Ryan safely away, Jessie continued to munch on her toast, enjoying the warmth from the rising sun on her bare arms and legs.

Keeping her face raised to the sun, loving its warmth on her skin, she sighed inwardly as the bench vibrated. Someone had sat down beside her and, expecting it to be one of Bravo Recon, she said teasingly, "Morning, asswipe."

She jumped out of her skin when unexpectedly the voice of Nick Ryan, amusement evident in his tone, replied, "Morning, Mac."

Eyes wide, Jessie jumped to her feet, spinning around to face the officer. Nick was leaning forward, hands between his legs, gazing up at her, an amused expression on his face.

"Shit!" she exclaimed. Her face burned, and she wished the ground would open up and swallow her. She squirmed with embarrassment, wanting to run for the privacy of her tent. "Sorry, Lieutenant."

"Sorry for scaring you, Mac," Nick said quietly. "I didn't think you scared so easily."

Jessie saw that he was smiling at her. That slow grin was enough to make her legs feel weak. Feeling like a complete fool, nerves frazzled and keeping distance between them, she sat back down on the bench.

"I don't scare easily, sir," she replied at last, her voice

husky. "You just crept up on me, is all." A small silence hung between them, then she asked politely and a little coolly, "How's your head, Lieutenant?"

Nick glanced down at his hands, frowning. "It's fine, Mac, and thanks again for your timely treatment. I guess I would be feeling a lot worse if it weren't for you."

"Glad to hear it," Jessie responded, "but I was just doing my job, Lieutenant. That's what I'm here to do. You'll have to come and see me later, so I can check the wound."

"All right, I'll do that. There'll be an AA security force coming in later this morning. They'll be joining us on future patrols and there'll be a briefing, so I'm not sure what time I'll check in."

Jessie glanced at him and noticed that he still looked pale, and blood stained the dressing on his forehead. Her persistent wayward thoughts turned to how dark his eyes and hair were in contrast to the pallor of his skin. Realizing that she was staring, she dragged her eyes away, glancing down at her hands, which she was twisting together nervously.

"AA, sir?" she asked, in a pathetic attempt to distract her thoughts from the animal charisma of the man.

"Afghanistan National Army," Nick replied at last. "We often get a small contingent of AA in to lend a hand with translation, to use as extra firepower and liaison with the locals. We're going out on a night patrol tonight, so their presence will be beneficial."

"Can they be trusted?" Jessie asked, still not looking at him. "I mean…security-wise?"

"Yes, they can be trusted," he answered. "Why wouldn't they be? They're vetted the same way for recruitment into their army as we are for ours, particularly as they're a security force, the same as we are."

"Well, I guess we'll know for sure once they're on the FOB, won't we?" Jessie retaliated, her voice a little chilly.

"Is everything all right?" Nick asked.

Jessie glanced at him at last. "Why shouldn't it be?" she

asked defensively. She was aware of Nick staring at her, a frown marring his face. His eyes looked a little hard. Jessie avoided his gaze and stood up. "Someone I…knew was shot and killed by an insurgent posing as AA. The…man managed to infiltrate an FOB. Well, the rest is history," she explained coldly.

"I'm sorry to hear that, Mac," she heard Nick say in a soft voice.

"Yeah, well, like I said, it's history. Do you want a hot drink, sir?" she asked, changing the subject. "The rabble will be awake in a minute, and you won't be able to move for the crush."

"Coffee would be great."

As Jessie boiled the enormous kettle and set out two plastic cups, chemlamps began to come on in the accommodation tents and the first unruly noises from her section began to break apart the early morning silence. As she finished making a coffee and her own tea then carried it to where Nick sat, Dingle and his entourage burst out of their tent and came toward them.

"Morning, rugrats," she called out, forcing a lightness into her voice that she didn't remotely feel. "I see you've surfaced at last."

"Morning, Mac, LT," the men chorused, and Mungo said, in response to Jessie's taunt, "Rugrats? I can't speak for my comrades, but I am deeply hurt."

"Oh, right," said Jessie, trying to smile. "Well, my apologies to your hurt feelings."

She noticed Shrek glance at her, then at Lug Nut, raising a bushy eyebrow. She realized that the man had taken note of the forced humor in her tone.

Nick also glanced at Jessie as he stood up.

"I'm off," he announced. "Work to do before our patrol tonight. PT at 0900 hours," and as this was greeted with low groans, he laughed. "'Nuff said. Form up out here. Rehydrate and don't stuff your faces."

From out of the corner of her eye, Jessie watched him

stride away. Sighing, she finished her tea, then rose to her feet.

"See you later, guys," she said. "I've got some stuff to do."

Lifting a hand in a wave, she strode off back to the medical tent, determined to stay inside until the PT session. She had a quick shower, washed her hair and plaited it, then went in search of her trainers, setting them ready for the planned run.

It was only 0730 hours when she finished, so after making her bed, she put on her iPod headphones and lay down. She intended to spend the next hour and a half listening to music and trying to relax. Tapping a foot to the heavy beat, she closed her eyes.

She was almost dozing when a voice said, "Mac?"

Jerking upright with the cable from her earphones becoming tangled around her arm and almost falling off the bed as she got to her feet, Jessie spun around to see Nick Ryan holding back the net at the entrance to her accommodation and watching her.

Wrenching off her earphones she said breathlessly, "Sir? Is there anything wrong?"

"There's nothing's wrong, Mac. I came for my check-up. That's all. I'm going to be busy for the rest of the day, so thought I'd better come by now."

Jessie flung her iPod onto her bed and approached him. "Okay. Let's get you sitting up on the examination table."

As she neared him, she stopped. He was standing in her way, and she couldn't get by him without brushing up against him or, alternatively, him moving out of her way. At present, he looked like he wasn't budging.

She noticed the expression in his eyes and warmth flooded her body. She felt both exhilarated and frightened at what his gaze was telling her.

Swallowing, she asked quietly, "Can I get by, sir?" She gestured at her tent entrance and he seemed to jerk back to the present, nodded then stepped back hastily.

Sidling past him, reluctant to have his body touch hers,

Jessie moved into the medical tent and to the supply table, as far away from him as possible.

Nick hoisted himself up onto the examination table, and she retrieved the clipboard, then went to stand in front of him. Placing it on the table, she said, "How're things, Lieutenant? Do you have any pain in the wound or a fever? Any other aches and pains that I should know about?"

Nick shook his head. "Negative. All good," he answered, his tone sounding casual.

Jessie made a note on the medical form. "That's great. I'm going to check you over and take the same vitals as yesterday. Then I'll re-dress your wound."

She hesitated, trying to control her churning inner emotions. Hoping and praying that her hands wouldn't tremble when she touched him, she checked his pupils. Next, she held his wrist between her fingers to take note of his pulse rate, then catalog the information on the form. Finally, she glanced at him and smiled slightly.

"Well, you're still alive and obviously kicking, Lieutenant. It's all looking good. Do you have any headache?"

"I'm glad to hear that, Mac," Nick answered quietly. "And no, there's no headache."

Jessie moved away to collect dressings for the wound. After laying them out on the table, she pulled on a pair of gloves then turned to him. Tilting his head back slightly, she gently pulled off the used dressing and, once it was removed, studied the long, livid furrow. It was clean with no sign of infection, and she smiled slightly in satisfaction.

"All looking good, sir," she announced.

She saw that he was watching her, and she had to suppress a shiver. For a second she forgot what she was doing. She released his head quickly, then disposed of the used dressing in the waste receptacle before she began to tear open a new one. She sprayed on more antibiotic then placed the fresh covering on his forehead. As she leaned forward, she felt the front of her thighs press against his knees.

She froze and before she could back away, felt his knees part and found herself standing within the space left by their separation.

Nick suddenly placed his hands on her hips and gently pulled her toward him.

"Lieutenant!" Jessie uttered a protest but her voice was nothing but a whisper, holding no admonishment or refusal.

His face was on the same level as hers and her voice locked in her throat as she watched his eyes roam her face. His gaze came to rest on her mouth and slowly his own moved closer. She closed her eyes, her body quivering as she waited with anticipation for his kiss. At last, his lips touched hers delicately.

They were firm and warm and Jessie sank into him, reveling in the intense sensations that the kiss was arousing in her body. Her own response was such that she could not withdraw it and no longer wanted to. She could feel his body move against hers and her hips involuntarily pressed into his groin, a tight knot of heat forming in the deepest regions of her abdomen.

She felt as if she were drowning in the tenderness of the moment. His mouth was hot against her own and the muscles of his thighs tightened as they straddled hers. He raised a hand and gently cupped the back of her head. With slight pressure, he brought it forward so that his mouth was firmer on hers.

Moving to the edge of the table, he pulled her forward, so that her lower body pressed firmly against his. She could feel his hardness against her stomach as he moved and her breathing quickened with the images it conjured in her mind.

She wanted him more than she had ever wanted a man before and she had to control herself not to kiss him harder and more passionately.

She suddenly wanted more, much more.

Jessie ran one hand up the back of his neck and gently ran

her fingers through his hair, feeling him shiver at her touch. She applied more pressure and their kiss became harder and deeper. She moved as close to him as she could and he moved his hand around to the center of her back.

Jessie uttered a small, sensual moan. She put both arms up around his neck then an image of Mark popped into her mind. Guilt immediately surged through her.

Chapter Ten

What in the hell am I doing?

She stepped back from between Nick's knees, her face burning, heart beating painfully hard in her chest.

"Jessie?" Nick questioned, his voice sounding hoarse and unsteady.

Grabbing blindly for the clipboard with the lieutenant's medical form attached to it, Jessie snapped in a strangled voice, "You're fine, sir. You can go."

Nick frowned. "What happened?" he asked, sounding annoyed. "What's wrong?"

Jessie felt her eyes fill with tears. Feeling overwhelmed by guilt, her emotions in turmoil, she forced a sarcastic and angry note into her voice to disguise how she really felt and how the last few moments had disturbed her, and she said, "What? Did you think we were just going to make out in the medical tent?"

"What the fuck?" Nick glared at her and Jessie saw that the color of his eyes had become darker. She had heard him swear before but never in the tone of voice that he had just used.

"Just go," she whispered, her voice shaking. "Please."

Still glaring at her, Nick jumped down from the examination table. Without a word, he strode to the entrance and, flinging aside the mesh netting and flap, he stormed out.

At his exit, Jessie slumped against the table, bending her head and closing her eyes. A small dry sob escaped her.

Shit! Shit! Why did I say that to him? He didn't deserve that. You are such a bitch, Jessie McAllister.

She winced, realizing at last why she had not held back when responding to the kiss. She could not possibly go on denying the feelings she had for Nick Ryan.

Jessie suddenly remembered the PT session and glanced at her watch. It was 0845 hours and no matter how bad she felt, she could not waste any further time mulling over what had just happened. She needed to report with the rest of the section. She quickly cleared up the discarded dressing wrappings, throwing them into the waste receptacle, and she straightened the paper covering. Going through to her sleeping quarters, she sat down on the bed to lace her feet into her training shoes, finally standing up then reluctantly leaving the tent.

Once outside, she found herself glancing around for sight of Nick but she didn't see him. Bravo Recon was on their way to line up, mock wrestling and, as usual, acting like fools, but she couldn't muster a smile in response to their antics.

As they formed up in a line—Jessie taking her place among them—Nick came out of his tent. She glanced at him from beneath her eyelashes when he came to stand in front of them to see whether he was still as angry as he had appeared to be when he had stormed from the medical tent. Her heart sank when she saw his thunderous expression, eyebrows drawn down, hands on hips, and when Shrek and Mungo continued to fool around, he yelled, "Shut up, the lot of you, and stand easy."

There was an abrupt silence, the men darting puzzled glances at each other at their commanding officer's apparent bad temper. Complete silence followed, and the section focused their attention on him, waiting for him to speak again. Nick glanced at Jessie briefly, then his gaze slid away, dismissing her.

"All right, six circuits of the compound. Get going," he ordered, and the men and Jessie turned to the left and in single file began to jog around the perimeter of the FOB. "And let's see some life in you. You're not dead yet," was his parting shot.

Lug Nut ran up beside her. "LT seems pretty pissed off today," he remarked. "That's not like him."

Jessie, keeping her pace even, shrugged and answered a little shortly, "Maybe his head is hurting him," then concentrated on her running.

The run seemed to go on forever and her legs became heavier, the heat intolerable. Dust inside the FOB began to choke them but Nick, jogging alongside them, ignored their groans, berating them when their pace faltered or they coughed and choked.

Trying to keep her breathing even, Jessie concluded that he was making Bravo Recon and herself pay for what had occurred between them in the medical tent. She wondered whether he was a man who did not like rejection. If that was the case, then he was just going to have to deal with it.

The run finally came to an end and she and the men staggered to a halt, panting and gasping for air.

Breathing easily, Nick snapped, "Oh, come on. You'd think I'd run you around there in full battle rattle. Get yourself showered, hydrate, then get some downtime. Mission briefing is at 2200 hours tonight, patrol at 2300 hours." With that, he strode away from them into his tent.

"Well, that was fun, I don't fucking think," Mungo said to Jessie, his voice hinting that it was anything but. "Fucking chickenshit Rupert!" He swiped sweat from his face, spat on the ground, then walked away to the accommodation tent.

Bending over with his hands on his knees, sweat soaking his hair, Wolf announced, "Well, I guess LT got out of the wrong side of his pit this morning."

Grunting his agreement, Shrek straightened and said, "I'm going to hit the shower and then I'm hitting *my* pit."

One by one, Bravo Recon staggered to their tent and disappeared inside. Wiping the sweat from her face, Jessie went to her sleeping quarters where she sank onto the bed and buried her head in her hands. She sat there for long minutes—her mind mercifully blank—worn out with exercise. Then, groaning, she rose and went to have a shower.

Dressing herself in shorts and a T-shirt then tying her thick hair high up on her head in a ponytail, she decided to write some letters to her parents and brother and she spent the next hour doing so. It was as she was sealing the last letter that she heard the sound of a helicopter approaching and remembered that the AA were coming to join them.

Deciding that its arrival provided a perfect opportunity to hand over her post, Jessie changed from her shorts into combat trousers then went outside.

The sound of the helicopter grew louder, and she turned and watched it come in to land beyond the FOB walls. As it did so, Nick came out of his tent and, without glancing about him, strode to the gates, signaling for the guards to open them.

Jessie watched as he stood by the open gate with his arms folded. She found herself admiring the way he stood, casual but alert. She remembered the kiss that had occurred between them and felt her lips tingle where Nick's mouth had been against hers.

Continuing to watch him, she eventually saw four members of the AA enter, accompanied by the co-pilot of the helicopter. Nick shook hands with them all, then the group began to head away from the gates to the operations tent. The co-pilot deposited a mail sack inside the gates, then waited his usual ten minutes for any outgoing items.

Jessie kept her eyes on Nick and the AA as they walked by her. One of the Afghans noticed her and turned his head to stare in her direction. She saw that he was a tall, handsome man with a swarthy complexion, black hair and dark eyes.

She held his gaze as he strode past and was startled to see a look of contempt and disgust cross his face. She stepped back as though he had verbally threatened her, but the moment passed as they walked on, Nick showing them into the operations tent.

Shrugging off the incident, Jessie clutched her envelopes and walked slowly toward the gates. She handed her post to the co-pilot and, with time heavy on her hands, made her way back.

Running into Dingle, Jessie took him back to the medical tent to check the wound on his foot. She found the gash healing nicely with no sign of infection, re-dressed it with a simple protective dressing and was happy to advise him that he was fit to resume his duties.

"I suggest you go see the Lieutenant and let him know you're okay to play with the big guys," Jessie told him teasingly.

"Great, Mac. Thanks," Dingle said, sounding relieved. "Looks like I don't have to be a fobbit anymore."

"Fobbit?" She raised a hand as Dingle opened his mouth, looking as though he was going to launch into an explanation. "I'll pass on its meaning. Thank me after patrol," she responded. "Now get lost."

She spent the next few hours carrying out an inventory of medical supplies and writing up a request for items that she needed from Camp Bastion. She joined the rest of the section for chow, knowing that it would raise her spirits to hear their somewhat childish banter and watch them playing the fool.

It was while she was sitting on a bench in the mess area, drinking from a cold bottle of water and feeling hot and uncomfortable, that she noticed a slight change in the weather.

It had become sultry and humid and when she glanced up at the sky, its normal pale blue color was gray with overcast, the sun a hazy orb. Jessie didn't like what she saw and hoped fervently that the weather wasn't going to deteriorate for the patrol that night. It would cause no end of problems if it rained. HUDs were notorious for malfunctioning in bad atmospherics, visibility would be considerably reduced and getting combats and boots soaked and having to wear them for any length of time would make life extremely uncomfortable.

As the day wore on, the temperature rose and a canopy of ominous, charcoal-colored cloud began to build up, pressing lower and lower to the ground, the air turning oppressive and stifling.

At 1600 hours, bored and filled with a nervous tension, Jessie decided that a little music might help her relax. Placing her iPod into the speakers and plugging it in, she turned it on and flung herself on her bed.

Within minutes, Dingle appeared, thrusting his head through the netting of her sleeping quarters and Jessie sighed, resigned to the fact that her peace and quiet was about to be disturbed.

"Is that music I hear?" he asked in a cheerful voice.

Remaining where she was on the bed, Jessie gave him a small smile, "I don't know, is it?" she replied.

"Well, don't be selfish and keep it to yourself, girl. Bring it outside and we can all listen to it. Maybe we can have a dance—a lark. You and I cutting the rug, so to speak."

"Really?" Jessie exclaimed. "At 1600 hours on a scorching afternoon? You've got your head up your ass."

"Oh, come on, Mac. We all need some fun now and again," Dingle pleaded, his voice taking on a wheedling tone. "It's like watching paint dry out here."

Jessie hesitated, reluctant to leave the relatively cool confines of her tent. She gazed at the child-like expectancy on Dingle's face and eventually shrugged. Huffing in mock irritation, she got up from the bed, turned off the iPod and followed the man outside, carrying the machine and its speakers.

As she approached them, she saw Bravo Recon languishing apathetically on benches in the mess area, could hear them bitching about the heat and the patrol that night. They looked up half-heartedly as she plugged in the iPod, but when the music blared out, they cheered loudly.

"*All right*," JR said, bringing the flat of his hand down on a table. "That's more like it."

He immediately grabbed Jessie's hand and dragged her away from the tables, starting to dance when they reached an open space. Feeling like an idiot, she tried to pull back in an effort to return to her seat but JR was having none of it. Keeping hold of her hand, he made her twist and turn and finally, laughing, she obligingly followed his moves.

Other members of the section jumped to their feet and joined in, laughing with high spirits and cavorting around like a bunch of monkeys.

Jessie loved dancing and her restlessness and wayward feelings acted like a catalyst. Forgetting for the moment where she was and her issues with Nick Ryan, she danced with enthusiasm, her ponytail bouncing as though it had a life of its own.

At one point, while dancing, she turned and happened to glance over toward Nick's tent to see him standing watching her. In the next second however, he had turned away to go back inside and suddenly her enthusiasm drained away and her energy flagged with it.

So, that was it.

Somehow, their kiss had served to drive a wedge between them. Her rejection of him—not for lack of any feelings on her part but through guilt and betrayal of her husband—appeared to have destroyed the fragile beginnings of what could have been something new and exciting for them both.

It was her fault, without a doubt. Nick was unaware of Mark and, therefore, must be feeling confused and let down by first her response to his kiss, then a withdrawal. It would be better for them both if she just tried to forget about what had happened and concentrated on getting through her deployment.

She continued to dance for a while longer but as early evening wore on, the temperature continued to increase, the clouds becoming more threatening. It became so dark—the natural light sucked from the world by the onrush of the leaden sky—that chemlamps and strip lighting started to come on inside the tents. There was a strange feeling in the air, as though static electricity had charged the very atmosphere and caused the hairs on Jessie's arms to feel as if they were standing on end.

Sapped of their energy, she and the men began to flag and, one by one, Jessie and Bravo Recon collapsed onto benches, wiping their faces and drinking water thirstily. As they conversed quietly, their voices sounding muffled and without any strength, a faint rumbling came from the direction of the mountains. They all fell silent.

"What the fuck?" Yeti exclaimed, cocking his head to one side.

Another rumble came again—not loud, ears had to strain to hear it—but a prolonged one, and Shrek and Mungo hurriedly got to their feet, instantly alert.

"It's all right, lads," Nick said, exiting his tent and striding toward them. "There's a heavy storm on the way. That's thunder you hear."

"Oh, fucking ace. Situation normal, lads, all fucked up," responded Lug Nut. "We get to go on patrol in the dark and in a fucking storm. I can't wait."

Reaching the group, Nick stopped and smiled at Lug Nut's remark. "Can't hack it, Lug Nut?" he asked.

Jessie thought that he appeared to be in a better frame of mind than earlier but noticed that he did not glance in her direction.

"I didn't say that, LT," Lug Nut answered. "I'm only too happy to put myself in the line of fire, either from the *mujis* or a bleedin' bolt of lightning. Count me in."

Rolling a water bottle between her hands, Jessie glanced at the Lieutenant, but seeing that he was grinning at Lug Nut's remark, she quickly stood up.

"Okay, guys, I'm off to catch a nap. Don't go without me," she said, offering them a small smile.

"We wouldn't dream of letting you miss out on the most exciting event of our day," Mungo said in a teasing voice. "You're going to love it, Mac."

Jessie lifted a hand in a brief farewell and made her way

to her tent.

Back in her quarters, she sat down on the bed and put her head in her hands. Now and again, she could hear a faint rumble of thunder in the distance – like some behemoth turning over in its slumber – and it filled her with fear.

She detested thunderstorms, had ever since she and Jake had been caught outside in one when they were children. As soon as thunder and lightning preceded a storm, she would lock herself in her room, turn on all the lights then draw the curtains, huddling on the bed until it passed.

She never dreamed that she would find herself in the position of having to go out in one. She hoped fervently that her courage would hold out and she would not end up squealing and flinching at every flash of lightning and crack of thunder, humiliating herself.

Lying back on the bed, she inserted the headphones of her iPod in her ears and turned on the music, blocking out all other noise except for the thundering beat.

* * * *

In conversation with Dingle – from out of the corner of his eye – Nick had watched her leave. She hadn't acknowledged his presence, had not even stayed to participate in the conversation, and he felt angry at her attitude. She had been giving him all the signals, so how was he the one in the wrong? Annoyed with her as well as himself, he sat down and tried to dismiss her from his mind.

The kiss between them hadn't worked. For reasons known only to her, Jessie had rejected him at the last minute, although he had been convinced that she had some feelings for him. As it was, he had to keep his distance. She was too much of a distraction and with what he had learned from the AA in the recent briefing, things were going to get a little hot around the FOB before much longer.

Bloody woman, I'm better off without her.

A small part of his subconscious called him a liar.

Earlier, when he had come out of the operations tent, he had immediately noticed Jessie dancing. He remembered that he had felt his body tense, his mind instantly full of the tantalizing images of their kiss and the feel of her body under his hands. He had let the memories fade, folding his arms and relaxing back against a tent pole, watching her every move.

His heart had seemed to stop, then speed on when she had thrown her head back — laughing, playing around with the men, moving from one to another, dancing with each one in turn. She looked graceful and beautiful and Nick accepted that without a doubt, he was deeply smitten.

He had found himself watching her hips move, then JR had come up behind her. He was an impressive dancer and as he and Jessie had moved to the music, the other members had stopped to watch, clapping their hands, whistling and cheering. Nick had found his gaze riveted on her and to his consternation, found that the way she moved had almost sent his blood pressure through the ceiling.

Nick had eventually straightened and withdrawn into his tent. He had had far more important things to be concerned about other than a very sexy and enticing medic, such as a bloody bad storm on its way to disrupt the patrol that night and a higher risk of making contact with hostiles as they would surely use the approaching inclement weather to their advantage.

Chapter Eleven

Jessie awoke abruptly from a shallow, restless doze. Her headphones had fallen off and she could hear a strange hissing sound coming from above her. It grew louder and louder, turning to a tumultuous pattering then a loud hammering on the roof, and she realized at last that it was the sound of torrential rain.

Glancing at her watch and seeing that it was 2100 hours, she quickly got up from the bed and hurried to the entrance. Pushing aside the flap, she glanced outside. Just as she did so, a flicker of lightning lit up her surroundings with strobe-like striations. A brief but loud rumble of thunder rolled across the sky directly above her, the storm announcing its arrival with ferocity.

Jessie cringed, fear suddenly lodging in her throat. The rain came down even harder from the black sky, a blinding curtain reducing visibility to a few meters. She could barely see the end of the platform and she frowned, then shivered. The patrol was going to be a nightmare.

Her heart pounding with a primal fear, she stumbled backward a few paces then stopped, biting her lip in agitation. She wanted to run to her bed, climb inside the sleeping bag and pull it up over her head. Instead, she knew that she had to occupy her mind with mundane trivia or actions and attempt to quash the nerves that were tying her stomach in knots.

Deciding to have a quick shower, she grabbed her toilet kit and, humming nervously beneath her breath, did that very thing. Once she had finished, she plaited her hair, pinned it up, then dressed in her combat gear. Before putting on her body armor, she quickly shrugged into her Gore-Tex wet weather jacket and trousers. Finally pulling on her combat gloves and helmet, she hefted on the medical pack, then picked up her rifle.

As she finished getting ready, there came another thunderclap, and she whimpered like a frightened child. She did not want to go outside and expose herself to the elements, but she knew that she had no other choice. Besides, pride would not allow the others to see her fear at something as minor as a thunderstorm.

She hesitated before venturing out, took a deep breath, then stepped reluctantly onto the platform. She almost jumped out of her skin when Dingle appeared out of the gloom.

"Hey, Mac," he announced loudly, obviously trying to make himself heard over the pouring rain. "Mission briefing is in the DFAC."

Jessie nodded. Her mouth was so dry that she could not answer him. Instead, she followed the man out into the torrent. Raindrops immediately pounded on the crown of her helmet like a timpani. Water trickled off the front in a miniature waterfall and managed to run down the nape protection inside the collar of her jacket.

She was halfway to the mess area when a flash of lighting — white and almost blinding — shot across the sky, followed instantaneously by a clap of thunder that sounded like an explosion. She jumped violently and squealed.

Dingle appeared to notice her reaction as he grasped her arm and brought her to a halt. "Don't tell me you're scared of storms, Mac," he shouted.

Breath catching in her throat, Jessie nodded and swallowed. "Terrified," she yelled. "Thanks for the thought, but I'm drowning here."

"You've got a problem tonight then, girl," Dingle continued. "Listen. Just stick with me. I'll try and get you through it."

They ran on to the DFAC, boots splashing through deep

puddles. In the short time the rain had fallen, water—unable to soak away into the concrete-hard surface—had started to form miniature shallow lakes across the FOB.

The rest of the section was waiting for them and as they found seats, Nick appeared from the operations tent in the company of two of the Afghan Army, then jogged across to join them.

"Everyone ready, Bravo Recon Section?" he asked.

"Yes, LT," the men chorused, Jessie noting that their voices sounded as glum as the expressions on their faces.

"Good. First of all, Sergeant Kabir Lizai and Sergeant Nabil Bannusi will be joining us on patrol tonight. They are here to act as liaisons and security enforcement for an indefinite period of time."

Jessie glanced at the AA and saw with a start that one of them was the Afghan soldier who had studied her so rudely on his arrival at the FOB. He was standing beside Nick with his hands behind his back, surveying everyone. A look of contempt twisted his features and she made up her mind that he was a most arrogant and dislikeable man.

He'd probably just as soon shoot us in the back as look at us.

"Okay," Nick went on, his tone brisk. "Let's get this mission briefing on the road. Tonight is going to be nasty. There is one bastard of a storm coming in, and it will be blacker than all hell out there. You'll get soaking wet, tired and cold. We will not be able to see a bloody thing, so you'll need to concentrate and focus much more than usual. Use your HUD maps to keep an eye out for the enemy, although the atmospherics are going to cause a lot of interference with incoming data.

"We will be patrolling five clicks up the mountain to Checkpoint Charlie and will remain there until 0600 hours when Charlie Recon will relieve us. Our AA friends have reported insurgent presence increasing, and they've been gathering around the CP location. As yet, intel has no idea why.

"Charlie Recon and the AA have tried to track them on a

number of occasions without much success. If a shitstorm is going to happen over the next few days, we need to know about it, which is one reason why we have to go out in this bloody weather. Are there any questions?"

Jessie noticed that the only response to his query were resigned expressions and the half-hearted shaking of heads.

Following Nick's words, a series of flickering flashes lit up their faces and, holding her breath, she watched forked lightning rip its way across the black sky. Following on the heels of the electrical discharge was the inevitable enormous crash of thunder. Rain pounded above them on the roof and hit the ground so hard that raindrops bounced up almost two inches from the surface. A few moments later, another roll of thunder came roaring in off the mountains and another sheet of lighting lit up the FOB with flickering, strobe-like whiteness.

Jessie jumped, then cringed. Dingle, seated next to her noticed. "Easy, Mac. You'll be fine," he soothed.

She turned to look at him and whispered, "Fuck, Dingle, I'm scared."

Dingle nudged her arm in reassurance. "You'll be fine," he repeated.

Jessie—not feeling fine at all—turned back to the briefing and saw that Nick was watching her and Dingle, an expression of annoyance on his face. Their gazes locked for a moment and she was mortified when another crash of thunder reverberated around the sky and she jumped violently. She saw Nick frown and look away from her.

"All right, let's get going," he ordered, dragging his eyes away from Jessie. He had noticed the expression of fear on her face and the way she had jumped at the crash of thunder. He realized by her reaction that she had some fear of storms, which meant that she was going to have a very difficult time.

A report from the Meteorology Center had advised that the bad weather was going to stay around for a few hours yet, and if she couldn't come to grips with her fears, she would be unable to focus fully on the mission. She could be scared into making errors of judgment and, as reluctant as he was to do it, this prompted him to decide to speak with her before they left.

"All right, lads. Load your weapons then form up at the gates. Face shields down, HUDs and night vision on. Keep your weapons as dry as you can, otherwise they won't be worth anything."

Nick watched as, with expressions ranging from reluctance to disgust, the men got up from their seats and hurried to the sandbagged safety area to load magazines and test fire their weapons. They then filed one by one out into the center of the FOB, disappearing into a curtain of rain after a few meters.

Jessie was about to follow them when Nick said, "Mac, a word."

She stopped dead in her tracks and turned to face him. "Lieutenant?"

Nick moved closer to her, shifting his weapon to a more comfortable position on his shoulder and asked, "Are you all right? Is there a problem?"

He saw her hesitate and before she could answer, there was another brilliant flash of lightning followed almost immediately by a crack of thunder. He watched her cower and saw her fear.

He leaned closer to her so that she could hear him above the raging storm. "You'll be fine, Mac. It's only a storm. You need to concentrate and get yourself through this. You think you can make it?"

He watched her raise her chin in a defiant manner. "I believe so, sir. Why shouldn't I?"

Nick smiled slightly. "I've never yet had anyone die in my charge from a lightning strike," he said.

Jessie replied in a solemn tone, "Well, there's always a first time, Lieutenant." With that last remark, she turned and ran out into the rain.

Squinting through his rain-lashed face shield, Nick watched her load her weapon and take up position in the formation in front of Dingle. He joined Sergeant Kabir Lizai and Sergeant Nabil Bannusi, the second member of the AA who was to join the patrol as tail-end Charlie, and they took their positions, boots splashing up sprays of water and sand. As Nick moved past the section, he shouted, "Everyone online."

Checking to make sure that everyone was ready, he caught sight of Jessie — barely visible through the sheets of rain — standing rigid, frozen in place. He felt a tug of remorse at the fact that she would have to face her fear of storms in the most inappropriate of environments but quickly dismissed the thought, the need to concentrate fully on the forthcoming patrol of more importance than a frightened medic.

Standing waiting to leave the FOB, Jessie was immediately drenched in the warm, monsoon-like downpour. It thundered down on the top of her helmet, raised pattering sounds on her wet-weather clothing and beat a rapid tattoo on the casing of her weapon, the barrel of which she held pointing down at the ground to avoid water getting into the delicate mechanism.

"Jumping Jesus fucking H. Christ," Jessie heard Shrek say loudly. "What a clusterfuck."

A roll of thunder sounded as if it was trying to rip the heavens open. It seemed to go on forever, followed almost immediately by forked lightning that filled the air with electricity and had Jessie closing her eyes. Another grumble of thunder — sounding almost sinister — rolled toward the FOB, becoming louder and louder before it faded away to a muted muttering.

She almost bolted for the medical tent. Instead, she gritted her teeth and forced herself to remain in position, keeping her eyes closed and waiting for the incandescent light display to fade away. She activated her HUD and quickly brought up her night vision and a schematic of their route, now outlined in red. Any hostiles would also show up as red blinking dots.

She glimpsed Nick through the curtain of rain as he signaled to the security guard to open the gate. As the section moved off, she slowly followed Shrek, glancing over her shoulder to watch as the FOB was sealed. She immediately felt as though she was leaving a haven of safety to venture out into a hazardous unknown environment with nowhere to run.

As the distance from the FOB increased, the pale gleam of the Hesco walls began to vanish into blackness behind curtains of rain until, as they reached the landing zone, the walls and security towers disappeared altogether.

The patrol moved at a slight angle across the sodden ground into what felt like an impenetrable wall of blackness. Jessie felt the darkness closing in around her like a solid, tangible presence, its intention to stifle and suffocate her.

Through her face shield, she could see green speckled rain and an equally green Shrek in front of her. Other than that, she was blind on all sides, and it must have been the same for the rest of the section. If any insurgents had had the courage to hide out in the bushes and behind rocks in the severe storm in order to watch their progress or wait to launch an ambush, she thought that Bravo Recon would be unable to see them.

The patrol was halfway across the landing zone — feeling their way carefully across syrupy, slippery ground — when another brilliant electronic discharge lit up the sky in a kaleidoscopic effect.

Jessie gasped and flinched, watching the striking display throw into prominence the mountains to her right, their serrated peaks outlined in sharp relief. Thunder crashed around the sky, so loudly it was almost deafening. Raindrops pounded the ground, the spray creating a knee-high mist that obliterated all possible sight of mines or IEDs.

Her progress, as well as that of the rest of the section, was slow as they struggled to keep their feet on the waterlogged ground. Every so often, someone floundered, then fell to their knees in the oozing, miring muck and there was much stopping and starting to haul them back to their feet.

Each crash of thunder and flash of lighting made Jessie want to cringe, and her fear at being so exposed was beginning to gain the upper hand. Strung out and nervous, she bit her lip until it was sore but kept up the surveillance of the surrounding area via her HUD.

The patrol finally reached the path leading up to the mountain pass, and there the going became much worse. What was, in fact, nothing more than a narrow track, normally consisted of small rocks embedded into hard-packed sand and soil. It was now nothing more than a small but fast-flowing stream. After the torrential rain of the past hours, the rocks, loosened by running water, rolled from beneath their boots and the ground underfoot had become treacherous.

On more than one occasion, a section member stumbled, slipped and went down on their knees. In the brief silences between the roaring thunder and through her comms, Jessie could hear loud, colorful curses and exclamations of pain. She had the feeling that she would be seeing quite a few of the men in the medical tent the next day with bruises and other injuries sustained in their falls.

As the path began its gradual climb — becoming more hazardous — there was no sign of the storm abating. Lightning flickered around the peaks of the mountains, accompanied by thunder that boomed in intense, artillery-like attacks, almost deafening. Water ran in narrow streams down the slope, small rocks, stones and broken branches tumbling and bouncing end over end to mingle with the miniature white-water cascade.

As they climbed higher, Jessie concentrated on keeping her footing on the slippery ground. Whatever humor she and Bravo Recon had found in the mission was markedly absent as they tried to conserve energy.

A nightmarish while later and much to Jessie's relief, they reached Checkpoint Charlie. Nothing more than two sandbag enclosures with the path running through the center, its walls rose to a height of about two meters. There was a lookout to the right where, in good visibility, a security team could keep watch over two hundred meters of scrubland to the foot of the mountains. At present, they and the surrounding terrain were invisible, blanketed in impenetrable blackness.

The men crouched, slumping wearily against the left-hand wall of the CP then raised their face shields. They huddled down into the collars of their wet weather jackets, trying to protect themselves from the harsh elements.

"Fucking bloody weather," Dingle moaned. "I feel like a wet sponge." He shook his head, water spraying from his helmet. The avalanche caught Shrek full in the face, catching him off guard.

"Watch it, you dick," he yelled. "I'm wet enough as it is. Keep your bloody rain to yourself."

Attempting to make himself more comfortable, he cursed colorfully when his boots slipped out from beneath him and he crashed down onto the soaking wet ground.

"Now my fucking arse is wet," he announced. "Who'd join the fucking bloody army?"

Feeling utterly miserable and soaked, despite her wet-weather clothing, Jessie glanced in Nick's direction and saw that he was striding toward where the men were huddled dejectedly against the sandbags. "Okay, lads," she heard him say when he reached them. "I want Shrek, Mungo, Wolf and JR to take positions at the lookout. The rest of you take a break and get some water."

The four chosen men struggled to their feet and moved to take their positions up against the sandbags. Lowering their face shields — flickering red schematics dancing across them as they faced out into the storm-swept blackness — they rested their rifles on top of the saturated wall.

Nick turned to Jessie. "Mac?"

Jessie started as Nick spoke her name and when she turned her attention on him saw him gesturing with his head for her to move off to the side away from the others. Negotiating her way over to him she said, "Lieutenant?" raising her voice above the splattering of rain on wet weather clothing and the ground.

In a voice just loud enough that she could hear it above the storm, Nick asked, "Are you all right?"

"I'll survive, Lieutenant," Jessie replied as lightly as she could, wishing she could see his face more clearly. She was tired and wet and suddenly experienced an intense longing to be in his arms where she was sure it would be warm and where he could protect her from the wild thunderstorm.

Nick remained silent for a minute and said, "All right, Mac. Get some water down you."

"Yes, sir," Jessie said nodding and joined Lug Nut, Devil, Dingle and Yeti where they were all attempting to shelter from the lashing rain. She positioned herself between Devil and Dingle, trying to shield her face, then lay her weapon across her knees.

Dingle nudged her. "You all right?" he asked.

Jessie nodded. "Yeah, a bit cold though," she replied. "It's not even a night for the ducks."

"You're right there," Dingle acknowledged. "I can't see a fucking thing. Fuck knows how we would detect any *mujis* in the area if they were here. They could just walk in and kick us in the balls." He paused. "Well, our balls you understand, not…never mind."

Leaning against the cold, wet sandbags, trying to get as comfortable as possible, Jessie felt her knee accidentally brush against Devil. She quickly pulled it away, muttered, "Sorry," and turned back to Dingle.

"I could murder a hot drink," she sighed, "and a hot shower, and my pit and hot food, even if it's cooked by you, Dingle."

Dingle laughed. "Dream on," he said. "You have approximately" — he pressed a button on his wristwatch illuminating the dial—"only four hours to go."

"Crap," Jessie muttered. "Four more hours of hell."

She was startled when Devil suddenly leaned in close to her, so near that the rim of his helmet almost clashed with hers and announced quietly, "I can keep you warm in more ways than one if you want, Mac."

At first not understanding what he was implying, Jessie tensed. She had never really gotten to know the man with the dark, saturnine face and powerful muscular body. He did not join in with the others and sometimes she had seen him staring at her. Whenever she caught him in the act, he neither turned away nor acted embarrassed that she had seen him. She was startled at the fact that he had now initiated a conversation with her.

"Fancy sliding off for a little bit of fun?" Devil continued when Jessie didn't respond to his first comment. "No one will know we're gone."

Chapter Twelve

Jessie shuddered, first with disbelief, then with a frisson of fear. Turning to him and seeing his face jus blur in the darkness, she asked, "What did you say?

At the moment of asking the question, there was a white-hot lightning that completely lit up the surrou mountainside and scrubland. The atmosphere sizzled with electricity, and Jessie felt the hairs stand her forearms and the back of her neck. In particula up Devil and she noticed that he had lowered his hea there was a leer on his face.

"Come on, babe. You heard what I said," he answ "We could have a good time, you and me. After al Marine girls are known for your...adventurous spirit

Stunned at the crude way the soldier was speaking Jessie felt the disbelief and fear begin to turn to anger

"Do me a favor, Devil," she spat angrily. "Dream or off and die, asshole."

She turned away from him with the intention of ign any further remarks he chose to make, but the obviously could not take the hint. To Jessie's horro placed a gloved hand on her knee and squeezed it. I she could stop him, he had trailed his fingers up the i of her thigh.

Jessie violently jerked her leg away, falling side against Dingle in the process.

"Get your fucking hand off me," she ordered, fury i her voice, "unless you want me to rip it off and ram it i your throat."

As she cannoned into him, Dingle turned to her. "

he fuck?" he exclaimed.

Jessie sprang to her feet and turned to face Devil, who had risen from his crouch. She brought her weapon up between them and spat, "You touch me again, you son of a bitch, and I'll break your face with this gun."

Dingle grabbed Jessie's arm, pushing the weapon down. "Whoa, what's going on here?" he asked.

Jessie remained silent, watching Devil, waiting for his response to her words. She was stunned when the man laughed.

"Stay away from me," Jessie ordered. "Don't ever come near me or speak to me again."

Dingle turned her to face him. "What's the problem?" he asked again.

Hearing concern in his voice, Jessie shook her head, not wanting to disclose what had just happened. She managed a smile. "Nothing," she answered. "Everything's fine."

Dingle touched her arm, "Are you sure?" he asked.

Jessie nodded again and crouched back down against the sandbags. She was relieved when Devil moved away from her but she still felt uneasy at the sudden onslaught of sordid requests he had made of her.

* * * *

The hours passed slowly. Two teams of four each stood two-hour watches, all growing stiff with cold under the onslaught of the storm. At 0300 hours in the morning, the rain began to slacken off and gradually the thunder and lightning abated. Most of Bravo Recon had become thoroughly wet and tired. Jessie had caught Nick checking on each of them periodically throughout the night, ensuring that none had started to suffer from exposure, reminding them to keep hydrated and eat.

By 0400 hours, the rain had stopped completely and the sky had begun to lighten over the mountains, the heavy thunderclouds moving away. The spirits of the section

rose as the storm retreated and the sun began to rise. With the exception of the incident with Devil, Jessie's humor had returned and there was some quiet joking and teasing between her and the men.

A few moments before the arrival of Charlie Recon, Nick called them together.

"You did well, lads, Mac," he announced. "It wasn't the easiest of nights. I'm sure you're all feeling like crap. You'll be ecstatic to know, I'm sure, that Charlie Recon will be here for a handover in about ten minutes, then we can be on our way back to the FOB."

There was a small resounding cheer at this news and before much more time had passed, the sound of boots approached them along the path and Charlie Recon appeared through the early morning gloom. There was much handshaking as the two sections greeted each other and ribald comments resounded in the cool misty air as Nick and the newly arrived commanding officer quickly debriefed each other.

Jessie and the men loitered wearily, smoking and cursing, as they waited for the two officers to complete their sitreps. Finally, they took their patrol positions and began to make their way back along the route to the FOB.

As the air warmed up about them, steam began to writhe up from the ground, swirling about their knees. Water dripped from vegetation and rocks and small rivulets ran down each side of the path. The surface underfoot remained saturated, a quagmire of sand and dust that had turned into something resembling liquid cement. The mountains to their left remained obscured by wraiths of mist that swirled and entwined about the trees and bushes like smoke.

Bravo Recon negotiated the path slowly and with a great deal of care, surveying the landscape even more intently now that it was getting light. At 0800 hours, they arrived back at the FOB and entered through its welcoming open gates.

Once inside, the men quickly shed their equipment. They

were all exhausted and wet, and Nick dismissed them quickly, ordering them to eat and get some downtime. Instead, all the men went straight to their accommodation, nobody bothering to go for food.

Jessie turned to head toward the medical tent, her own feet stumbling with weariness until Nick called out her name. Stopping in her tracks, shoulders slumping, she turned to face him. Although she was exhausted and still slightly shaken by the altercation with Devil at the checkpoint, she couldn't help but feel that *if* they were away from the FOB and out of Afghanistan, *if* she wasn't still in love with her husband and *if* she knew for sure that Nick felt the same as she, she would walk straight into his arms. As it was, it appeared that the problems inherent in their turbulent relationship were insurmountable.

"What was going on out there between you, Dingle and Devil?" he asked abruptly.

Noting that he was watching her intently while he waited for her to respond, Jessie hesitated. If she mentioned the incident that had occurred at the checkpoint, there would inevitably be repercussions for her and the two men, as the charge she would make would possibly have nasty consequences for Devil. It would entail an investigation and there was no way that she wanted to go down that route.

"Lieutenant?" she queried. "I don't know what you mean."

Nick glanced down at his boots then back at her. "I'm not blind, Mac," he continued. "I was watching what took place between you three. What was going on?"

Jessie shook her head. "Not sure what you're getting at, Lieutenant. It was just some joking and larking around." She tried to keep the evasiveness out of her voice but wasn't sure that she had succeeded.

A frown creasing his forehead, Nick shook his head in exasperation. "It didn't look like any larking or joking around that I've ever seen, Mac."

As Jessie's eyes met the chocolate brown gaze, she

remembered the kiss they had shared the previous day and her legs suddenly felt weak. Her stomach began to flutter with nervous reaction and she had a strange feeling of drowning in the darkness of his eyes. She had to forcibly drag hers away from his.

"Nothing happened, sir," she repeated, her voice sounding a little shaky with emotion.

"Okay, Mac," Nick acquiesced, his tone sounding cool. "I suppose I'll have to take your word for it. Go get some sleep. You look all in."

"Thank you, Lieutenant," Jessie said, and with a last look at him, turned then walked slowly toward the medical tent.

She wearily entered and went straight to her sleeping quarters. Dropping her combat equipment on the floor, she drew the blinds at the window then turned on the fan, the cool breeze slightly dispersing the warm air already building up inside.

Grabbing her toilet kit and nightwear, she went to shower, washing her hair quickly. Then she spent a few minutes toweling it dry to remove some of the moisture. Afterward, she hunted until she discovered some nylon cord. Then, collecting her wet combats together with her saturated boots and socks, she went out onto the platform. Stringing the cord between two tent posts, she hung her combats up to dry, placing her boots and socks in the sun.

Almost asleep on her feet, she gave one last glance over her shoulder toward Nick's tent and was startled to see him walking across the FOB toward the chow area. As if he sensed her staring at him, he glanced in her direction and their eyes met. Jessie saw his gaze move from her face down her body to her tan legs and back up again. She shivered with a delicious awareness of his eyes on her body and the sexual frisson that flowed between them.

Cheeks flushing, she quickly moved back inside the tent, went to her sleeping quarters then threw herself down on the bed. She moaned slightly with the bliss of being able to relax and a few minutes later, she fell asleep.

* * * *

At 1400 hours that afternoon, Jessie awoke, hot and thirsty, in a tent that had become very warm and airless. She lay for a moment on the bed, still dazed from her deep sleep until, yawning, she opted to go for another shower to see if it would not only wake her up but also cool her down.

Once back in her sleeping quarters, she tied her hair into a ponytail and pulled on a clean pair of combat trousers, T-shirt and shower sandals. She went to the tent flap and drew it back, fastening it open with its cord to let some air into the interior then went back to her sleeping quarters. Within the space of a few minutes, there was a slap on the canvas and Yeti thrust his head—moose-like—through the opening.

"Mac, you decent?" he yelled.

Re-entering the treatment room, Jessie laughed at what appeared to be a bashful expression on his face. "Why, Yeti, are you concerned about my modesty?" she asked and laughed again as the soldier blushed.

"Huh?" he frowned, as though he had no idea what she was talking about.

"Never mind," Jessie said, shaking her head. "What's up?"

"Well, er...last night on patrol I tripped on that shitty path and put my hand on a sharp stone. It tore through my glove and ripped my palm," he explained. "I wondered if you would have a look at it."

Jessie nodded. "I can do that. Come in and jump up on the table."

Yeti obliged her and, once seated, held out his hand. Jessie took his wrist and had a close look at the wound.

"Ouch," she said. A triangular flap of skin had been levered up and away and had hardened into a ridge, leaving raw tissue exposed to the elements. She could also see debris in the wound and knew that it needed a good cleaning out.

"That will have to be soaked to get that piece of skin softened and the crap out of it."

Jessie glanced at Yeti, watching him nod his head. Dropping his hand for the moment, she collected the supplies that she needed, including a large bowl of water mixed with antiseptic, and placed them on the examination table. Setting the bowl on his lap she said, "Put the whole of your hand in there, palm down, and leave it there until I tell you to take it out. I'll look at it afterward to see if it's clean."

As she was saying this, there was another tap on the outside of the tent. Glancing up and seeing Mungo's head looking in, she said, "My, I am popular today. Come in, Mungo, and make yourself comfortable."

Mungo obeyed and gingerly leaned against a wall with his muscular arms folded. "What's old Yeti done?" he asked.

"It won't kill him," Jessie remarked. "He's being a big, brave boy."

Yeti wrinkled his nose. "Well, thanks for that, Mac. I appreciate the compliment."

Jessie laughed and, picking up his wrist, turned his hand over to look at the wound. "Okay," she began, "this might hurt…a lot. I've got to clean it out."

She spent the next ten minutes easing out minute bits of gravel and sand as gently as she could. Once she was satisfied that it was as debris-free as she could get it, she dried the area, sprayed it with antibiotic, then covered it with a dressing. She kept this in place by winding a thin layer of bandage about his palm and wrist.

Once she had finished, she patted the tattoo on his head and said, "There you go, Yeti. Keep it dry and clean. You'll still be able to fit your glove over the bandage, but if you have any problems, come back to see me."

Grinning, Yeti flexed his hand, said, "Thanks, Mac," and jumping off the examination table, punched the other man in the arm as he passed him and left.

Jessie, left alone with Mungo said, "Let me guess. On the

patrol last night, you fell and hurt something?"

"Yep," Mungo said, "my knee."

"Okay, drop your trousers," Jessie ordered, waiting for the protest from the soldier, which wasn't long in coming.

"Oh, hey, Mac. I don't just drop my kegs for anyone, you know," he exclaimed, his face coloring slightly.

Folding her arms, Jessie tried to keep the smile from her face. "You drop 'em, soldier, or I won't be able to look at your knee. I'm not just *anyone*, pal. I'm your medic. Look on me as…your mom."

Mungo looked at Jessie's face, an expression of doubt on his. "My mum?" he echoed. "You? You're nothing like my mum, and I don't think anyone in their wildest dreams would be able to picture you as their mum."

"Mungo, just get them down and let's get this over with," Jessie reiterated impatiently. "I promise I won't look anywhere but at your knee."

Embarrassment in every movement of his body, Mungo jumped down from the table and began to undo the Velcro fastenings on his combat trousers.

"Sheesh. I'm shucking off my trousers in front of a strange female. If the lads could see this…" he muttered. "I'll never live it down."

Watching him push his combats down around his ankles then hop back up onto the table, Jessie said, "So, I'm strange. That's a first. Well, I won't tell anyone if you won't. Your secret is safe with me."

Even though he was wearing cotton shorts, Mungo laid a hand across his lap, as though shielding himself from her gaze, and Jessie had to struggle to stop herself from laughing. Bending forward, she lifted his leg and took a close look at the graze on his knee.

Sometime during the patrol the night before, Mungo must have slipped, causing his knee to come into contact with something hard and solid. The whole joint was a swollen, livid bruise with a large raw area of shredded skin in the center.

Eyeing him, Jessie asked, "Can you bend your knee for me?"

Mungo nodded and proceeded to vigorously flex the joint backward and forward, proving that the limb was still functioning.

Holding up a hand Jessie said, "Okay, okay, I get the picture."

Skillfully, she bathed the wound, using a fresh bowl of antiseptic solution. Then she put a dressing on the graze and strapped the knee up with an elasticized bandage. Once she had finished, she gestured for him to put his combats back on and said, "Right. If the knee swells any more or gets worse, you'll need to take a trip to Camp Bastion. You should really have an X-ray but I think it's just damage to soft tissue. You're okay to go."

Fastening his combats, Mungo nodded, gave her a brief smile and said, "Thanks, Mac," then left the tent.

A few minutes after he had left, Lug Nut appeared with a cut elbow. Once she had treated him, she was finally able to complete all the medical forms and tidy up the supplies she had used.

She knew that she could not put the inevitable off any longer. She needed to speak with Nick about finding extra beds and chairs. Today had been a case in point with three casualties. If the injuries had been more serious or all three casualties had arrived together, the medical tent would have been crowded and that was just not good enough. She was reluctant to speak to the Lieutenant, but it was time to put their personal differences aside as it was for the benefit of the FOB.

Smoothing her hair back and tucking her T-shirt into her combat trousers, she went outside. Pausing on the platform, she glanced around to see if Nick was out around the FOB, but there was no sign of him. She really did not want to venture into his tent. That would be his territory, and she would be at a distinct disadvantage. There was no other way of getting the equipment she wanted though, and so, taking a deep breath, she stepped down off the platform and made her way reluctantly toward her destination.

As Jessie approached, she found her footsteps growing slower and slower, her stomach becoming more tense. Pausing before entering, she raised a hand, hesitated then, gritting her teeth, slapped the palm against the side.

Nick answered immediately, "Yes."

Feeling sick to her stomach, Jessie went inside. She found him sitting in a chair with one ankle propped on his knee, a pile of papers on his lap. A look of surprise crossed his face as he saw her, then an indecipherable look appeared in his eyes. He did not offer her a smile of greeting. He only said, "Mac. Problem?"

For a moment Jessie remained silent, taking in the fact that there were faint dark circles beneath his eyes and he looked tired. She had a sudden urge to take the papers away from him and throw them aside, sit on his lap and gently brush back his hair that had fallen in waves across his forehead.

Quickly shaking her head, she swallowed, and answered, "Nothing's wrong, Lieutenant. I've had a few visits today from some of the guys with scrapes and bruises from the patrol last night. There were no major injuries, although Mungo might have to take a trip to the CTH at Camp Bastion if his knee gets any worse."

Nick nodded his head, then continued to stare at her, waiting in silence for anything further she had to say. "And?" he finally asked.

"Lieutenant, I was wondering if I could have a couple of beds and chairs for the medical tent. If we have more than one casualty, it's going to get kinda difficult, like this morning when I had three patients. We need somewhere for them all to sit while they wait."

Feeling extremely uncomfortable under the man's scrutiny, Jessie wished that he would say something — anything — to relieve the tension that was building up between them.

Nick glanced down at the paperwork then back up at

her. "It's not a doctor's surgery, and I don't think the lads would collapse from exhaustion if they had to wait for a few minutes, but I think that can be arranged, Mac," he replied. "We already have the equipment stored on the FOB. I'll get a couple of the section to bring the requested items over to you."

"Thank you, sir," Jessie said, a small smile creeping across her face. Then, because she had an uncontrollable urge to make things better between them, she decided to deal with the problem directly and added, "Sir? I'm sorry."

There was a small silence following her apology with Nick's face remaining inscrutable. "Sorry for what, Mac?" he asked at last.

This man wasn't making things easy for her and Jessie blushed. "For…the misunderstanding between us in the medical tent," she eventually said, floundering slightly.

"Misunderstanding?" Nick queried, a frown appearing between his eyebrows, and Jessie's heart sank. "Well, if you want to call it that, fair enough, but I would have called what happened between us something other than a… misunderstanding." He looked away from her and down at the paperwork on his lap, as though dismissing her.

Feeling weak at the knees with her stomach knotting, Jessie took a step backward. "Yes, Lieutenant. I'd better go."

"Yes, you do that," was the last comment she heard as she spun around and almost ran out of the tent.

Once outside, she took a deep breath, cursing silently. She had only made matters worse with what she considered now was a pathetic apology. She felt ten times worse than she had following their kiss yesterday. Raging inwardly, she stormed across the FOB to the medical tent, went straight in and, finding her innocent combat helmet on the floor where she had dropped it, booted it across to the opposite side of the tent.

Back in his tent, Nick uttered a loud groan, his emotions

warring between anger at Jessie's choice of words and frustration at his inability to stop himself feeling what he did for the woman. The words she had used to apologize – labeling the kiss a misunderstanding – had strongly annoyed him.

If she could describe his feelings – and hers for that matter – in that way, then she obviously deeply regretted the mutual decision to kiss, and she felt less for him than he believed she did.

As Nick had watched her leave his tent, he wished that he had called her back, regretting his response and wanting to delve more deeply into what he had witnessed up at the checkpoint during the previous night's patrol. He knew that something had gone on between Jessie and the two men. He'd seen the altercation and observed the expression on Mac's face when she was having the conversation with Devil, but he had no idea what it had been about. When it appeared that she might have been having problems with the two men, he had wanted to intervene and punch the culprit who'd had the nerve to cause the anxious expression on her face.

He'd found himself watching her whenever he saw her. He'd been impressed with the methodical and competent way she carried out her duties and the way she'd treated his wound. Whenever he heard the sound of her voice or her laughter, he experienced all manner of very imaginative thoughts and feelings that he could no longer deny and, more to the point, no longer wanted to. Jessie McAllister was beautiful, feisty and stubborn but gentle and soft and she was seriously affecting his ability to concentrate and focus on his job.

He still could not dismiss his feelings for her. It was beginning to feel like some form of torture to see her, be in her presence and not talk to her or touch her, as he wanted. He was even tempted to request a transfer out of there, but if that were to occur, he would never see her again and that was something he could not tolerate. He was a stubborn man and wasn't about to give up so easily.

Chapter Thirteen

Her eyes gritty and aching from lack of sleep, Jessie exited her tent clutching her empty thermo cup. Her sole aim was to make her first cup of tea of the day and a strong one at that. She had discovered that she was never fully alert until she'd had a hot drink, but this particular morning, after the night patrol with its accompanying raging thunderstorm and the incident with Nick in his tent, her self-confidence and self-esteem needed some boosting, even if it was from the brief rush of a large dose of sugar.

Her body ached in places she had never dreamed it could. She mused that she could quite happily go back to her accommodation, crawl into her sleeping bag and sleep the day away.

The day before had been downtime and she had spent most of it with Bravo Recon, treating minor injuries that had occurred during the patrol, then spending the rest of the day with them. Later that same day, Dingle and JR had turned up at the medical tent with two folding cots and chairs, together with mattresses, blankets and pillows, which were now stored away, ready for use when required.

Jessie had gone to bed early the previous night but had spent most of it awake, tossing and turning restlessly, her thoughts in turmoil about Nick Ryan. She knew she had definitely been in love with her husband, but now—hating to admit it—she doubted whether it had been the kind of intense and passionate love that books wrote about, when your life revolved around one person and there was no room for anyone or anything else. The feelings that she'd had for Mark had never been as intense or bittersweet compared to those she had for Nick, and that had increased her guilt threefold.

Always brutally honest with herself, she now knew that she had fallen in love with her commanding officer. This revelation had come abruptly in the early hours of the morning and had both warmed and frightened her at the same time. The kiss between them in the medical tent had caused her confused and wayward feelings to consolidate and become clearer.

She wanted to be with him, have him kiss her again and touch her. She could clearly remember the feelings that he had stirred in her, and not only did she want to experience the exquisite sensations again, she wanted even more.

Sighing, Jessie made her way to the mess area. As she passed Nick's tent, she glanced in that direction, hoping to see a light through the blinds at the window, showing that he was awake. It was in darkness with the entrance flap closed. She turned her attention to her immediate surroundings, just on the off chance that he was already up, but nothing moved.

She glanced up at the nearest tower and her heart stopped for a brief moment before racing on, beating harder and faster. She recognized Nick's tall figure, silhouetted dimly against the faint golden backdrop of the rising sun. He was standing as still as a statue, his head held in his own unique, alert way, his gaze focused completely out onto the still-dark countryside.

Jessie slowed her pace, keeping her gaze turned on him, hoping he would notice her. She was disappointed when he continued to remain motionless.

Reaching the mess area, she stopped by the kettle and checked to make sure that there was enough water in it before turning it on to boil. She stood waiting, pensively and distractedly nibbling at her bottom lip, glancing every now and again back up at the tower.

She wanted — *needed* — to talk to Nick again, to hear his voice, even if it was just for him to indicate his disapproval at something she had done or to argue with her. Having admitted her feelings for him, she had an almost unbearable longing to be near him. An idea – impulsive and reckless and one that would quite clearly show Nick her obvious interest in him – slammed into her mind with the force of a blow.

Pushing all thought of possible repercussions aside, she collected a plastic cup from the stack beside the kettle, made her own cup of tea in it and coffee in the thermo cup. Not knowing if he took sugar, she poured a small amount of the white granules into another plastic cup, put a spoon in it, and started walking toward the tower.

On reaching the foot of the wooden steps leading up to the platform, she glanced about her to make sure there was nobody around, then hesitated. She was unsure that what she was about to do was such a good idea after all. She could not picture what Nick's reaction might be at her appearance. She might well be on the receiving end of a roasting, or he might ignore her altogether.

The urge to be near him overcoming any doubts, Jessie shrugged and began to climb the steps, moving carefully, the containers of hot liquid wavering precariously in her trembling hands. When she had almost reached the top, she called softly, "Lieutenant?"

There was a brief silence, then a faint exclamation floated down from the darkness. Nick leaned over the side of the platform, looking down. Jessie was unable to see the expression on his face – the light was still faint and his helmet threw its own black shadow over his features – but she heard a casual tone in his voice when he asked, "What are you doing here, Mac? Is something the matter?"

Reaching the top step, Jessie stopped and nervously replied, "No, Lieutenant, there's no problem. I'm probably breaking every rule that your army has in doing this, but I thought you might like a coffee. I have sugar, if you take it."

Beginning to feel slightly foolish, she wished wholeheartedly that she had never followed the direction in which her wildly beating heart was forcing her.

Never again will I throw myself at a man. What a dipshit!

There was another small silence, which seemed to Jessie to stretch into eternity before Nick replied in the same emotionless voice, "Yes, you are breaking every rule in the army, Mac, mainly because I'm on duty, but never mind. Come up anyway…and thanks."

Relieved that he had not actually told her to disappear or, more drastically, thrown her down the steps, Jessie climbed up to join him on the platform. She found him waiting for her, holding out his hand for the coffee. When she gave him the thermo cup, he took a sip and nodded.

"That's good," he said and when she gestured with the cup of sugar, he shook his head.

Shy and tongue-tied and not sure what to say to him now that she was with him, Jessie bent and stood the small container of sugar on the floor. Straightening up, determined not to look in his direction, she rested her elbows on the security barrier and, to cover her embarrassment, sipped at her own hot drink.

She stayed silent, watching the sun coming up, its weak rays blazing a wispy trail across the dark blue sky, faded stars still twinkling through the wraiths of dawn light. A cool breeze wafted against her bare arms, and she breathed deeply of the chilly air. She could just make out the dim outline of the barren landscape and the peaks of the looming mountains close by, the ruggedness outlined in lemon-orange light as the sun began to make its appearance.

Her thoughts scattered and she felt the involuntary tensing of her body as Nick came to stand beside her. His arm brushed against hers and she had to quell the shiver that ran up to her shoulder and down through her body like an electric shock.

She was acutely aware of his closeness as he leaned an elbow on the barrier, continuing to drink his coffee in silence. She tried to drag her chaotic thoughts away from the man standing beside her and drew in another deep breath.

"I love this time of the day. Everything is so fresh and clean." She was grateful that her tone held just the right note of friendliness and betrayed nothing of her inner feelings – or so she hoped.

"Me too," Nick answered in an equally friendly manner. "Even the countryside looks good."

Jessie tossed back her hair when a mild gust of wind blew it into her face and she continued sipping her tea.

Dammit! This is harder than I thought it was going to be.

Noticing the gesture, Nick suddenly had an urge to run his hands through the lush thickness. He mentally shied away from the thought. He had been startled at Jessie's appearance and was completely at a loss to understand what game she was playing. He felt irritated at the conflicting signals she was giving him. He wanted desperately to iron things out between them, but he wondered that if he made a tentative approach to do this, she would dismiss it without a thought. He was a different person when in her presence, as gauche and nervous as a schoolboy, and he hated the feeling.

Clearing his throat, he asked, "So, what are you doing up here, Mac?"

A second's silence lengthened into a minute as he waited for her response. At last he heard a murmured, "I don't know what I'm doing here. Perhaps I thought...I needed to..." Jessie's voice trailed off into silence.

Nick felt his irritation rise another notch. "What the fuck is going on with us, Jessie?" he asked. "That kiss we had. I thought –"

"There was...is no *us*, Lieutenant," Jessie replied quickly, a tremor marring her voice. "I came up here because it's not going to do the section or us any good if we carry on the way we are. The guys will sense that something is up. They're not stupid."

Nick felt acutely disappointed at her answer and even

more frustrated because he sensed that she was lying. He straightened up from her side.

"You're right. We need to put everything other than a working relationship aside. It looks like there's nothing more to be said on the subject. Thanks for the coffee." He stepped back and away from her.

"Do you want me to go?"

The words were low and husky, and Nick tensed as she turned to face him. Her face was a pale blur in the brightening light of the new day, but he could see that she was watching him, her eyes glistening slightly as she held his gaze.

His senses sizzled. Her very presence was doing all manner of things to him and he wanted to grab her and pull her roughly into his arms, to kiss her until she begged him to stop, force her to acknowledge what his intuition was telling him that she felt for him. He suddenly remembered that she had asked him a question and said abruptly, "What?"

"I ought to leave," Jessie stated but didn't move.

Nick stood motionless, watching her.

"Will you stop fucking playing with me, Jessie? None of this is a game. You came up here for a reason. Tell me what it is."

While he waited for her answer, Nick stayed silent. His resistance to this woman was almost gone. He struggled to hang on to the shredded remnants of his control and as a last desperate measure, moved farther away from her.

As though sensing his reticence, Jessie also moved back from him and said in a voice that held an element of hurt, "I'd better go."

She turned to descend the steps and, seeing her retreat, he realized that he could not keep away from her any longer and he didn't want to. He quickly propped his rifle against the security barrier and, throwing all caution to the wind, said, "No! I don't want you to go. Jesus Christ, Jessie…"

Holding his breath, he watched as she stopped, then

turned back to face him.

A long silence flowed between them full of meaning and promise, if only one of them would take that first step.

Jessie took a single pace forward.

Nick watched her move hesitantly toward him. The ethereal light bathed her in a misty citrus glow and his breath hitched in his throat as spangled streaks caught the golden highlights in her hair and showed up the soft gleam in her eyes. This irresistible woman had totally ensnared him, and it was exhilarating.

She stopped mere inches from him. His heart racing, he ran his eyes down her body, aware of the heat coiling like a dead weight in his lower stomach. Even though she seemed encased in shifting cobwebby shadows, he could see her full breasts outlined in the tight white vest and her long legs encased in combat trousers. His breath grew tight in his throat and, quickly removing his helmet and letting it drop to the floor, he leaned slowly forward, bending his head close to hers.

Nick tasted her lips, feeling the soft moistness of her mouth under his and her pliant, responsive body under his hands. Grasping her hips, he pulled her closer and, as he did, found part of his mind stunned that this was happening.

He had dreamed about this one thing until it had nearly driven him mad, and now here she was, returning his kiss passionately. She felt warm in his arms, her body firm against his, her hips not shying away from his rigid, aching hardness.

He roamed his hands up her back and, on reaching her luxurious silky hair, clenched in the strands, caressing her scalp with his fingers. He knew that she could feel how hard he was—it being only too evident—but she did not move away from him. In fact, by her response, she seemed to welcome it.

At last, reluctantly stopping the kiss, his breathing ragged and uneven, Nick gently took Jessie's face between his hands and, in the quickly brightening morning, studied her lips, already slightly swollen from his rough kisses.

"Christ, you're driving me mad," he murmured. "And I think we are truly fucked." His voice was husky with emotion. "We're on full display here in the tower and that means nothing less than a court martial for the both of us."

"Like I care...sir," Jessie murmured, clasping her hands up around the back of his neck.

Nick pulled her in closer to him, arms tightening about her waist, and ran his tongue sensuously along her lips. His breathing ragged and uneven, he gently nipped her neck before saying, "If we were alone..."

Jessie's arms tightened around his neck. "If we were alone...what?" she asked, her voice sounding throaty and sensuous.

"Well..." Nick kissed her neck again then trailed soft kisses up to her mouth. Before he kissed her once more, he finished, "I certainly wouldn't be standing here not doing my job because I am completely distracted by a stubborn, insubordinate, beautiful medic." Then his mouth met hers again and he was kissing her hard and passionately, the kiss deep and hot, his tongue finding hers as she opened her mouth to welcome it.

At that precise moment, chemlamps began to come on in the tents below and muffled voices sounded from their interiors. Nick instantly drew back from Jessie, his arms dropping from around her waist.

When he next spoke, his tone was strained and devoid of the sensual emotion that had been present earlier. It was now formal and that of a commanding officer.

"Get going, Mac, and thanks for the coffee."

Jessie stared at him astounded. She straightened, took a step back from him and, flushing at his dismissal, said, "Yes, Lieutenant."

Nick silently handed her the thermo cup and she turned to start her descent to the ground. On the third step down, she turned and looked back at him. He jerked his head, a gesture for her to get moving and emphasized it by saying quietly, "Get going."

It was the hardest order he'd ever given.

He watched Jessie descend the wooden steps of the tower, wanting to call her back and explain that he wasn't rejecting her. He had seen the expression of hurt and bewilderment on her face when she had turned to look at him as she paused after leaving the platform, and he knew that she did not understand his change of mood.

He had only done it to protect her. If they had been seen together, her life on the FOB would have been intolerable. Lone women on the frontline were vulnerable and therefore easy bait for many service men in Afghanistan, and he did not want her exposed to crass and vulgar comments. The lights coming on in the tents and the sound of voices had pulled him back from the brink of becoming embroiled in something that would have irrevocably changed their working relationship.

He needed to focus on the men in his charge, as well as Jessie herself, and he could not in all honesty allow a woman to create such a problem, no matter how deep his feelings were for her.

Nick turned to look back out at the mist-enshrouded landscape. Although his eyes, by years of training, continued to search for dickers and insurgents or any anomaly that appeared out of the ordinary, his thoughts were of Jessie and what had just occurred between them. He stirred uncomfortably as he remembered their passionate and uninhibited kisses and he closed his eyes for a brief second, groaning softly.

Chapter Fourteen

Jessie and saw on her watch that she had fifteen minutes before the mission briefing in the operations tent. Seated on a chair next to the examination table, fully kitted out, medical pack ready and leaning against her leg, weapon lying across her lap, she was already hot. The temperature was high, even so early in the morning, the air back to its usual arid dryness.

The mission briefing was set for 0700 hours, the patrol for 0800. For now, she sat with eyes closed, her mind not focused on the upcoming patrol at all but exclusively on Nick. He was all she seemed to think about nowadays, but what she had allowed to take place between them earlier should not have happened.

Since their meeting in the tower, she had seen no sign of him. Whether he was avoiding her or tied up in operational briefings, she had no idea. There had been no opportunity to ask him why his mood had changed, no way of easing the pain that haunted her at his sudden withdrawal. The fact that she felt such pain was proof of how she felt about him and how deep her feelings were.

Whenever she thought of him, she shivered inside. She still remembered the heat of his kisses, the strength of his arms about her and the feel of his erection, proof of how much he wanted her. She wanted to make love with him anywhere they could find privacy, wanted to feel him hold her and show her what he felt for her. Nevertheless, somewhere deep inside her there remained an element of guilt about Mark. She had tried to suppress it — gave herself any number of reasons and answers for what she was doing. Sometimes it worked and the confusion dissipated, sometimes the guilt almost tore her apart.

Jerking herself back to reality, Jessie glanced quickly at her watch again. With five minutes to get to the mission briefing, she got to her feet, slipping her arm through the shoulder strap of her weapon then grabbing for her pack. She hurried out of the medical tent and strode across to operations, wrinkling her nose at the stifling heat that greeted her.

She found both Bravo and Charlie Recon Sections already standing around a long metal table covered with a large, laminated map. As she entered, everyone turned in her direction and she colored a little when she met Nick's eyes. Lieutenant Marshall, the commanding officer of Charlie Recon, was also in attendance, and she was embarrassed to discover that Major Hayward was also present, as were four members of the AA.

"Glad you could make it, Corporal," Nick announced, his voice sounding neutral. He gestured with his head for her to join them.

"Sorry, sir," Jessie murmured and inserted her body between Mungo and Wolf. Mungo whispered out of the side of his mouth, "Good one, Mac."

Jessie pulled a face at him and, placing her pack on the floor, she took a notebook and pen from a pouch on her body armor. She tried to relax and get herself focused on the briefing but felt that she only partially succeeded as her body still felt tense.

Nick began, "Because of a change of orders, we'll backtrack over the intel we have for the benefit of Mac. The ISAF are to attend a *shura* in the town of Khavak, twenty clicks from our location. For the uninitiated, a *shura* is a council made up of elders and a *mullah*, who is a local official of some standing. A *shura* is normally Taliban-controlled but Khavak is now under ISAF control and there have been no Taliban sighted in that area for some time.

"The problem lies in the fact that it's not uncommon for

elders to agree to a *shura* in order to lure Coalition forces into a pre-planned ambush. Elders and civilians will usually disappear or fail to show up at the meeting, allowing as much as several hundred insurgents to attack a patrol from houses in the town.

"Their strategy is to fortify and open fire from a complex of buildings overlooking the planned location. You should all know by now the strategies insurgents use and the way they work, but we'll quickly go over the danger signs. The Taliban sometimes warn civilians before carrying out ambushes near populated areas. I say *sometimes* because they also take innocent civilians to cover their attacks, knowing that Coalition forces will not openly make contact with hostiles who are holding hostages.

"We need to keep eyes on for departing civilians or an empty town or marketplace. This is usually indicative of an impending attack, sometimes followed by men of fighting age arriving in pickup trucks or on motorcycles. Insurgents make regular use of forward observers, usually unarmed men standing on rooftops or driving around on bikes, using cell phones to warn them of a patrol's approach. Some observers are local children, as sick as that is. Insurgents can use referee whistles to communicate with fighters nearby, or they may use the whistles as a way of communicating without revealing their position.

"Insurgent tactics used are fire, maneuver, cover and concealment. They will also use command-wired IEDs to get around counter measures used by British troops."

Nick paused and studied all section members. "Any questions so far?" he asked. He watched as they all shook their heads.

"Excellent," he responded and leaned forward, planting a finger on an area of the map where there was a red meandering line culminating in a red circle. "This is our route, running parallel to the mountains. The Watchkeeper has done a recce over the route and data has come back that the area is clear. As you know, this intel can change minute by minute, so a Watchkeeper will fly over our location periodically and our central information systems will receive updates every ten minutes.

"There is only one route in and out of the town, northwest to southeast. The *shura* buildings are in the center of the town." He stabbed his finger in the middle of the red circle. "They face southwest and border a marketplace. There are buildings on three sides of the area facing north-northwest, north-northeast and east-northeast.

"The marketplace creates a chokepoint in the middle of the ingress and egress, so we cannot drive the M-ATVs into the area. This means that we'll have to dismount at the marketplace, secure the area, then a small team will attend the *shura*. The mission is classed as high level as there is maximum risk of an ambush."

At this, there were a number of grunts and curses from the men, and Jessie looked up from making notes on her pad directly at Nick. He glanced at her briefly and she felt her cheeks go warm as an instant vision of their passionate meeting in the tower forced its way into her mind. She bit her lip hard to force the images away.

"All right, let's have some quiet," JR yelled. "Shut up."

The men became quiet, allowing Nick to continue. "Bravo Recon will come in from the northwest, and Charlie Recon will circle around and come in from the southeast. When reaching the marketplace, we'll seal off both routes. Security teams will maintain perimeters around the vehicles. Keep HUDs online at all times and keep weapons locked and loaded."

Nick turned to Major Hayward, who had been standing with his arms folded throughout Nick's briefing.

"Sir?" he said, an enquiring note in his voice.

Major Hayward nodded and stepped forward. "Lady and gentlemen. I have nothing more to add to Lieutenant Ryan's briefing except that both he and Lieutenant Marshall are experienced officers in the field and excellent under hostile conditions. Listen to them, obey their orders and think.

Never let your vigilance lapse or lose concentration. Keep your minds on your mission. *Do not* become distracted. Good luck."

He nodded at them all and, moving past Jessie and the rest of the group at the table, marched out of the operations tent.

"Any questions?" Nick asked. He turned to Lieutenant Marshall, who shook his head, then he turned back to the sections who were also responding in the negative.

"Shall we get this done?" he asked, raising his voice. Jessie knew it to be a tactic to provoke in them a sense of purpose, enhance their resolve for the mission ahead.

"Yes, sir!" came the loud, almost adrenaline-fueled chorus from the men.

"Excellent," Nick answered nodding his head slightly in satisfaction at the sound of eagerness and enthusiasm in their voices. "Form up outside. Go!"

Without wasting any time, Bravo and Charlie Recon got to their feet and with much coarse laughter, shrugged into their packs and, after picking up their weapons, jostled each other to get outside the tent.

Jessie stashed her notebook and pen and rose to put on her own pack. As she turned to go, she thought she heard Nick call out her name, but she moved quickly outside the operations tent into the sultry burning heat of the day.

Squinting in the bright sunlight — already feeling hot and sticky — she followed the men making their way toward the two M-ATVs, now parked one behind the other in front of the gates. Bravo Recon formed up at the back of the lead vehicle with Charlie Recon taking the one at the rear.

Jessie joined the highly strung section members and, while waiting to board, studied the huge vehicle in which they would be making the journey.

The M-ATV was a new design and able to carry three crew and eight to twelve troops. She also knew that it could transport a great deal of mission equipment and was capable of off-road mobility over any type of terrain. It had the benefit of being multi-mission ready and allowed crews whose roles could rapidly change to have the right vehicle to perform any mission.

The roof-mounted turret sported an M230LF chain gun, a far more advanced version of the Apache auto-cannon, able to fire two hundred rounds a minute. It could be operated from the turret by a single gunner or remotely controlled from inside the cabin via a common remotely operated weapons station — CROWS.

Of far more importance to Jessie was the fact that the M-ATV had its own heating, ventilation and air conditioning system. The vehicle did have windows, but they were protected with armor-plated shields, so without the HVAC system, conditions inside would have been extremely uncomfortable for her and the section as they traveled to and from Khavak.

"Enough of the antics, Bravo Recon," Nick shouted, as he joined them, accompanied by two Afghan Army, startling Jessie from her reverie about their transport. "Get yourselves onboard."

She glanced sideways at him but he did not look in her direction, and he moved off to take his place in the passenger seat of the driver's cab.

The last one to climb aboard, Jessie took a seat closest to the pneumatic double suicide doors — rear hinged — and made herself comfortable by kicking her pack beneath her seat. She stood her weapon on its buttstock between her legs then tried to relax.

The seven other members of Bravo Recon were boisterous and loud. The briefing had obviously stirred in them a heightened enthusiasm for the mission ahead. Whether they were nervous or not, Jessie couldn't tell, but she felt dread coiling insidiously inside her.

There was no real reason for her to feel anxious. The Watchkeeper had thoroughly reconned Khavak, and the drone's data had clearly shown that there was no sign of any insurgents along their route or surrounding the town.

As this was her first major mission, she was bound to feel anxious. A bout of nervousness would keep her on her toes, adrenaline fueling her nervous system, allowing her to think clearly and boosting her energy levels. However, no matter how much she tried to convince herself that nothing was going to happen, she couldn't help but feel that it was more than nerves she felt. It was more like a foreboding that the mission was going to go pear-shaped in a very bad way.

Someone kicked her foot, jerking her from her doom-laden thoughts. Glancing to the seat opposite, she saw Dingle smiling at her, and she nervously returned it.

"Christ, Mac. You look like you're heading for a firing squad," he announced.

"It's hardly going to be a tea party, is it?" Jessie snapped, a little irritated by his statement.

"We'll have your back, Mac, sweetheart," Shrek sang out, his voice full of confidence and, when she turned her attention to him, he winked at her.

"Yeah, I'm sure you will," Jessie answered, a sour taste in her mouth. "I'll remind you later that you said that."

She looked to her left toward the cab and saw that Nick had turned to glance over his shoulder at her. His eyes met hers and she saw him smile very slightly and wink reassuringly, as if he knew how she was feeling. Some of her agitation dispersed and she felt a warm feeling spiral in her stomach.

"All right, Bravo Recon. Yeti, get yourself on the CROWS. Everyone take it easy and try to relax."

Jessie watched as Yeti turned to the control mount set up behind the passenger seat. He turned on a display monitor and with fingers darting over switches, activated the CROWS remote weapons system and manipulated a joystick, which resembled the control used in playing a video game. He tested the sight package, which included a daylight video camera, thermal camera and an eye-safe laser rangefinder.

"All online, checked and ready to go, LT," Yeti finally announced.

"Copy that," Nick announced and spoke in an undertone to JR, who was the designated driver.

The M-ATV started with a roar, the engine finally settling down to a loud rumble and within a few minutes, they were on the move.

Jessie found herself jolted mercilessly as they proceeded along a road that felt uneven and full of potholes. Although the huge tires negotiated the rough terrain with ease, she hoped that the rest of the route was not going to be as uncomfortable, as she could see herself becoming physically ill.

There was nothing of interest inside the vehicle that she could focus on to occupy her mind except for the sweating faces of her section mates, so Jessie closed her eyes. The journey would take approximately thirty minutes, barring any problems on their route. She hoped fervently that there wouldn't be and they could reach Khavak without incident.

She opened her eyes again, her attention focusing on the four members of the AA. They sat with expressionless faces and in silence, not participating in the ribaldry that came from the other men. Jessie felt uneasy at their presence. She knew the reason for her reticence, wished she could trust them as Nick did. A member of the Taliban posing as a member of the AA had cruelly killed her husband, and she could, therefore, never allow herself to regard them as part of the ongoing operation to make Afghanistan a safer place for its people.

* * * *

Jessie jerked awake from a light doze as Nick's voice sounded over the comms system in her helmet. She was surprised that she had finally relaxed enough to be able to sleep, and she straightened up in her seat, glancing around self-consciously.

"We're coming up on Khavak. Everyone get ready."

There was eager movement inside the M-ATV as everyone checked their weapons and settled down to await further orders. The vehicle slowed gradually, trundled along at a greatly reduced speed for a further ten minutes before it swung to the left, then stopped.

"Security teams, prepare to dismount. Report back to me with a sitrep as soon as you've checked out the area."

Shrek, Mungo, Wolf and Devil, designated security teams one and two, each team accompanied by a single AA, quickly unstrapped themselves from their seats. They queued in a line, waiting to dismount and Jessie saw that they now appeared nervous, checking their helmets and weapons, their feet shifting around aimlessly, unable to keep still.

The pneumatic doors hissed open and they jumped down, each team disappearing around either side of the vehicle, one taking up position to observe the route they had just traversed, the other reconnoitering the area to the front.

The rest of Bravo Recon sat inside and waited in silence, fidgeting nervously until at last, Shrek's voice came through their helmets, giving the all clear. Immediately, everyone released themselves from their seats and, one by one, they dismounted.

The first to jump down, Jessie was instantly alert, acutely aware of her surroundings and where the rest of the members of her section were in relation to herself. As soon as her boots touched the ground, she crouched slightly and glanced about.

The M-ATV, positioned at an angle across the narrow road that served as the main thoroughfare into the town, sealed off the route into the marketplace. The second M-ATV had carried out the same maneuver opposite, on the road leading out of the village. There was now no access to the area from either direction.

Jessie quickly studied the small, square marketplace in front of her. She was looking for anyone acting suspiciously or anything that looked out of place or out of the ordinary. She assumed that the dirty tan-colored building to her left was where the *shura* was due to take place. Directly opposite and to her right, beyond the jumble of market stalls, she spied some rundown buildings, their glassless windows looking down onto the townspeople as they went about their business.

She was relieved to note that the civilians of Khavak seemed to be going about their daily lives as if unaware of the arrival of the British army in their midst. If they were unafraid, then surely there could not be any insurgents in the area.

On rare occasions, the Taliban warned civilians of an impending attack, but there was always the chance that other insurgents turned a cold shoulder and had no sympathy for ordinary people caught in the crossfire. That meant there was no guarantee that because things looked normal within the town that they, in fact, were.

Nick joined the four remaining members of Bravo Recon who were to attend the *shura* with him.

"Gather around, you lot," he ordered and once Jessie and the men had done so, he continued, "We'll walk the perimeter of the marketplace just to check things out, make sure the area is clear, then we'll make our way to the meeting. Charlie Recon will cover the other side. Let's move out."

With Nick taking point, he moved casually away from the M-ATV, gesturing for the section to follow. Putting distance between the vehicle and themselves, they moved slowly into the marketplace and along the stalls. Careful to appear friendly, the motto *'hearts and minds'* uppermost in their thoughts, they all made a point of interacting with the locals, who greeted them, smiling and chattering loudly.

Jessie maintained her vigilance, part of her attention focused on the townspeople, but keenly searching areas of the buildings for hidden movement that might precede an attack.

A group of children began to gather about her, tugging at her combats and babbling in a language that she wasn't able to understand. She smiled at them, stopping now and again to reach out a hand to rub silky black hair and stroke smooth skin, thrilling to their dark eyes and wide, beaming smiles.

She stopped at a couple of stalls, fingering brightly colored material and luxurious, handcrafted Afghan blankets, shrugging in helplessness when a couple of the stallholders spoke to her.

I definitely need to learn Pashto.

She was just beginning to relax and enjoy her surroundings — lulled into a false sense of complacency — when there was the sudden sound of a gunshot.

No!

For a moment Jessie froze, unable to believe that she had actually heard the sharp retort. Everyone stopped moving, heads turning this way and that to try to locate where the shot had come from, people looking at each other with fear and confusion on their faces. Silence fanned out across the marketplace, disturbed only when a small child cried out, frightened at the sudden tension in the air.

All hell suddenly broke loose.

A sudden barrage of both small arms and automatic gunfire broke the shocked silence, and the screaming started. Men, women and children began to flee, their panicked cries rending the air. Women hoisted up the long skirts of their *firaq partūgs* and grabbed or dragged young children toward the backs of the stalls, as if the flimsy partitions could prevent the lethal bullets from thudding into their vulnerable bodies.

Jessie saw one man grab the woman with him about the waist, lift her feet from the ground then run at a lumbering sprint toward the M-ATV. A cacophony of shrieks and screams resounded through the air and she could almost taste the fear that had suddenly appeared like a tangible cloud within the town.

Her mind completely numb with shock, she saw Nick run past her toward the M-ATV and she got herself moving, following at a dead run. From out of the corner of her eye, she saw a man stumble, throw up his arms then collapse face down on the ground. Jessie stopped abruptly then turned to go to the man's aid, all thought of her own personal safety vanishing.

A woman, tugging a small child by its arm with one hand, ran holding up her voluminous skirts with the other until suddenly the toddler tripped and fell, unable to keep up with its mother. The woman stopped, hoisted the child up by its top, and hauled it to safety behind the M-ATV.

As she ran toward the supine figure of the man, Jessie glimpsed dust and sand spiral up in miniature tornados about one meter from her boots and fear lodged in her throat when she realized that the strafing was getting ever closer to her own body.

She heard her section mates shouting, the screams from the unprotected civilians seemed to rise to a crescendo until suddenly there was a massive explosion. She felt a hard shove in the small of her back, then she went flying, her feet leaving the ground as she literally flew through the air for a few meters. She landed face down on the ground, the front of her helmet smashing into the unyielding cracked earth, the wind knocked from her lungs.

Chapter Fifteen

Jessie heard the sound of her own harsh struggles to breathe and she grunted in an attempt to fill her lungs with oxygen. For what seemed like an eternity, she lay prone. Dust coated her face and she spat it from her mouth. The gunfire had ceased as suddenly as it had begun and, for a brief moment, silence surrounded her. It was as though the world had stopped and all life with it. Then moans and screams interspersed with panicked pleadings suddenly flooded in, assaulting her ears, and she squirmed with fear.

I need to get moving and see to the injured. Move your ass, girl!

Halfway to her feet, she was promptly knocked flat again by a further explosion. She curled into a fetal position as the ground shook beneath her. There was a rumbling noise that grew in intensity before dwindling away, and she heard the crash of falling masonry and splintering wood.

Jessie lay still, hardly daring to breathe, as though one single intake of air would create another, more lethal, explosion. Aware of the need to see to what sounded like numerous casualties, she staggered to her feet, her body tensing. Almost before she was standing upright, she gasped in horror at the scene of destruction that surrounded her.

She coughed violently from the clouds of choking dust hanging motionless in the hot air that partially obscured her view of the scene. From what she *could* see, the marketplace was littered with bodies, some ominously still, others writhing in agony. Most of the stalls were now splintered wreckage, brightly colored canopies and items that had been for sale mixed in with splintered and torn wood.

Without thinking of carrying out triage, assigning

priorities or her own personal safety, focusing entirely on the thought that she had to help the casualties, Jessie quickly got herself moving, jogging toward the first man she had seen collapsing to the ground. Releasing her medical pack, she dropped to her knees beside the prone figure, noting immediately that the man was conscious and mumbling incoherently.

"Listen to my voice. You're going to be okay."

She carried out a hasty body assessment and found a bullet wound in his upper thigh. It was bleeding heavily but not spurting, as it would have been if there were arterial damage.

She quickly found a pair of nitrile gloves in the front of her body armor, put them on then proceeded to pull out Kerlix gauze and emergency trauma bandages. Ripping open the various sterile packages, she first made a bulky dressing from the gauze, layering it across the wound. She then wound a bandage tightly around the thigh and fastened the end down with an elasticized gripper.

"You'll be fine. Keep focused on my voice." The litany of soothing words poured from her as she dressed the wound. "We'll get you out of here. Don't worry."

Hating to leave the casualty alone but knowing that there were numerous others that she needed to attend to, possibly with far more serious injuries, she moved on to the next one.

For the next hour, Jessie moved from casualty to casualty, assessing, treating the wounds, reassuring those still conscious and offering comfort when it was required. At last, she stopped when it appeared that she had tended to the last casualty. Her gaze rested on the four pitiful, lifeless bodies then she assessed the area to see if there were any more injured or dead.

Some members of Bravo and Charlie Recon were clearing the market area of rubble while others of her own section monitored the injured, as she had instructed them. The security teams had moved position and were enforcing a perimeter around the edges of the marketplace.

She searched the area for a sign of Nick but couldn't see him. She felt a brief moment of fear as she wondered if he was safe. She jumped as he spoke over her comms.

"Jessie."

She was so relieved to hear his voice that it barely registered that he had used her first name.

"Are you all right? What's the situation? How many casualties are there? Three combat trauma flights are on their way. ETA ten minutes, and they need a casualty count."

Jessie tiredly rotated her head on tense shoulders and answered, "I'm fine, sir. We have four non-hostiles dead and eight non-hostile casualties — two Cat As, status urgent, two Cat Bs, surgical urgent, requiring stretchers and four Cat Cs — status priority, all ambulatory."

"Good job, Mac."

She felt a small thrill at Nick's praise, but when she again checked the area, she felt sick at the sight of so many injured. She frowned when she saw something lying beneath an overturned stall and without thinking, grabbed her pack and jogged across to the wreckage.

Her heart almost stopped for a second, then galloped on when she saw a hand protruding from beneath a pile of splintered, gouged wood entwined with swathes of brightly colored material.

Kneeling down, she began to lift up and throw aside the debris until she laid bare the still body of a young woman, lying face down. With her head turned to the side, the dark brown eyes stared up at her, wide open and lifeless.

Jessie pressed two trembling fingers against the carotid pulse and her heart sank when she could not find a faint beat. She let her eyes run along the woman's body until she found the cause of death. She had received a bullet wound in the back that had ultimately killed her.

"Fuck," she murmured brokenly.

She gently turned the woman onto her back and as the

body toppled away from her, she let out a moan of utter horror. Lying beneath her was a baby.

The sounds around her faded away until all she could hear were the thudding of her heartbeat and the rush of blood in her ears.

Quickly, she picked up the child, who could have been no more than three months old. Despite the heat of the day, the little body was cold. She quickly checked for a pulse while studying its face. She noted a tinge of cyanosis about the bow-like lips, the pallor, and she saw that the little chest did not rise and fall.

She thought that the mother—shot—had fallen forward and pinned her child beneath her. The baby had suffocated. It was a tragedy brought about by the murderous acts of the Taliban.

Holding the little form in her arms, Jessie's eyes filled with tears. "You poor little thing," she whispered. "I'm so sorry."

She bowed her head over the small body and a tear trickled down her face. It was so cruel and unjust. None of the people in Khavak had deserved what had happened to them that day. This mother and child had been murdered. The child—an innocent—would never play, attend school, get married or have children of its own. Its little life had ended the moment its mother had died.

Jessie felt the hot coals of rage start to burn deep inside her. She allowed the embers to catch fire and it spread throughout her body, burning like lava.

"Sir," she announced, her grief suppressed now but her voice flat with unexpressed anger. "I have an update on the casualty status. I have two dead bodies, a female and young child, approximately three months old."

There was a short silence then Nick responded softly, "Fuck! Copy that. Are you—?"

Jessie cut him off. "Out, sir."

She laid the baby next to its mother, tenderly straightening its clothes and running a gentle finger down its cold cheek.

Staring at it for a final moment, she rose to her feet. Clasping her weapon tightly in her hands, she turned slowly, again surveying the scene.

The frightening aspect of the whole incident was that she now felt nothing but a deep rage. If she sighted a target, she would not have hesitated to aim her weapon and fire.

She closely surveyed the buildings on the opposite side of the marketplace that had obviously concealed the insurgents while they waited to ambush the platoon. She wondered if they were still in there, watching them all, perhaps waiting to attack them again. She felt her body tense when she sighted movement as someone left one of the buildings to hurry along the edge of the market square. She suddenly felt a surge of triumph.

Payback!

Jessie could not tell from that distance whether it was male or female, but by the way the person walked and the black clothes that included a woolen Pakol hat, she was almost sure that it was a man.

With icy calmness, she activated her HUD and brought up her present location, all the while keeping her eyes on the figure that appeared to be moving quickly and keeping close to the wall of the building, as though it was trying to keep as low a profile as possible.

Without hesitation—fueled by her fury—she began to run across the rubble-strewn ground toward the figure. She thought she heard someone shout out behind her but ignored it, her sole aim being to catch one of the people who had caused the atrocity in Khavak.

She continued to watch the insurgent until he turned a corner, disappearing into what looked like a narrow alleyway. Fully aware that she was acting irrationally but determined that the person in her sights would not get away from her, she ran faster, keeping on the balls of her feet so as to not give herself away.

Reaching the building, she slowed her pace and, keeping parallel to the wall, jogged along its length. Stopping, she peered carefully around the corner, scanning the narrow street and she saw the person approximately halfway down. As she was about to follow him, he suddenly ducked into a hidden doorway.

"Fucking bastard. I'll get you!"

Jessie moved slowly down the street, hugging the walls of the houses, studying each doorway and window for signs of anyone observing her, holding her weapon at shoulder level, ready to pull the trigger.

She reached what she hoped was the entryway the person had ducked into, then stopped. Holding her breath, she listened carefully for any sound that might lead her to them or confirm that she was on the right track. A faint crunch of gravel heard from deep inside the building was her reward, and she knew she had located the person she was after.

Stealthily, placing her feet heel to toe to make her footfalls lighter, she moved inside. She sidled along the left-hand wall for a few paces, then quickly stepped across to flatten herself against the opposite one. Again, pressing herself back against the cracked surface, she moved along the short corridor, stopping only when another doorway appeared, preventing her from going any farther.

Quietly lifting her weapon — finger on the trigger — she moved the final few inches to the door jamb, rested her cheek against the splintered wood and cautiously edged her face forward so that she could peer around its edge.

The small room beyond was strewn with rubble but empty. Jessie noticed another doorway to her left and oblivious to everything around her — totally focused on what she was about to do — she stepped inside and hurriedly moved to hug the wall again, making her way toward the door frame.

Once there, she peered into the room and her body went rigid when she saw the man she was pursuing standing in its center, facing away from her with a satellite phone in his hand.

Jessie hesitated. For a moment, she felt fear at what she was about to do, then once again, anger took over and she crept up behind the man and raised her weapon, aiming it at the back of his head.

"Get your fucking hands in the air," she commanded quietly and watched as the man stiffened. "I said…raise your…fucking hands," she ordered again, "unless you want me to blast your pathetic brains all over the wall."

Her finger hovered over the trigger as the man slowly began to turn. He still did not raise his hands and, when he finally faced her, she was stunned to see a smile spread across his swarthy face. He said something incomprehensible and Jessie shook her head.

"Shut the fuck up, you piece of shit. And wipe that smile off your face before I wipe it off for you."

Then she recognized him, and, for a split second, she felt as if the ground actually moved beneath her feet. The world spun dizzily about her.

It was Sergeant Nabil Bannusi, the Afghan who had been a member of the AA who had joined them at the FOB, supposedly to act as security, and the man who had studied her with such contempt on his arrival.

"*You!*" she exclaimed. Hate and rage boiled up inside her, and she nearly lost it. Struggling to regain control of the situation, she said with venom in her voice, "You fucking traitor. I should have known."

The Afghan continued to stare at her, his expression one of contempt with an element of amusement in it. Jessie knew that he might not understand her — or at least pretend that he couldn't — but it didn't stop her verbally venting her outrage.

She jerked the barrel of her weapon down toward the ground. "Get down on your knees."

When the man did not comply, Jessie felt the rage coil in her chest like an inflamed chancre and she repeated, "I said, down on your goddamned knees." She gestured downward more forcefully with her weapon.

The man continued to glare at her with impenetrable black eyes, the expression of contempt now replaced by a look of insolence.

Goaded, Jessie took two paces forward. She tensed, wary that the man might suddenly launch himself at her, alert for the faintest sign of movement from him. She raised her weapon to point it directly at his head once again.

"You want me to blow your brains out, motherfucker? Or maybe I should shoot out your knee caps." She lowered her assault rifle and aimed it in the direction of his concealed legs.

Pretending that she was thinking of alternatives, she suddenly said, "No. Wait a minute. How about if I blow your balls off? If you have any, that is."

She glared at the Afghan, feeling a sneer cross her face. A small part of her mind protested vehemently at her actions but she could not stop now, even if she had wanted to.

I'm losing it. I'm close to the edge. I could really do it. I could kill this son of a bitch. Wipe him off the face of the earth. No great loss.

It didn't matter, so Jessie didn't care. She couldn't stop herself from continuing on to whatever the final outcome would be. She took another pace forward, now only about a foot or so away from the insurgent.

"I'm gonna count to three, and if you're not groveling on your knees, I'm gonna reduce that brain cell you possess to nothing. You'll be *finito*, pal."

Retaining a hold on her rifle with one hand, she held up a finger of the other, then a second. "One. Two…"

The Afghan's gaze switched to her gesturing finger, darted back to her face then focused back on her hand. Finally, Jessie noticed a fleeting expression of fear cross his face. It appeared that he finally understood her intentions.

He suddenly dropped to his knees and raised his hands in the air, his black gaze still holding hers.

Jessie returned her hand to her weapon. "Excellent. Now we're getting somewhere."

Bending forward slightly, she calmly pressed the barrel end against his forehead, hard enough that the skin surrounding the rigid plastic puckered.

"I would love to reduce your brains to shit," she began, her voice low but full of venom. "I've scraped better things off of my boots, you fucker. You don't deserve to fucking walk out of here. I should make you crawl, make you suffer as you made that mother and child suffer."

Jessie choked on her words and paused, struggling to regain her composure. She tensed when she thought she heard the soft sound of a footfall from one of the other rooms. When she didn't hear it again, she continued, "What gives you the God-given right to murder innocent people? What *fucking* law says that you can blow people up, destroy them and deprive them of their lives? Huh? Answer me, you fucking monster."

She shouted the last words and thrust the barrel of her weapon forward hard so that the man's head jerked backward.

"I'm going to kill you." Her tone was matter of fact and her finger hovered over the trigger, almost caressing it. "You don't deserve—"

"Lower your weapon, Mac," Nick ordered from behind her.

Jessie did not respond to the firm voice, continuing to stare at the insurgent kneeling before her, hate for the enemy becoming a white-hot flame inside her.

"Lower…your…weapon…Corporal."

Again, Jessie did not acknowledge the order but continued to mull over what she was going to do to the man kneeling in front of her. Her finger continued to stroke the trigger, the tip of it, now and again delicately increasing the pressure on it then releasing.

"I am giving you an order, Corporal McAllister. I will *not* give you another one. I *will* have you removed by force if necessary."

Jessie found herself suddenly paying attention. The voice, although both low and calm, insinuated itself into the fog and numbness that had enshrouded her brain, compelling and persuasive. She found herself absentmindedly pondering his words, then, without warning, her anger dissipated and she suddenly felt empty of all emotion, exhausted.

Silently, she pulled her weapon away and stepped back from the man. Stumbling, she staggered to the wall then slumped against it. She watched as Nick moved toward the Afghan, finally noticing that JR was with him. He stopped by the prisoner, who had remained on his knees and stared down at him.

"Put him in flexi ties and get him the fuck out of here," Nick said to JR.

The section leader obeyed, withdrawing a set of plastic ties from a pouch on his body armor and moving around behind the Afghan. He roughly brought the prisoner's arms up behind him and fastened his wrists together. Finally, he jerked the man's arm.

"On your feet, shit for brains," he ordered.

Once the man had struggled upright, JR gestured for him to walk ahead, following behind with his weapon pointed at the insurgent's back. They left the room.

Once they were alone, Jessie turned to Nick. "Sir –" she began.

Nick raised a hand and her words dried up. Gazing at his face, she saw that he was furious. He was glaring at her, his eyebrows drawn down over eyes that were so dark they looked almost black.

"What the fuck? Have you lost your fucking mind?"

Nick's words were low but the tone cut her to the core. He had never spoken to her like that before.

"Lieutenant –" she began again, and for the second time, he shut her up.

"Don't speak, Corporal. I don't want to hear your explanation as to why you took it upon yourself to leave your casualties and your section to go running off after a person who could have killed you. You've not only endangered everyone here but also yourself, and it's the most irresponsible act I have ever come across."

His words were like daggers in her heart and Jessie swallowed, praying that she would not cry.

"Get out of here. I'll deal with you back at the FOB. You're in deep shit, Corporal."

With a last ferocious look at her, Nick turned and walked from the room, gesturing for her to follow him.

Feeling as though her whole world was falling apart, Jessie took her place behind him as they went through the empty rooms and back out into the street.

What did I expect would come of this – a medal or a bronze star, a pat on the back? I am in a whole world of hurt here, and I'm the only one to blame.

Following in Nick's wake, all her hate and outrage now vanished, she felt lost, empty of direction. For a few minutes of revenge for those who had been hurt and for the grief that she had felt at the death of the mother and child, she had brought the wrath of the man she loved down on her head.

I deserve everything I'm going to get for this – a court martial, demotion or losing the man I love.

As the last thought crossed her mind, Jessie felt a sharp stab of pain. She couldn't lose Nick because of her own stupidity. He needed to see why she had done what she had. She needed to justify it to him, then hope that he could see beyond the loss of control to the compassion and sadness behind it.

As she crossed the market square, she noticed that a large area was clear of rubble, obviously in preparation for the arrival of the CTFs. The casualties were grouped together, ready for extraction. The townspeople who had survived were thronging the edges of the marketplace, members of Bravo and Charlie Recon Sections keeping them away from the makeshift landing zone. As she followed Nick toward the M-ATV, she heard the distant sound of helicopters approaching Khavak.

On reaching the vehicle, Nick turned to her. Pointing to a spot by the driver's door—as though she were a child in need of direction—he said in a cold voice, "Stay there and *do not* move," then he left her without another word, heading in the direction of Lieutenant Marshall, who was heading up the perimeter security teams.

Jessie stood with her head bowed until Dingle's voice announced itself from beside her, "Jesus H Christ, Jessie!"

Glancing at him, she immediately saw a look of disgust mingling with concern on his face.

"Have you lost your fucking mind? I've seen some frigging daft things in my time but yours takes the biscuit."

"Okay, okay," Jessie answered impatiently. "The lieutenant has already let me know in no uncertain terms that I am gonna be hauled over the coals. I don't need you to corroborate the fact that I'm an idiot."

The conversation came to an abrupt end as two Wildcats and a Blackhawk came into view overhead. One started to descend slowly toward the clearing. As it neared the ground, clouds of dust and minute particles of debris soared up into the air, and everyone shielded their faces as the huge helo's undercarriage touched down and the rotor blades slowed slightly.

"All right. Let's get the most urgent casualties on board. Move it!" Nick shouted.

Knowing that she had to give a report to the combat trauma teams, Jessie moved toward the casualties. She watched as the CTT dismounted from the helicopter, carrying stretchers, and she jogged toward them. One man, the CTT doctor—a Major—strode toward her and proceeded to question her as to injuries sustained and the type of treatment given.

Not having had time to complete field casualty cards, Jessie proceeded to give the officer a verbal report, detailing procedures she had followed and medication given. Once she had finished, he nodded, then strode off to join his team.

Quickly and efficiently, the CTT assessed each casualty, then the first four cases were loaded on board the helicopter. Within a few minutes, the Wildcat's blades sped up and it gradually rose into the air, banked to the right then sped off.

The second CTF, which had remained on station, came in to land and the remaining casualties were loaded aboard, then it too, took off.

Once the Blackhawk had come then gone, Nick ordered, "Everyone load up. Let's head back."

Feeling tired, hot and miserable, Jessie headed back to the M-ATV. She waited for the men ahead of her to climb aboard, then she took the same seat as she had on their outward journey. The atmosphere was filled with tension and whenever she glanced up, she found one or more of her section mates staring at her and began to feel uncomfortable under their scrutiny.

She wondered what the men were thinking. They were obviously aware of what had happened, but their expressions were inscrutable. She couldn't figure out what they thought of her actions. She closed her eyes, withdrawing into herself.

The journey back to the FOB seemed to take forever. For the whole of that time, Bravo Recon remained quiet, their usual humor markedly absent. Nobody spoke or bothered Jessie and on their arrival back at the FOB, she was up and out of the M-ATV before anyone else. All she wanted to do was get inside her quarters and remain there to lick her wounds.

She was about to make her way there when Nick's voice stopped her. "Go and get yourself cleaned up, then report to me."

"Yes, sir," Jessie replied in a low voice and continued in the direction of her tent, aware that Bravo Recon was still standing by the M-ATV staring at her.

Oh, fuck it! Let them stare. What do I care?

She pushed through the flap then dropped her equipment to the floor just inside, roughly removing her helmet and releasing the pins on her body armor. She stood motionless for a few seconds, her body aching with fatigue, thoughts scattered and incoherent. Finally, she made her way into her quarters and tiredly began to undress.

As she rid herself of her combats, she grimaced when she discovered that the legs of her trousers were soaked with blood, as were parts of her combat shirt. Red stains smeared her hands and grime and crimson caked her fingernails thickly, even though she had worn gloves. Shuddering, Jessie found her toilet kit and hurried into the shower tent.

She spent some time beneath the water, scrubbing her skin over and over until it tingled and grew red. She felt that if she washed herself hard enough, she might obliterate the events of that day and what she had done.

She finally remembered that Nick wanted to see her. She had wasted enough time in the shower. He was already angry with her, and she was in enough trouble as it was. She had probably only made things worse for herself, taking so much time.

She quickly dried herself, plaited her damp hair and pinned it up then dressed in fresh combats and a white T-shirt. Feeling slightly better but not looking forward to the meeting with Nick, she laced her feet back into boots that were liberally spotted with blood, and left the tent. With the exception of the security guards on duty, the FOB appeared deserted, although she could hear loud voices coming from the men's accommodation tents.

Jessie stopped outside Nick's tent and, taking a deep breath, preparing for the worst, she slapped the flap.

Chapter Sixteen

"Come in."

Nick — still furious with her — watched Jessie enter, walk smartly to stand to attention in front of his desk and stare at a point over his right shoulder.

There was a short silence while he stared at her. At last, "Let's cut the crap, Mac. There's nothing remotely of interest at the back of my tent, so look at me," he snapped.

Jessie lowered her gaze to his and he saw her cheeks flush red, two hectic patches on her face, which was the color of cream. Her dark blue eyes had lost their sparkle, the expression in them blank.

He had seen men who had been involved in incidents such as she and he recognized the expression of someone who was shell-shocked and traumatized. He gritted his teeth trying to quell the sympathy and concern that he felt.

"What's the story?" he asked without preamble. "And make it a good one."

"I lost it, sir," she replied at last. "It's as simple and as stupid as that. When I found the mother and baby…I was so angry I couldn't think straight. It seemed so unfair. I saw the insurgent leave the building and took the opportunity. When I recognized him, it got even worse."

Nick saw her hesitate then take a deep breath.

"There's something else," she began, and her voice shook slightly. "That man I told you about, the one who was killed by an insurgent posing as AA? He was my husband. We'd only been married for six months. I know that's no excuse for doing what I did… I just thought you should know."

Nick looked down at his hands, feeling sympathy coil

insidiously in his stomach. However, for all that he felt her pain, he couldn't let her actions go unacknowledged.

"Is that it?" he asked, forcing his tone to remain cold and angry, a feat that he was finding extremely difficult when all he wanted to do was knock the table aside and take her in his arms. "That's your explanation?"

"That's it, sir."

"Well, you fucked up big time, Corporal. No one on my watch puts lives at risk because of a need for revenge or because *they* think they know better. What were you thinking? You could have gotten your section killed. More to the point, you could have gotten yourself killed. No matter what pressure we find ourselves under, we *never* let it get the better of us."

Nick paused. He hated the words that spilled from his mouth. He remained shaken from the incident at Khavak. Even more than that, he had felt frantic when he realized that Jessie had gone missing. He should have realized that something was wrong after her brief comms message advising him of the discovery of the mother and child. There had been something in her voice, a cold and emotionless tone that had set off alarm bells in his head.

Once he had seen that she was gone, he had immediately started a hasty, unorganized search, bringing himself up short when he noticed the puzzled expressions on the faces of his men. Trying to calm himself down, he had scanned his HUD and saw her ident heading toward the buildings on the opposite side of the market square.

Now he stared at her, noting her pallor and the beginnings of faint dark circles beneath her eyes. There was an expression of sadness in them together with stubbornness. He could understand where she was coming from.

It must have been traumatic to discover the body of the woman and child, and now that she had explained what had happened to her husband, he was well aware of the reason behind her actions, not just in the village but also during the past days. However, he needed to make her understand the danger she had put herself in. When he had found her with her weapon pressed against the prisoner's forehead, his reaction had been to kill the man himself. If the insurgent had attacked Jessie, he would have done so without hesitation. This was only one of the problems that arose when you fell in love with someone in a war zone. He was angry with her for a number of reasons, not least because he now realized that he *did* love her and that he could well have lost her.

Jessie waited for Nick to speak. She knew that he was right in everything he had said, but it didn't make her feel any better. The events of the day had sent her emotions into a turmoil of anger and sadness, and she was now burdened with the knowledge that humans — no matter what side they were on — could be merciless when it came to war.

"I've spoken to the Major about the incident," Nick announced, his tone softer. "Also, both Bravo and Charlie Recon came to see me. Dingle as spokesperson on your behalf was very eloquent, as usual. He persuaded me not to go any further with this. Major Hayward agreed with me — and them — so it looks like you get away with a warning… this time."

He stopped speaking, stood up and came around the table to stand in front of her.

Jessie found herself trembling as silence enveloped them both. Nick suddenly made a move toward her, reached out and pulled her roughly against him.

"Jessie, don't *ever* do that again. I was out of my mind when I found out you'd disappeared."

Pulled into the circle of his arms, Jessie placed the palms of her hands flat against his chest. She studied his face and saw that what he had told her was the truth.

"I'm sorry, Nick," she said softly. "I shouldn't have done what I did."

Nick pulled her in tighter against him. "No, you shouldn't have. Your behavior was well out of order. I should kick you out of the section, get you transferred out of here so you don't cause any further trouble. The only problem is I didn't realize how much you meant to me...until I discovered what you'd done."

With those words, he kissed her, and she felt all the pent up emotion that he had been feeling, released in that kiss.

Jessie moaned as his tongue entwined with hers and her own parried and entangled with it. He ran his hands down her back and clasped the cheeks of her backside, pulling her hips in toward his.

Jessie lightly trailed her fingers up the warm skin of his arms to his shoulders, conscious of the way his muscles rippled and flexed beneath his T-shirt. Her hands moved on up to the back of his head, where she clenched her fingers in his thick hair.

At last, Nick pulled away. "You do know I love you, right?"

Jessie, her breathing as rapid as his, was startled at his admission. She leaned back in his arms and saw the truth of what he had said in his face.

"You do?" she asked breathlessly.

"I do," Nick reiterated, kissing her nose. "You're obstinate, stubborn, headstrong and bloody insubordinate. You're going to turn my hair gray with the way you put your life on the line, but...yes, I love you more than my life, Jessie McAllister."

"I love you too," Jessie responded, feeling a brief but intense upwelling of joy, then she was kissing him and he was returning her kiss hungrily until he pulled away again.

She suddenly felt his body stiffen against hers. Seeing the wary expression appear on his face, she was about to ask what was wrong when he put a finger to his lips, bent his head toward hers and whispered, "Keep your voice down. I think I heard someone outside."

Holding her breath, Jessie listened intently for somebody moving around outside the tent but heard nothing suspicious and eventually, she felt Nick relax.

"Enough," he ordered, although his words sounded reluctant. "You need to go and relax. Get some rest. You've had a rough day."

"Will I...see you later?" Jessie asked shyly.

Nick raised an eyebrow and smiled. "Come to your tent? Naughty," he teased, his voice low. "I might just pop in and let you give me the once-over."

"Don't keep me waiting, Lieutenant," she said, her voice equally low but seductive. She could hear the words, the sensual quality of her tone but, for some reason, she felt nothing and it frightened her.

"Now go," Nick ordered, "before the rumor network finds something to talk about."

Jessie nodded and stepped back from him. Giving him a brief smile, she turned and left, making her way across to her tent. On entering, she went straight to her quarters and, feeling emotionally exhausted, sat down on her bed, unlaced her boots then kicked them off. She lay back and closed her eyes.

Nick's admission that he loved her had lifted her spirits for a short time. She still couldn't believe that he had actually said those words to her. The thought exhilarated her, filled her with a soaring hope for their future. If she could obliterate the thoughts of the attack that had happened that day in Khavak and the images of those killed and injured, she would have been the happiest girl in the world.

Now that she was alone, the killings at Khavak haunted her. As a result of the incident, something had happened to her. Somewhere inside was a hollow numbness that felt like a ball of ice. There was something wrong. The anger and hate that had manifested itself at the marketplace at the futile killing of the mother and child had destroyed some of her zest for living, for believing in good and for what the ISAF had been trying to achieve in Afghanistan. The fact that she had wanted to kill the Afghan was a case in point. She had wanted to wipe out his life as he had done to the civilians and her husband. If Nick and JR had not interrupted her? Well…she thought she might have done something that she would have deeply regretted. It made her no better than those whose intent was to destroy a country and her people.

A dry sob suddenly escaped her. She wanted to relish and absorb Nick's love for her. Any other woman would have only had thoughts of the man she loved in turn. She wanted to feel human again — but for the moment, felt…nothing.

She lay staring up at the ceiling, feeling distant from her surroundings. She wanted to sleep, needed to, but her brain was teeming with mixed up images of maimed and bleeding bodies and Nick holding her in his arms. She wanted to escape into oblivion and wipe out the memories tormenting her.

Jessie abruptly sat up and swung her legs over the side of her bed. Putting her hands over her face, she bowed her head.

"Jessie."

She jumped, startled at the sound of Nick's voice and looked up to find him standing just inside her quarters.

"What's wrong?" she asked. She noticed that he was holding a satellite phone and wondered what he was doing with it. The question skittered away as he came in and crouched down in front of her.

Setting the phone down on the floor, he placed a hand on each of her thighs and squeezed them gently.

"Are you all right?" he asked gently.

Jessie bowed her head again and then glancing up, shook her head. "No," she answered in a small voice. "I keep remembering…what happened today at Khavak. The thoughts won't go away. Some of me feels…dead inside, Nick, and it frightens me."

Nick gently ran a finger down her cheek, then cupped her chin, tenderly stroking a thumb over her lips.

"I know it's hard," he said softly. "I've been where you are. An incident occurred on my first tour out here. I was on a search and rescue mission and I came across one of our men, not from my platoon, who had been tortured then mercifully killed. Following on from some intel, we caught up with and captured the insurgents responsible. To cut a long story short, I was alone with one of them and…he tried to jump me and I killed him."

Nick lapsed into silence and Jessie stared at him, feeling a little stunned at his admission.

Nick continued, "When I killed him, I felt the same rage, hate and lack of remorse that you felt. It was only after I came to my senses — and I admit that I might have been a little off my head — that I went numb. The numbness is just the body's way of protecting you from too much stress and pressure until you can come to terms with what's happened. The grief and anger that you felt during this incident are the human part of you.

"If you ever get used to killing and death and the unfairness and injustice that goes with it and if you ever become one of those people who get to enjoy it, then that would be a bad thing, Jessie. Part of being a sensitive and caring human being is allowing yourself to feel anger and grief, even over the loss of people you don't know.

"Some people judge us for doing a job that involves the destruction of human beings. It doesn't make us monsters. We care enough to travel thousands of miles to godforsaken places that we've never been to before. We work with, defend and protect complete strangers. That's who we are. Never lose that humanity, Jessie. If you do, you'll never regain it."

Jessie nodded. "I hear you," she replied in a small voice.

She put a hand on the back of his neck and with a slight pressure, brought his head toward hers then placed a light but moist kiss on his mouth. Nick's grip tightened on her chin and he increased the firmness of his kiss for a few more seconds until he drew back a few inches and she saw that he had a gentle smile on his face.

"As much as I love the distraction," he said, "we'll have to continue this later. I'm sorry to be the bearer of bad news, but I'm going to give the lads some downtime tomorrow. Unfortunately, *you* are to act as medic for Charlie Recon on a mission. Their medic is injured and needs to rest for a couple of days. A helicopter will be dropping you just outside Darbart, where the section will do a recon, then you'll be extracted."

Jessie grimaced, her humor returning slightly. "Great!" she exclaimed. "I am *so* in the mood for something like that."

Nick laughed. "Secondly," he began and picked up the satellite phone, "give your parents a ring."

Jessie looked at the phone and then at Nick. "Call my mom and dad?" she echoed, surprised.

"Yes. It will do you good. They'll be able to put things into perspective for you, which is what you need right now. Just dial your home number. The call will be relayed via satellite, so they'll be a few beeps and boops and strange noises, but it will go through."

"I'm not sure," Jessie answered slowly. "I don't really want to bother them with it or even feel much like talking about it."

Leaning forward, Nick placed a warm kiss on her mouth. "Do it, Jessie. That's an order." He got to his feet and, with a last lingering look, said, "I'll see you later, if I can make it," and left, leaving her alone.

Jessie sat on the bed, holding the satellite phone in a trembling hand, staring at it. She was desperate to speak to her parents. She needed to somehow release the guilt and unhappiness she felt at what had happened at Khavak, but the thought that she would disappoint them held her back.

The rational part of her protested at this thought. She knew perfectly well that her parents would never think of her in that way, would love her no matter what mistakes she made. The fact that she was furious and disappointed with herself for losing control was uppermost in her thoughts and distorted her perceptions of what people, including her own family, might think of her.

She tapped the phone against her thigh, her thoughts in turmoil. Finally, she made a decision and hesitantly dialed the international code for the United States then the telephone number of her home.

Her heart was thundering in her chest as she listened to the distant sound of static interspersed with, as Nick had explained, a few weird noises as the call went through the various satellite relays. Eventually, the telephone at the other end began to ring.

Her mouth went dry as she waited. Her heart jerked in her chest as at the other end, the husky deep voice of her father spoke.

"Hello."

She almost dissolved into tears at that point, but choked them back and swallowed. In a husky voice she said, "Dad? It's Jessie."

"Hey, sweetheart! How are you? It's great to hear your voice."

Jessie closed her eyes, hearing the delight and happiness in his voice. She swallowed again, trying to clear the lump in her throat.

"Wait just a second, honey. Let me call your mom. She'll kill me if I don't. I'll put you on speaker. Don't go away."

Jessie heard his voice shout, "Honey, it's Jessie."

From somewhere in the house she heard a faint, "Really?" then a beep and her mom's voice, sounding excited, spoke, "Baby girl, is that you? How are you?"

"I…I'm fine, Mom, Dad." Jessie winced as she heard the shakiness in her voice. Her parents knew her too well and would detect there was something wrong instantly. She was right.

"Honey, is something wrong?" her father asked, his tone sounding casual but concerned.

Jessie hesitated but the ache in her heart was too much. "Mom, Dad? I screwed up, big time."

There was a short silence during which she held her breath. At last, her father said, "It's okay, honey. We're not going anywhere. We're here if you need to talk."

"You know you can tell us if you want to, sweetheart. Take your time," her mother responded, her tone gentle and soothing.

Jessie instantly began to feel the balm of her mom's voice enfold her like a warm blanket. The sadness and guilt eased slightly but the tears still threatened. She coughed and said tremulously, "We had to go out on a high-level mission yesterday. I can't say too much, but there was a pretty strong risk of an ambush. When we reached our location, everything seemed normal. The area was clear, or so we thought.

"We made contact with insurgents who were hiding out in some buildings in the area. They had pretty heavy firepower, the works. For quite a while we were pinned down and then...then they detonated some IEDs. The civilians bore the brunt of it. There were a lot of casualties. None of my section was hurt and neither was I, but..."

Jessie paused, unable to go on. A tear trickled down her face and she forced back a sob.

"Go on, honey. We're listening. It's okay."

The caring tone in her father's voice was nearly Jessie's undoing. She wanted to be taken into her dad's strong arms and hugged, to be soothed and gain strength from him. She wanted to hear him say that everything was going to be all right.

"I found a mother and child. The mother was shot and killed. I think she tried to save the baby by throwing herself on top of it, but by the time I found them both, the baby was dead."

Her last words choked her so she could barely force them out, and finally the tears began to fall fast from her burning eyes.

"Daddy, I tried to save them both, but it was too late. I felt so angry and sad, then I saw someone run out of a building and I *left* my casualties and *left* my section and ran after the man. He didn't know I was following him. He slipped into

168

a building, and I went in after him.

"Mom, Dad. I nearly killed him. I was so angry that I couldn't think straight. I had him on his knees with the barrel of my gun pressed against his forehead. I ranted at him, Dad. I came that close to blowing his brains out all over the wall. If Nick—Lieutenant Ryan—and a section buddy of mine hadn't found me, I would have killed him."

Jessie took a deep breath. "I lost control. I've let everyone down, including myself, and you and Mom." By the time she finished speaking, she was sobbing.

"Hey, Jessie, honey. Take it easy now. Easy, sweetheart," her father responded calmly.

"Jessie!" Her mother's voice spoke gently but firmly. "Listen, baby girl."

Feeling that she was losing herself to her grief, Jessie gritted her teeth. "I'm listening, Mom," she answered in a watery voice.

"Terrible things happen that are beyond our control," her father continued. "First of all, you haven't let anyone down, and you can't blame yourself. The only one getting a beating over this is the one you're giving yourself. Are there going to be repercussions?"

"I was hauled over the coals," Jessie replied, "but apparently my section went and pleaded my case to the lieutenant, and he's decided to overlook it, although I was given a warning."

"Good man," her father responded. "Listen, sweetheart. I've been where you are. Your mom has as well. Combat is never easy. I tore myself up so many times over things that I could never change. It's a terrible side effect of war. You need to let it go. Grieve for those people, rant at the injustice of it, go kick the hell out of something but don't hang on to it. Guilt has a way of digging deep into you and once it's there, it's a helluva nightmare to get rid of it. Trust me, honey. I know.

"As for losing control, it's what's called being human, honey. If you didn't feel anything, if you felt numb when something like that happens, then I would be worried. Blowing one of those bastards' brains out would have been too easy on him. That's just revenge on your part and revenge is just as bad as guilt. I know it's tough, honey, but you need to let it go. I understand that it's easy for me to say all this and right now you probably feel like you're in hell, but go talk to your section. Hash it over with them. Let them know how you feel."

Hearing her father's words, Jessie felt some of the heavy weight lift from her shoulders. Wiping her wet face, she sniffed and said tearfully, "I miss you and Mom so much."

"And we miss you too, sweetheart," her mother said, her own voice sounding a little emotional.

"I gotta go," Jessie announced. "Thank you, Dad, and you too, Mom."

"You be strong, honey. Stay safe, and remember... Let it go."

"Love you both," Jessie said.

"Love you too, baby girl," her parents said together, then there was a snap as Jessie pressed the button and disconnected the call.

Chapter Seventeen

Just after midnight, Nick quietly stepped into the medical tent and stopped, listening to see if he had disturbed anyone or had caused the security teams to notice him as he moved from his tent to Jessie's. His heart was beating nervously, and he felt as though he was a teenager who had snuck out of the house in the middle of the night.

He had spent most of the evening deliberating on whether to visit Jessie once the FOB had gone quiet, swinging indecisively from giving in to the craving to be with her to feeling uncomfortable that he would be breaking regulations.

He had at last concluded that this might be the one and only time that he and Jessie could be together and to pass up the opportunity would be to regret it. He came up with the forlorn idea that if caught, he could just lie and say he was unwell and seeking the medic for treatment. His thoughts had made him laugh as he realized that his days of sneaking into girls' rooms were not over.

Hearing no sound from outside, Nick glanced around the treatment room. He saw that Jessie had left a chemlamp burning, almost as if she was leaving a beacon alight for those who might need comfort or a place of safety in the dead of night.

Feeling almost tense with anticipation — eager to see her — he made his way toward her sleeping quarters. Quietly sweeping aside the flap in an effort not to disturb her, he peered in.

He saw her immediately. Faint moonlight fingered its way through the slats of the blinds at her window and painted her in striations of silver where she lay face down on her cot, her gorgeous hair fanned out over the pillow.

As he walked to stand at Jessie's side, Nick's breath caught in his throat. She remained deeply asleep, her face beautiful, a small smile curving her full lips. As he crouched, then knelt on the floor, he wondered how he could have gotten so lucky to have her love him. Leaning forward, he tenderly kissed the corner of her mouth, hoping that it wouldn't startle her into making a noise if she woke up. Drawing back, he was startled to see that her eyes had opened and she was staring at him, a small smile playing about her mouth.

"Hey, Lieutenant," she greeted softly. "You're out of bounds."

Nick smiled in return. "Tell me about it. I'm trying to destroy a long and fruitful army career, just to try something different."

Jessie's smile widened. "You don't have to stay, you know. We can always take a rain check."

Hearing that her low tone was halfway serious and halfway teasing, he gently touched her face, trailing one finger down her cheek and across her mouth.
"Not fucking likely," he whispered.

Jessie sensuously licked the tip of his finger. "Well then, if you're staying, are you going to join me here? It could get kinda uncomfortable if you intend on staying down there."

Without waiting for a response, she turned onto her right side and moved so that her back rested against the tent wall. She watched him impatiently, wanting him lying beside her so that he could hold and touch her.

At last, Nick rose from his crouch, sat on the cot, then lay down, turning to face her. She moved closer to him and lifted her head so that he could put his arm about her. Once she had rested her head on his shoulder, he pulled her in tightly so that the full length of her body pressed against his.

Resting the palm of her hand on his chest, Jessie laughed softly. "Your heart is racing," she whispered teasingly.

"You don't say," Nick answered. "It's the shock of finding myself in here."

Raising herself and leaning over him, Jessie slowly kissed his mouth. "Want me to calm you down?" she asked.

Nick grasped a handful of her hair and tugged gently. "Calm me down?" he echoed. "There's no way on this earth that being near you can keep me calm."

He pulled her head down and kissed her gently. Jessie sucked at his tongue when he thrust it into her mouth and as she sensuously entwined her own with his, pressed her body against his and heard him groan softly.

Nick suddenly pushed her over onto her back and crushed his hot mouth against hers, no longer tender but almost painful. Jessie gently traced her fingernails along the powerful muscles of his arms, which caused him to shiver slightly. Reaching his shoulders, she put her hands up behind his head, burying her fingers in the thick springiness of his hair.

Her thoughts disintegrated into sparkling shards of want as Nick left her mouth and began to kiss her neck. She tossed her head back with reckless abandon, allowing him to have easier access to the suddenly hypersensitive skin. He licked a swirling trail along and around a small pulse beating fast and delicately beneath her skin, eliciting a quiet moan from her and sending a series of volcanic shivers rippling through her body. She could feel his hardness against her thigh and she wanted him — was desperate for him — to forget foreplay and make love to her — hard.

God, I want him so much.

As he captured her lips again, Jessie moved her hands from the back of his head down to the waistband of his combats. She tugged out his T-shirt and thrust her hands up beneath it, pressing her palms against the smooth, warm firmness of his stomach. She sensuously glided them down his sides then curved back in along his stomach, eliciting a strong contraction there and the ripple of muscles as he moved.

Tenderly, she trailed her fingers down to the waistband of his combats and slowly — taking her time — she unfastened the Velcro, then grasped the zip. Nick caught her hands in his and shook his head quickly.

She grasped the waistband of his trousers and tugged him closer. She could feel how hard he was and gently moved her hips in small circles, rubbing her groin against his. He moaned softly and trailed a hand up her stomach to one of her breasts. Urging him on, Jessie pressed her hand hard on top of his.

Nick tugged her T-shirt out of her shorts and thrust his free hand up inside, laying the warm palm against her skin. Her stomach quivered at his touch.

His hand moved on until it came to rest on a bare breast and he clasped the fullness of it, his thumb gently circling her erect nipple. Jessie gasped and raised herself to kiss him but Nick pushed her back. Leaning over her, he licked her nipple.

She arched her back, clenching her fingers in his hair in response. Nick circled her nipple with his tongue, then he took it into his mouth, teasing the hard bud. He moved away from the firm mound, leaving gentle kisses on the way, licking a swirling trail down her stomach.

Exquisite sensations coursed through Jessie's body at his touch. Wanting him so much, she writhed and, reaching down, grasped the waistband of his combats and attempted — with small tugs — to get him to move on top of her.

She heard Nick laugh softly as he moved to look into her face. "In a hurry?" he asked against her mouth.

"Yes," Jessie answered without artifice, her voice husky with arousal. "I want you, Nick."

"Christ, I want you too," Nick answered and his hand went to the waistband of her shorts.

Jessie rested a gentle hand on top of his, stopping him

from completing what he was about to do.

"What's the matter?" he asked.

Without answering him, Jessie pushed him onto his back and raised herself up slightly so she leaned over him. She rolled up his T-shirt and gently kissed his chest, feeling muscles twitch at her touch. Smiling to herself, she placed the palm of her hand on his lower stomach, once again feeling his abdomen contract.

Raising her head, she stared at him, noting that he was looking at her with an intense expression in his dark eyes. Slowly and sensually, she moistened her lips with the tip of her tongue, lowered her head and trailed it up to his nipple, swirling it around once before raising her head again. She recognized the expression on his face, understanding almost telepathically what he was thinking and what he wanted.

Nick stayed silent and motionless as she lowered her head again to place more tiny, moist kisses across his chest, interspersing them with delicate nibbles and swirling licks. She heard him make a small sound of response but she continued with her actions.

Her body made whispering sounds against the sleeping bag as she slid gracefully down his body, tongue and lips teasing the tan skin of his stomach. She traced random circles with her fingertips on his lower abdomen, also moving lower and lower until they reached the waistband of his combats where they came to a stop. Her mouth reached his lower stomach and she felt his hips move, as though in anticipation of what she was about to do next. She bit his stomach gently then raised her head.

"Expecting something?" she asked breathlessly, her own heightening sexual tension causing her nipples to harden into buds of arousal.

Nick cleared his throat. "Me? No." His voice was hoarse and deep. "Why? You offering?"

"Depends," Jessie responded. Glancing at him sideways, she ordered softly, "Lift your hips."

After he had obeyed her, Jessie swiftly slid the combats down his legs to his knees. When she turned her head slightly, she saw the rigid outline of his erect cock through the material of his shorts and she moved her hand so that her palm rested against it. She could feel his hot hardness and she squeezed him gently.

Nick groaned softly and his hips jerked.

"Depends on what?" he asked after a small hesitation, his voice sounding strangled.

Jessie left a moist trail with her tongue across his stomach, from one side to the other, just above the waistband of his shorts.

"Depends if you're willing to offer something in kind," she said, her voice low and seductive. "Fair's fair."

"Oh, I'm willing," Nick responded, arching his groin slightly so that his cotton-encased cock brushed against her face.

"Careful, big boy," Jessie teased in a low voice and, after rubbing her cheek against his erection, suddenly put her mouth over the bulging crown and breathed out. The clinging material became moist and the heat from her breath must have penetrated through to him because he groaned out loud.

She squeezed his turgid, straining shaft and said huskily, "In that case..."

One-handed, Jessie swiftly but smoothly lifted the waistband of his shorts and pulled them away and down from his cock, releasing it from its confinement. She followed up this action by lifting herself slightly and leaning over him. Lowering her head, she paused, deliberately teasing, then sensuously and tantalizingly slowly licked up the full length of him, her tongue creating intricate circles along his skin until, reaching the glans, she quickly took the crown in her mouth, sucked briefly once, then released him. Panting slightly, she glanced sideways at Nick again, loving and wanting to see his reaction to her ministrations. Again, he was watching her and their gazes locked, the sexual tension between then heightening, both knowing what each other wanted, both anticipating and lusting.

Giving him a last wanton look, Jessie turned and again licked the hot length of him, the feel of how hard he was and how his hips bucked to meet her mouth, causing her to want him with a deep and erotic craving.

He moaned, a deep and meaningful sound.

Without pausing, Jessie grasped him and moved her hand slowly up and down, intermittently squeezing and releasing. She took the tip of his cock into her mouth and sucked gently, using her tongue again to lash at the hot skin.

She heard Nick's breathing suddenly speed up, sounding harsh and guttural, and his hips began to move rhythmically.

Jessie tasted the faint salty tang of him. He was so hard and filled her mouth. She gently stroked his balls, cupped them in her hand and marveled at how tight they had become.

Aware of her own desire, she moved her mouth on Nick faster, alternately lapping at him with her tongue, and rhythmically moving her hand until she heard Nick suddenly exclaim quietly in warning, "Jessie…"

Jessie immediately stopped and gently released him from her mouth. Nick grasped her arm and drew her, almost roughly, toward him. Her own breathing was ragged and uneven and, as she reached him, she quickly rid herself of her T-shirt and shorts then climbed gracefully astride his groin.

Settling herself on him, she felt her cleft make contact with his hot cock. She moaned and rubbed herself against him, her hot juices mingling with the saliva already moistening him.

Nick's hands immediately went to her breasts. Placing her own over his, she clenched them tightly so that he, in turn, squeezed her breasts almost cruelly.

Nick felt the heat of the firm mounds and wanted her

with every fiber of his being. He wanted to be inside her, feel her slick moistness and her tightness grasping his cock.

He moved his hands and grasped her hips, gasping as the feel of her heat enveloped his cock and the friction of her movements created an intense coil of pleasure in his groin.

He watched Jessie's face. Her cheeks were flushed, the skin of her neck and chest rosy with arousal. Her dark brown nipples were hard buds, beckoning to have his lips around them.

He sat upright and began to kiss each breast in turn, then impatiently took one of the nubs almost savagely into his mouth. He heard Jessie moan and she arched her back and buried her hands in his hair.

He nibbled and sucked until he lost patience. Clutching at her hips, he raised her up and, understanding what he wanted, Jessie reached down, grasped him then guided him into her.

On feeling her tight wetness, Nick gritted his teeth. Slowly he began to push himself in deeper. He felt her lithe body jerk in response, then he was sliding silkily upward, her internal muscles clenching delicately around his cock.

For a few moments, they were both still, Nick trying to control himself. He ran his hands up her slim back, then she bent forward and her moist, full lips were kissing his neck and moving on up to his mouth. They met and entwined their tongues and Nick tasted her breath and crushed her mouth roughly with his own. Her hands gripped his shoulders, then she was moving, gliding up the length of his cock, pausing for mere seconds then plunging back down. He met her movements with his own, thrusting his rigid length up as far as it would go without hurting her.

Her movements quickened and he felt the heat of her breath against his face. Familiar exquisite sensations of pressure started to build up in his balls, in his cock and in the lower regions of his stomach. Jessie's moans quickened and grew louder, and he watched her face, knowing that she was close to her orgasm, wanting to watch her come, knowing that in synchronization with her own, he would join her.

He pounded into her and she returned the movements smoothly and rapidly with an equal force of her own, until suddenly she tensed, arched her back, digging her nails into the muscles of his shoulders. Her internal muscles clenched about him and instantaneously, he came. He could not have controlled the exquisite consummation, even if he had wanted to.

Jessie slumped against him, nuzzling his neck, and Nick enveloped her in his arms. He kissed her damp forehead, loving her beyond words. Sometimes the strength of his feelings made him uneasy. At other times, he reveled in the hot wanting and loving that he had for her.

When his breathing nearly returned to normal, he said softly, "Hello?"

Jessie groaned and kissed his neck. "Pooped," she responded, her voice muffled.

Nick laughed. "Christ, that sounded romantic," he said, kissing her neck. "I make love to you once and already I'm losing my touch if you start to fall asleep on me."

He felt her shoulders shudder slightly and realized that she was laughing silently to herself. He shook her lightly.

"Are you laughing at me?"

Jessie raised her head to stare at him. Her dark blue eyes were almost luminous in the dim light, and she had a small smile playing about her lush lips. She raised a hand and stroked his cheek.

"You could *never* lose your touch with me, Nick Ryan," she announced. Her voice was full of sensual connotations and Nick's cock responded immediately.

"Uh huh," he replied. "I hope it stays that way." He paused. "You are one hell of a woman, Jessie McAllister."

Jessie placed a gentle, moist kiss on his mouth, followed almost immediately by a teasing, sexy lick.

"And you, Lieutenant, are one hell of a man."

Nick tightened his arms around her, loving the feel of her

naked body under his hands, the firm but feminine muscles beneath her skin, and, grinning, he said, "Well, Corporal. I need to make a quick and clean getaway before our luck runs out, so, if you don't want to go another round with this 'ere Lieutenant, I need to get some sleep as well."

"Oh, have I worn you out, honey?" Jessie giggled girlishly, the warm rich sound disturbing the shadowy silence of the tent.

"Nope. Now, release me, woman."

"Oh, hell. Go on then."

With a lithe movement, gracefulness in every line of her body, she slid off, allowing him freedom to get off the cot.

Jessie turned on her side and propped her head on her hand. She watched as Nick pulled up his combats and fastened them, admiring the way the muscles flexed in his body, his powerful legs and the firm sculpture of his backside.

As he turned while tucking in his T-shirt, Nick pulled a face. "Are you eyeing me up, lady?"

Jessie laughed. "Yes. Do you have a problem with that?"

"Nope. Feel free…but another time. I really have to go."

Sighing, Jessie sat up then reached for her T-shirt and shorts to quickly put them on. Standing up, she stretched out her hand to take his, then led him into the main tent. "I'll see you out," she announced.

They both came to a stop at the tent flap and Nick turned her toward him. He nuzzled her tousled hair, then, lifting her chin with one finger, said softly, "I'm sorry I have to rush off. I don't want us to get caught and this night to be ruined."

Jessie smiled at him. "I understand," she answered. "I'll see you later."

"You will," Nick agreed and gently kissed her. "I love you so much."

"Me too," Jessie responded.

Nick suddenly stiffened.

"What…?" Jessie began but stopped herself from saying anything else when Nick held up a hand.

"Someone's coming, heading in this direction," he exclaimed.

"Shit!"

Jessie glanced wildly around her then, grabbing his hand again, tugged him toward the examination table.

"Get yourself up on that. Pretend you've been ill," she whispered.

While Nick jumped up onto the table, Jessie searched quickly for the clipboard with medical forms and grabbed for the ear thermometer. She quickly stabbed the digital earpiece into Nick's ear, hissing an apology when she jammed it in too deep.

There came a slap on the outside of the tent and the flap was pulled back to reveal Dingle.

Trying to act as naturally as possible, Jessie withdrew the digital readout and glanced at it, as if reading the result. She tried not to laugh when she saw that, hilariously, Nick's temperature *was* elevated.

I know why he has a raised temperature.

She quickly made a note on the medical form then glanced in Dingle's direction.

"Hey," she said as casually as she could. "You're up early, or late, as the case may be. Are you ill?"

"I couldn't sleep and noticed movement in here. I thought you might need some help if someone was sick," Dingle replied after a slight hesitation.

"Thanks for the thought," Jessie said, taking Nick's wrist so that she could pretend to take his pulse. Again, she had to bite her lip to stop herself from giggling when she took note that his pulse rate was far from normal.

"What's wrong with LT?" Dingle asked.

Jessie stared at him when she noticed a strange tone to his voice.

Does he know about me and Nick?

"Our lieutenant has a gippy tummy, bless him," she

explained. "But it's nothing to worry about. Probably a virus or something he's eaten."

Dropping Nick's wrist, she again pretended to make a note on the form. "Okay, sir. You don't have a fever and everything else is normal. You're to have nothing to eat for twenty-four hours and drink plenty of fluids. If things get worse, come back to see me."

"Thanks, Mac. Sorry I woke you at this ungodly hour." Nick slid off the bed and with his hand resting on his stomach, said, "I'll be off. Come on, Dingle. Let's leave the lady alone to get some sleep."

"Yes, gentleman, if you would be so kind. I am exhausted and I have a mission tomorrow... No, later today," Jessie said.

She watched Nick's retreating back and wished that they could have been together for a while longer. She raised a hand at Dingle's muttered "Goodnight," and once the men had left, wearily made her way to her quarters.

I'll be lucky to get a couple of hours' sleep, if that.

She saw that it was 0200 hours and she groaned. Flinging herself down on her cot, she pulled her sleeping bag over her. She thought briefly back over the last few hours, remembering how she and Nick had made love.

Hold that thought.

Jessie fell asleep, a small smile of contentment on her face.

Chapter Eighteen

Jessie lay in her sleeping bag, unable to stay asleep. She glanced at the luminous face of her watch for what must have been the hundredth time. The hands had only crept on a few minutes from the last time she had looked — 0400 hours. She was going to be shattered for the mission in a few hours and that was not going to be a good thing.

Sighing, she plumped up her pillow and turned on to her side. Determined to sleep, she closed her eyes and again Nick's image popped into her mind. She groaned softly but allowed the thought to come.

Her mind filled with sizzling memories of their lovemaking earlier that morning. She could not stop thinking about him, and it was driving her crazy. Through no fault of his, Nick was seriously affecting her concentration, and if she didn't get her act together, she was going to make mistakes and get people hurt.

Opening her eyes once more, she threw herself over onto her back then sat up. Her sleeplessness was not going to cure itself while she lay in bed dreaming of a certain charismatic lieutenant. Irritated, she flung aside the sleeping bag and got up. She stumbled around in the dark, trying to find the chemlamp by feel, then, giving up on that, her shower sandals.

"Fuck and damn it!" she muttered beneath her breath as she earned herself a stubbed toe and bruised shin for her efforts.

Finally coming across them, she slipped the sandals on then made her way outside. With the exception of the dim lights in the security towers, by the gates and in the mess area, the rest of the FOB was in darkness. The night was hot and humid and, for a moment, she paused on the platform, glancing up at the night sky.

It's like someone's thrown a handful of sugar onto a black canvas, she mused as she admired the billions of stars above her. The moon was a huge, cream-colored orb surrounded by a misty halo and although beautiful, she knew that anyone out on patrol that night would need to be extra vigilant.

Jessie glanced around, taking note of the two soldiers on duty at the gates and the four soldiers in the towers. The FOB was silent, as usual, and she stealthily made her way to the mess area where she started the process of making herself a cup of tea. It was as she was pouring hot water onto a teabag that a voice said quietly from the shadows, "Can't sleep, Jessie?"

Jessie almost let out a small scream only stopping it from peeling forth by clamping a hand over her mouth. She spun round to see Nick coming toward her, a thermo cup in his hand.

"Oh, Christ, Nick," she gasped, heart pounding. "You scared the crap out of me. I thought you were the Terries or something."

Smiling slightly, Nick cocked an eyebrow. "Come on, Jessie? Do I look like a *muji*?"

Jessie let her eyes travel slowly up his body to his face. She took in the fact that he wore nothing except for combat trousers and boots, his well-muscled chest bare. His hair was untidy, as though he had been running his hands through it, and he looked nothing like the officer he presented during the day.

She cleared her throat and forcefully drew her eyes away from him. They were out in the FOB and there was no way that she could allow thoughts of what had happened between them in the medical tent, to influence how she acted with him now.

"Guess not," she replied huskily. There was a small silence, then Nick took a step toward her.

"Can't sleep?" he asked again. "Still thinking about the incident at Khavak?"

Wishing that he would move away from her because his closeness was doing all manner of things to her breathing, Jessie shook her head. "No, Lieutenant. I spoke to my dad and he put things into perspective. I'll work it out."

Nick nodded. "I'm glad, Jessie. You father sounds like a good man."

"He is, sir, the best. My mom is too."

There was another small but tense silence and Jessie cleared her throat.

"What about you? Having trouble sleeping?"

Nick nodded his head. "Too much on my mind," he answered slowly.

Jessie, pretending that she understood, asked, "The mission? Do you think there'll be any trouble?"

"No problems there," he answered. "You'll be fine." He stopped talking abruptly, as though he were considering something then continued, "I can't get you or this morning out of my mind. I feel like I'm going mad."

Jessie could see that he was staring at her, the color of eyes almost black in the dim light from the strip lighting. He seemed to be waiting for her response and when she stayed silent, Nick swore and ran a hand through his hair, making it more unruly.

"Shit. Look. This is out of order, but I really wish you weren't going out with Charlie Recon on that mission. I don't want to let you out of my sight. At least in my charge, I can keep you out of trouble."

Jessie smiled. "Why, Nick Ryan," she chided gently. "Are you worried about my safety?"

She placed her cup down on a table and stepped toward him, so that they were only a short distance apart.

Nick smiled slightly. He closed the space between them until he was standing a few inches from her.

His nearness made her pulse race, and she ached to be in his arms. "Is that why you can't sleep?" she asked in a low

185

voice.

"That...and other things keeping me awake," Nick answered.

They were still not touching each other. Jessie's breath caught in her throat as his eyes roamed her body, clad as it was in her nightwear of clinging strappy T-shirt and mid-thigh, tight-fitting shorts.

The silence that flowed between them was full of tingling sexual tension.

"What things?" Jessie asked at last.

"Do you want me to tell you...or show you?" Nick asked, his voice husky and full of meaning.

A tingling warmth began to coil in Jessie's stomach, spreading outward until her whole body felt flushed with sexual arousal. Her heart began to pound with anticipation.

"Definitely show me...please," she answered her breathing quickening.

Nick placed his hands on her hips and pulled her gently toward him. Jessie went willingly and stood in the circle of his arms. His hands moved around to her back, his touch burning through her T-shirt to her skin, and he pulled her in against him. Her heart beat painfully fast as she felt his body press against hers, and she thrust her hips against his groin, relishing and yearning for the hardness that she felt there.

"You are so beautiful," Nick began, reaching a hand up and running it through her hair. "I can't take my eyes off you. You do things to me that no woman has ever done before. I love and want you so much. I have since I first laid eyes on you."

Jessie ran the palms of her hands up his bare arms to his shoulders and thrilled inside when he shivered. She felt the warmth of his skin and the way his muscles rippled and trembled as she touched him. She ran her fingernails slowly down his chest, her breathing becoming more rapid when he groaned at her touch, and she felt his arms tighten about her body. Daringly and ever more slowly, she continued to run her fingers down to his stomach. She felt the muscles there flinch and contract.

"Jessie," Nick whispered hoarsely.

"Mmm?" she murmured questioningly. "Were you going to say something?"

"No," Nick answered.

"You were going to show me something though," she murmured. "So show me. Please."

Nick needed no second prompting and his mouth came down on hers, kissing her hungrily.

Jessie kissed him back, her arms going up around his neck. She cupped the back of his head and pulled it down so that the pressure of his mouth increased against hers. The passion that had previously arisen so easily between them flared white-hot.

Nick moved his hands from her back down to her backside then pulled her against him hard and Jessie went eagerly, wanting to feel all of him against her body, aching to feel that hardness. His rigidity pressed against her, straining through his combat trousers, and she rubbed herself sensuously against him.

"I want you," he said against her mouth.

His hand went to her breast, which he cupped gently, his thumb circling her erect nipple and Jessie moaned, dragging her mouth away from his, throwing her head back as the exquisite sensations flowed through her body.

"I want you too," she whispered, "so much."

Nick suddenly lifted her up and without thinking, Jessie swung her legs up and around his hips. Swinging her around, he rested her back against the tall industrial fridge, crouched slightly, and pressed himself against her between her legs.

Jessie was drowning in the heightened eroticism that was quickly spiraling out of control between them.

"Make love to me, Nick," she murmured. "I want to feel you inside me. I want it so much."

Nick kissed her again, this time his mouth rough on hers,

almost bruising her lips. She didn't care. She clenched her hands in his hair and sucked his tongue when he thrust it into her mouth, her own tangling with his. She could hear his breathing, rapid and uneven, and moaned softly.

A male voice suddenly sounded close by, and they both froze.

Jessie immediately rested her face against Nick's chest, trying to quiet her rapid breathing. She listened intently to the static noise of a radio, then silence fell once more.

"Fuck!" Nick swore softly and straightened up. Lowering her feet slowly to the ground, he buried his face in her hair.

There was a charged silence. Jessie felt shaken at the intensity of the passion that had flared again between them. Her pulse and heart were still racing and she felt more vitally alive than she had ever been before in her life.

"Jesus Christ." Nick kissed the top of her head. "Saved by the bell," he said quietly, his voice hoarse, chest rising and falling rapidly.

Raising her face to his, Jessie asked solemnly, "Relieved?"

Staring at her, Nick cupped her chin in his hand and stroked the skin of her cheek with his thumb. "Fuck, no," he answered, a serious note to his voice. "I could have and I would have. I love you, Jessie."

Jessie nuzzled his chest then sensuously licked his hot skin. She felt him flinch. "I know," she responded, "but it's so difficult."

"Tell me about it," Nick said. "But it will happen. We *will* be together. We just need to wait it out."

Looking up at him, Jessie felt herself smile. "Really? You mean that?" she asked.

"What? Did you think that this was going to be the kind of relationship that just flares up in a combat zone, burns itself out and won't last?" Nick asked, tracing her lips with a finger. "I told you, Jessie. I love you. Believe it. But this isn't the time or the place."

Jessie shrugged, then shivered at his touch. "I wasn't sure," she began tentatively.

"Well, be sure," Nick said firmly. "Now, I think you should go to bed."

Jessie made a small moue of reluctance then smiled teasingly. "Want to come back to my tent?" she asked in a sensuous voice.

Nick stiffened then said, "Don't tempt me. Want to come to mine?"

"And have Major Hayward catch us in the act?" Jessie responded, laughing quietly at the image that spawned in her mind. "I think we've used up all our luck."

Nick grinned. "All hell would break loose," he said. "Now, go to bed, Jessie McAllister, before I change my mind. You are too enticing and you need to get some sleep."

"Is that an order, Lieutenant?" Jessie asked teasingly.

Kissing her lightly on the lips he murmured, "No, it's a suggestion. Now, get going." He turned her around, slapped her on the bottom, and glanced around the FOB before guiding her out from the shadows. "Be at that mission briefing at 0700 hours, knackered or not. Copy?"

Walking slowly away, Jessie glanced over her shoulder and smiled at him, "Copy," she whispered, "I love you," and she hurried off toward the medical tent.

* * * *

Jessie was up by 0530 hours and had finished her breakfast by 0630. She reported to the operations tent at 0700 for the briefing, joining the six members of Charlie Recon Section — and herself — who had been selected to go on the mission. Lieutenant Marshall, commanding officer of Charlie Recon, spoke for twenty minutes, then Major Hayward gave a parting speech, after which he dismissed them to stand easy outside to wait for the Wildcat to arrive.

Jessie stood with the men as they milled around. Although she was acquainted with some of them, Bravo and Charlie Recon Sections had not had much interaction and, although they were friendly enough to her, she was not an integral part of the section.

Feeling a little lost, she gazed aimlessly around the FOB, wishing that she had someone to pass the time with, and she saw Nick exit his tent. He noticed her instantly and came toward her. Stopping a few paces away, he beckoned for her to join him.

Remembering what had taken place between them earlier that morning, Jessie felt her cheeks flush and knew she was blushing.
"Sir?"

Nick could remember – all too well – the feel of her body under his hands, their lovemaking and her passionate response to his kisses in the mess tent and he felt himself harden. He had hardly slept for the rest of the night. The temptation to sneak back to her tent to finish what they had begun for the second time was almost a craving, but the thought that his luck might run out and one of the guards might see him was something he could not risk.

He noticed Jessie's flushed face as she reached him and he knew what she was thinking. A small, knowing smile played about her mouth and the one word she had spoken curled around his senses, her voice soft and seductive.

Clearing his throat, he asked, "All set?"

"Yes, Lieutenant. Just waiting for the helo."

"You be careful, all right? *No* heroics. You hear me?"

"Copy that, Lieutenant. I hear you. Don't worry."

"I want you back safe and sound, Jessie. I mean it." Nick tried to emphasize the uneasiness he was feeling at her imminent departure. After what had happened between them, he didn't want her out of his sight and was feeling the effects of these new and challenging emotions.

Jessie laughed sensuously. "I promise."

Nick cocked his head to one side. "The helicopter is coming in. Stay safe."

He saw her giving him a last lingering look before she turned and went to join the others. Nick watched her go, wanting to call her back and take her in his arms. Knowing that that was impossible, he went back to his tent and stopped outside it, unable to prevent himself from watching her departure.

The gates opened, the security team carried out a brief recce of the area, then Charlie Recon Section formed up and jogged out of the FOB. As Jessie exited the gate, he saw her turn to stare in his direction. Nodding his head slightly in acknowledgement of her farewell look, he waited for the gates to close. A few minutes later, he saw the Wildcat take off, bank to the left and fly off into the early morning haze. He would not feel comfortable until she was back at the base and safe. It was going to be a long day.

Chapter Nineteen

A bright, white mist hung behind Jessie's eyelids and panic welled up inside her. She moaned, the noise sounding pitiful to her ears.

I can't see! I'm blind!

On the heels of that thought, came another. *I'm so cold.*

Trembling took control of her body and although she gritted her teeth, she was unable to control the shaking of her muscles and limbs. She felt icy water splattering the left side of her face and heard a dull, muted pattering as it hit her helmet and body armor. Her combats were soaking wet, her fingers stiff and cold in sodden combat gloves.

Her throat was dry and her tongue felt swollen to twice its size. There was no saliva in her mouth and she coughed—a dry raspy sound—and winced as pain lanced through various parts of her body.

"Oh, fuck," she murmured in a hoarse whisper.

What the fuck's happened?

Her right hand, pinned beneath her, was full of pins and needles. She needed to release it and, to do that, she had to roll onto her back. Holding her breath, her body involuntarily tensing up in preparation for pain, she gingerly moved her left leg. Pent-up air left her mouth in a hissing sound as, apart from a twinge in her hip, there was no major discomfort.

With an effort, she rolled her body backward, landing flat with a splash. Bruised and strained muscles protested at the sudden movement, but she relaxed slightly when the aches and pains faded. Shaking and flexing her right hand, she wiggled her fingers, opening and closing her fist to try to rid it of the annoying prickling.

Okay. I'm still in one piece, or, at least, it feels like I am. What in the hell happened?

The right side of her face felt uncomfortable. Despite still wearing her helmet, the skin there felt covered in a thick glutinous substance that also adhered to her eye. She tried to open both her eyes and her heart seemed to plummet into the depths of her stomach.

The left one opened with ease but the right refused to cooperate. Feeling the onset of panic, she raised a shaking hand and touched the side of her face. The substance was thick and cold and, by its texture, she suspected that it was a covering of sand and mud.

She gently touched her eye, but even with the lightest probing, sharp pain flared instantly around the eye socket. With cold fingertips, she explored the side of her face and found it to be swollen and tender to the touch.

It feels like I have a black eye, or, worse still, a fracture.

Her teeth began to chatter as though they had a life of their own and, try as she might, she couldn't stop them. As her body began to tremble from the cold, she realized that whatever her situation, if she didn't move and try to get warm, her body temperature would begin to plummet — if it hadn't done so already — and she would start to suffer from hypothermia.

Gritting her teeth, she plunged both hands into the cold, syrupy mud beneath her and pushed herself into an upright position. For a few seconds she sat motionless, waiting for her joints and muscles to stop protesting. When she felt able to, she ran her hands down her legs and arms, searching for any injury that hadn't manifested itself yet. Relief flowed through her when she confirmed definitely that she had not sustained any broken bones.

Having completed her personal medical assessment, she raised her head. The first thing she noticed was the silvery sheets of rain falling from a charcoal-gray sky. Her vision, already compromised by her injured eye, combined with reduced visibility, severely restricted the sight of her surroundings to no more than a few meters.

To her left, she could just make out the beginnings of a rock-strewn slope with a gentle gradient, bare of all vegetation except for a few stunted and gnarled trees clinging precariously to narrow ledges.

She frowned and glanced around at the unfamiliar landscape. In front of her, desert merged into murky grayness with misty images of rocky outcrops and teetering piles of boulders disappearing into the silvery curtains after a short distance. The only sounds were the pattering and splash of rain and the trickling sound of water.

Jessie turned to look back over her shoulder and froze with stunned disbelief and horror. A few meters behind her lay the wreckage of a helicopter. The Wildcat was lying in two buckled pieces, as though ripped apart by a terrible force. Its tail with rotor blades still attached rose almost vertically into the overcast sky. The cockpit and cabin, torn almost surgically away from the rear, reclined at an angle on the muddy ground. The massive curved rotor blades—still connected to the hub—remained attached to the rotating mast on the cabin, the blades splintered and buckled, some warped and twisted like broken fingers. The landing gear lay upside down close by, completely sheared away from the body of the helicopter.

Oh my God. What…

The trembling already assailing Jessie's body increased as shock took hold. She couldn't believe what she was seeing, was unable to comprehend the nightmare that was lying scattered on the sodden ground.

I can't remember. Why can't I…

As she studied the macabre scene, her memory returned in a rush and she bent double from the waist and shut her one good eye, as if she could wipe out the horrifying images that were suddenly flickering across her mind like an old black-and-white movie.

She remembered the obscene howling of the helicopter's

engines, metal rending and splintering, someone screaming over and over again and yells of panic. The words *Mayday Mayday* sounded repetitively in her head, the words calm but riddled with tension. There was the endless roaring of a wind followed by…blackness.

Jessie clamped muddy, shaking hands over her mouth before she could scream.

We crashed! I was with Charlie Recon Section. Lieutenant Marshall, the guys. Are they all dead?

Hating what she had to do but knowing that she had no choice, Jessie lowered her hands and forced herself to look at the wreckage. She saw large and small chunks of jagged and torn metal glistening with rainwater, littering the site. She identified a pack, a single helmet and a boot, the latter lying on its side against a boulder.

Feeling a stealthy numbness infiltrating her mind, she continued to study the scene and a moan escaped her when she saw two bodies lying in contorted postures on the ground a short distance from the wreckage.

Without thinking, she scrambled unsteadily to her feet, boots slipping and sliding out from beneath her twice before she was finally able to remain upright. She immediately shrieked when she put weight on her right leg. Excruciating pain shot all the way to her thigh, and her ankle threatened to give way beneath her.

Ignoring the discomfort, dread clamping her in its grip, Jessie spun lopsidedly in a circle. She saw nobody moving about the crash site and she appeared to be completely alone. She was reluctant to call out, in case any Taliban who had seen the crash were making their eager way toward her location to see what they could scavenge from the wreckage or to take any survivors prisoner.

She needed to check the two lifeless-seeming bodies and search for survivors. Somebody *might* still be alive and she had wasted enough time. She could not believe that everyone was dead. She needed to believe that she was not alone, that there might be at least one person alive, if not more.

It was not only her responsibility to treat casualties but to keep them safe. As exposed as they were, she needed to get them away quickly. With visibility as bad as it was, any hostiles could sneak up on her at any moment, and she would never see them until it was too late.

Jessie shivered violently, the cold seeping deep into her bones. Her wet combats clung to her body and her feet felt like chunks of ice in her boots. She longed for a hot shower and a warm drink but knew that it was probably going to be a long time before she could avail herself of such luxuries.

Before she started to search for casualties, she needed to transmit her location. The signal strength from her comms would not travel for any great distance, and information to her central information system would not update unless a Watchkeeper drone passed overhead. Nevertheless, she had to try.

She activated her comms system and, clearing her throat, said hoarsely, "Anyone on this net. This is a priority transmission to anyone on this net. Charlie Romeo Tango one seven is in need of immediate assistance. I say again, Charlie Romeo Tango one seven is in need of priority assistance. Cat A status — urgent. Medevac required for eight — repeat — eight casualties."

The response to her words was a muted background whine and the harsh hiss of interference, and she knew that such a noise was not meant to come from the complex piece of equipment. Her comms were obviously down, and Jessie felt panic. She realized that she was definitely on her own and, feeling a surge of desperation, she repeated the transmission once more but received the same response.

Temporarily defeated, she bowed her head. The right side of her face thrummed with pain, as did her leg and various other parts of her body. Making her feel even worse was the fact that she was not only alone but also lost as well. Not knowing the location and, therefore, the co-ordinates of the crash site, she could not bring up the appropriate map on her HUD. For a moment, she wanted to scream with rage at her predicament.

Trying to get her feelings of fear under control, she straightened and said through clenched teeth, "Fuck this. I *will* get out of here alive and kick some ass along the way. Nick wouldn't leave me out here. They're probably looking for me right now."

The act of giving her backside a mental kicking served to boost her confidence and resolve. Not wanting to waste any further time, she limped painfully across to the cockpit of the helicopter and moved around to the pilot's side. Glancing inside, she immediately took a step backward, covering her mouth with a trembling hand.

"Oh, God," she whispered and leaned for support against the cold, slick metal of the fuselage as her legs threatened to give way beneath her.

The pilot was still in his seat. Sitting bolt upright, hand curled like a claw around the cyclic grip between his legs, he appeared to be trying to control the helicopter's downward plunge, even in death.

His head was missing. The stub of his spine — severed almost surgically — protruded up through the collar of his overalls, which were no longer khaki in color but a deep, almost crimson-black. His free hand seemed to clutch a jagged piece of propeller blade against his chest.

Nausea roiled in Jessie's stomach and she retched twice, swallowing bitter bile. Scrunching her eyes shut, she hoped that by doing this, when she opened them again the horrendous scene would have disappeared.

Her stomach settling, she took a deep breath and opened her eyes.

The co-pilot was slumped over his controls with his head turned toward her. His eyes were wide open, staring at her as though begging for clarification as to why a needle-like sliver of metal had pierced his helmet, penetrating his skull, which had obviously killed him.

Feeling an overwhelming sadness, Jessie knew that there would be no point in checking for any sign of life. The man was motionless, with no sign of his chest rising and falling.

Ohmygod. Jesus Christ. This is a nightmare. It has to be. I'll wake up in a minute and Nick will be with me, and he'll hold me and love me and everything will be fine.

Common sense told Jessie otherwise. The terror caused by what she had seen so far and the situation she found herself in suddenly manifested itself physically. Bending forward, hands resting on her knees, she gagged, then retched violently again, her stomach finally ejecting burning acidic bile from her stomach. She wanted to curl up in a ball somewhere, shut her eyes and make everything go away. On the verge of hysteria, a small voice in her mind began to berate her.

Get a grip, bitch. Nick is not here. He probably doesn't even know where you are yet. You can't depend on anyone coming to save your sorry ass. You need to do this yourself. Get out of here before you get your body canned by the fucking Taliban.

Sheer determination made her straighten up. She would *not* give in. Averting her eyes, Jessie limped slowly to the front of the helicopter and around it to the opposite side. She promptly tripped over something lying in her path. Overbalancing and flailing for a handhold but finding none, she toppled face first onto whatever it was that she had stumbled over and lay there while pain flared up her injured leg.

She glanced down to see what she had fallen over and uttered an involuntary squeal. She was lying prone across a dead body, hands buried in a liquid gruel of mud, rainwater and bloody guts that had trailed from the man's torn-open stomach.

Jessie shut her eyes tightly, hearing herself whimpering in a forlorn, pathetic way. The shock of seeing someone she knew ripped apart, his life fluids slathering her gloved hands, brought on a fainting darkness that threatened to tip her into unconsciousness.

One, two, three, four…

She slowly counted to ten, trying to breathe deeply and evenly, conscious of her head swimming with dizziness and her stomach churning.

The dizziness eventually receded and she clambered unsteadily to her feet, standing on one leg as the other throbbed achingly. She felt dazed and was now so cold and wet that her body trembled persistently. She clasped her arms about herself and squeezed, attempting to warm herself. All she succeeded in doing was smearing blood and body tissue onto her body armor and combats.

She needed to get moving, search the site to see if anyone was alive, get them and her out of the area before they all succumbed to the elements. A thought entered her head. As reluctant as she was to carry it out, she needed to. She had to do it for each member of Charlie Recon Section and the pilot and co-pilot.

Gingerly, she bent down and, grimacing at the sticky mess on the man's combat jacket, blindly felt around his neck until she found his dog tags. Wrenching the chain free, she grimly pulled one metal tag from it and thrust it into her pocket. The other tag she pushed down inside his boot. She tucked the chain inside a pocket on the body then frantically scrubbed her hands down the legs of her combat trousers.

She was becoming sluggish and sensed that it was probably due to the fact that the cold was playing havoc with her senses, but she knew that if she gave up and sat down, she would fall asleep and probably never wake up.

I need to get out of here.

With rain lashing down even harder than before and every bone in her body aching, Jessie got herself moving.

She began a slow inspection of the crash site, her first action to check the two bodies she had seen first. Hobbling to them, she dropped to her knees in the mud and placed numb fingertips on each of their carotid arteries. She could feel no pulse in either of them. They were so severely mutilated. Any one of their injuries was incompatible with life. They lay with their eyes open, staring sightlessly up into the falling rain.

Jessie hadn't known either of the two men very well but it still wrenched at her heart to know that their lives had ended in such an unforgiving and unjust way.

"I'm sorry," she whispered softly. "I'm so sorry, guys. You didn't deserve this."

She gently closed their eyes, blinking away hot tears, then ripped off each man's dog tags, hiding one in each boot and putting the others into her pocket.

As she struggled tiredly to her feet, she murmured, "We'll come and get you. You won't be alone for long. I promise."

Continuing with her search, Jessie discovered two more bodies thrown some distance from the helicopter. Each one had also suffered terrible injuries, the ground beneath them a quagmire of crimson, watery liquid. Again, she checked for any signs of life and on discovering none, closed their eyes and retrieved their dog tags.

She found the final body, that of Lieutenant Marshall, lying in a contorted and broken heap like a rag doll. By this time, she could not stop the tears from trickling down her cold cheeks to mingle with the rain and blood on her face. Sobs shook her shoulders.

Exhausted, she finally made her way back to the wreckage, dragging her injured leg, gritting her teeth at the excruciating pain that was now encasing it. She was shivering violently, teeth chattering like castanets, the bone-chilling cold sinking like needles deep into her bones.

She wanted to sleep, but daren't. There were two further bodies that she needed to deal with before she could rest, then there was the prospect of another hunt for a weapon, water and perhaps dry clothing.

Mustering what little strength she had left, she dealt with the pilot and co-pilot in the same way that she had the others, pocketing their dog tags, then she rested against the side of the helicopter. Her body was a seething mass of pain, but she knew that if she remained exposed to the inclement weather for much longer, her condition would worsen considerably and she might not be able to leave at all.

Her combats and her boots, liberally splashed with blood, had taken on a crimson-brown color and despite the refreshing smell of rain, the coppery essence of blood stung her nostrils. She wondered if she would ever forget that smell, and her stomach suddenly churned with the odor.

"Oh, please," she murmured. "Someone come and find me."

Taking a deep breath, Jessie circled the crash site again. She found a pack and, on opening it, discovered that it contained two precious bottles of water and a poncho. Quickly taking off her body armor, she put on the poncho, with her protective equipment over the top.

She decided to take the pack and spent a few minutes sorting through it. She discarded the things that she would not need and kept a few MREs, ammunition, a sleeping pad and some basic medical supplies, including painkillers. She quickly popped two tablets from their protective packet, threw them into her mouth, then, unscrewing the top of a bottle of water, drank two mouthfuls. She hoped that the analgesic would kick in and give her some respite from the pain in her leg and face before she made her move to leave.

Continuing with her hunt, she discovered a weapon, half mired in the soupy ground. Its barrel had come to rest on a flat rock so, apart from a small amount of rainwater that might possibly have infiltrated its mechanism, Jessie thought that it might still work when it dried out. Whether it did or not, she couldn't pass it by. A weapon was one of her priorities.

She had one final thing she had to do before she left. She needed to find something with which to make a signal. When she and the medevac teams came back to extract the bodies, they would be able to locate the spot.

A small voice in the back of her mind wondered if it was

a good idea. Any Taliban arriving at the location would see the signal and know that there was someone alive. She had made a promise, however, to come back, and on her life, she would not break that promise. Whether insurgents came after her or not, she needed to do this.

With her ankle and leg aching like rotten teeth and her shoulders slumping wearily, she paced the site for a third and final time. After what seemed like hours to her quickly tiring body, she found what she was looking for. A white sheet of polyethylene had somehow escaped from inside the Wildcat and had snarled itself around a twisted tree trunk.

Jessie spent precious minutes unraveling the material, uttering a string of curses as it caught and snagged on every piece of uneven bark. Finally, it came free and she proceeded to drag it away some distance from the helicopter wreckage to a flat piece of ground. Laboriously spreading it out, she weighted down each corner with small piles of stones until it was reasonably flat and would not blow away unless there was a gale force wind.

With her whole body stiff and aching, she knew that the time had come for her to move out. Before she did so however, she needed some sort of plan. Finding herself a large boulder on which to rest at the foot of the slope, she activated her HUD, praying that apart from her comms, everything else would work.

Okay, where were we heading?

Jessie brought up the schematic of their mission details and route and studied it all carefully. The plan had been for them to drop just outside Darbart, a village in the Kunar Province of the Korangal Valley, some twenty clicks from FOB Elabat. From there, the section was to hump a few clicks and do a recce of that area before extraction back to the FOB.

Jessie located the village on a map, then stalled in her search as she realized again that she had no means of knowing where they had crashed. Flight time from the FOB to Darbart was thirty minutes and, if she guessed right, they had been in the air for approximately fifteen of those minutes before something had gone terribly wrong and the Wildcat had dropped out of the sky like a stone.

Dismissing the nightmarish images of the crash that seemed to pop into her mind at random intervals, she ground her teeth together—her dentist was going to be thrilled if she kept on doing it—and backtracked the best she could from Darbart along their flight route.

"Okay," she murmured. "By a rough estimate, that puts me about…here, right by some low hills. So, if I find the closest FOB, I might be able to hump it."

She quickly spoke her roughly estimated coordinates and waited for the appropriate schematic to appear on her face shield. She spoke a number and a list of forward operating bases appeared, overlaying the map of the Kunar Province. There was a solitary active FOB. She was lucky.

FOB Bostick, occupied by the US Marines, had been deactivated and handed over to the Afghan Army in 2012. It had only recently gone active again because of a recent increase in hostilities in Afghanistan.

She calculated a rough distance and was a little dismayed to note that she would have to walk about twenty clicks, just over twelve miles, to safety. Hoping that her watch was still working, she chanced a glance at it and saw that it was a little after 1000 hours. If she moved at a brisk pace, she might make FOB Bostick before nightfall. Being stranded and alone after dark in occupied territory was something that she did not want to happen.

Jessie sighed. She needed to head east-northeast and was grateful that her HUD would keep her on the right route. She input her destination and what she estimated the distance to be and watched as a map inscribed itself on her face shield. A meandering bright green line ended in a pulsating green dot, her final destination, and a glowing green dot at the opposite end of the line represented her. There was no sign of anything representing the Taliban between her present location and what she hoped was FOB Bostick.

The sight of what might be the final end of her journey gave her a sense of determination and resolve, and she felt her spirits lift a little. She was hurt, cold and tired but with enough strength and resoluteness, she was convinced that she would make it, barring bumping into any insurgents, of course.

Jessie slid gingerly off the rock and turned to face the wreckage of the helicopter. "I'm so sorry, you guys," she murmured. "But I'll come back, and we'll get you home."

She lingered for a moment longer, bowing her head and briefly closed her eyes. At last, she turned and began to walk away, thrusting her arms through the pack as she went. Once it felt comfortable, she positioned her weapon across her chest, finger resting lightly on the trigger, and with her heart thundering painfully in her chest, set out on what seemed like an endless march to safety.

Her injured leg instantly started to protest vehemently at the enforced exercise but Jessie continued hobbling away from the crash site, her mouth dry with fear.

What if I run out of water or collapse from exhaustion? I won't make it. Nick will never know where I am. I'll die out here in the desert.

The fear suddenly turned to terror.

Maybe I should go back, stay close to the helicopter. At least it will protect me from the weather. Friendlies might already know where the Wildcat went down. The Taliban might also know, though, and already be on their way. If I wait here, they'll find me.

Jessie stopped walking and turned to look uneasily over her shoulder. She was torn.

Do I take a risk or the coward's way out?

She saw something that almost sent her scurrying back to the wreckage. Since leaving the site, her passage was marked clearly in the wet mud and sand of the desert. No one could fail to discover the faint boot prints that she had left. All she could do was pray that the heavy rain would wash away any trail before the insurgents discovered it. If not, then they would track and find her.

Stiffening her shoulders, Jessie moved off again, trying to get herself into a rhythm where she could maintain an even pace, even though her leg screamed at her to *sit down, why don't you?*

As she left the relative protection of the low hills, a cold wind blew in chilled gusts, attacking her already freezing body, stiffening her saturated combats so that they chaffed the vulnerable parts of her body and lowering her body temperature even further. She had to concentrate hard to stop the occasional shudders that wracked her body. The poncho beneath her body armor had prevented any further rain from soaking her but she was already drenched and it did nothing to warm her.

The rain — still coming down heavily — reduced visibility to about five meters, so she would be unable to see anyone until they were almost upon her. The ground beneath her feet was a quagmire of sand and dust. It clung to her boots, adding weight to them, causing further strain on her injured leg. The farther she walked, the more painful it became, but she refused to stop.

She had planned that she would rest for five minutes each hour, take on board water and eat some of the MREs. Except for her comms, her HUD appeared to be functioning perfectly, and she checked her route every five minutes, ensuring that her green dot was keeping to the green line.

As time moved on, the rain showed no sign of abating and daylight started to fade quickly. Jessie was worried. With the bad weather, darkness would come early. The going was already hard, particularly with her injuries and with decreased visibility. There was no way that she was going to be able to use a light. Any illumination would act like a beacon for anyone near her location to see. She would have to rely on her night vision and hope that she didn't fall down a hole or trip over something, adding other injuries to her list of those present.

Jessie continued with her march. Now and again, she had to climb low rocky outcrops and over boulders and stones when they materialized in her way, sometimes having to deviate from her course, or backtrack a few meters to find a safer, easier route.

She attempted to increase her pace but her injuries and the difficulties of the half-seen terrain prevented her from doing so. At one point, she brought up the illuminated digital clock on her face shield and saw that she had been on the move for almost an hour. It was time that she found a safe place a little off her route where she could rest. It had to be somewhere that offered her protection from the rain and where she could conceal herself as much as possible.

She glanced around, looking for rocks big enough to provide some sort of hiding place, but she was disappointed. She debated searching the area then denounced that idea as being foolhardy. It was at that moment that she thought she heard a sound. It was difficult to decipher what it was above the pounding of rain on her helmet. Straining her ears, she felt a different kind of cold seep into her veins as she made out the sound of an engine in the distance.

Chapter Twenty

Turning in a circle, she tried to pinpoint the exact direction from which it was coming, hoping that it was friendlies from the crash site hot on her trail to rescue her. On the other hand, it could be Taliban on their way to investigate the downed helicopter. If it was, then they would have to pass her first and she needed to hide herself.

She had two alternatives – hide and stay silent in case it was the enemy or try to issue a radio transmission in case it was friendlies, alerting them to her whereabouts. If it was hostiles, they might be able to pick up her frequency and she would find herself in trouble. Any of these alternatives was full of imponderables, so she was in a catch-22 situation.

Desperately, Jessie glanced about her, indecisive and frightened. She needed to know if the vehicle was heading directly toward her and would inevitably cross her path or whether it would bypass her, missing her completely.

She saw two headlights approaching her from dead ahead, shining dimly through the rain. The vehicle would run right into her if she did not get out of its path. She did not recognize the shape of the headlights and therefore knew that they did not belong to any Coalition military vehicle.

I need to move…now!

Jessie turned quickly, ignoring the sudden flare of pain in her ankle, and ran as fast as she could off to her left, hoping that the pale camouflage pattern of her combats was sufficient to allow her to blend in with the leaden sheets of rain.

As she ran, lurching on her bad ankle, the growl of the

engine grew louder and she realized that there was no way she was going be able to find somewhere safe before whoever it was came upon her.

Breath hissing harshly from a throat dry with terror, Jessie released the quick release pins on her body armor, which allowed it and her pack to drop from her body, and she threw herself to the ground. She turned around so that she faced back the way she had come and could get a visual on the oncoming threat.

Partially sighted as she was, she peered through the murk, her one good eye straining to see what was approaching. She wriggled her body into the soft watery sand and mud, using her legs in a running motion together with her elbows to hollow out a shallow pit beneath her body.

Lowering her head almost to ground level, she watched with an almost primal terror as the vehicle grew nearer. If it did not deviate from its course, then it would pass her at a distance of approximately four meters. Horror struck her when she realized that she had probably left tracks in the sand, which would lead whoever it was right to her pathetic hiding place.

God, help me!

Resting her chin on the waterlogged surface, Jessie watched closely, squinting through the somber light. As the headlights expanded in her vision, she realized that her weapon was pinned beneath her left side. Holding her breath, she eased it out and carefully brought it forward so that it its barrel rested on the slight incline of the shallow dip. Her trembling finger hovered over the trigger. If the vehicle stopped and whoever it was dismounted, she would shoot to kill without hesitation.

Time seemed to stand still. Jessie's body began to grow numb from her enforced position and the cold and rain. Her whole focus was on the growl of the engine, growing ever louder. She heard male voices and was at first unable to make out whether they were speaking English or Pashto. Finally, she heard the language of Afghanistan and her skin prickled with icy goosebumps.

She hunkered down even farther into her makeshift foxhole and watched as the vehicle grew level with her. She could finally make out that it was a truck, its bed crammed full of Afghans leaning over the sides and over the top of the cab, shouting and waving what looked to be weapons in the air.

She knew that they were heading for the crash site. Once there, they would find the signal she had left and know that someone was alive. They would then come after her.

Hardly daring to breathe, she waited until the truck had disappeared into the gloom and jumped to her feet. She quickly put on her body armor and pack, then picked up her weapon and, giving one last glance over her shoulder in the direction the truck had taken, she slammed her face shield into place and began to run.

Her ankle flared instant pain but she kept up the pace, knowing with a deep primal instinct that the Taliban would be on her tail as soon as they had the opportunity. She darted her eyes briefly to the map of her route, wanting to get back on the trail, and she felt a little safer once her green dot merged with the green line.

Twenty minutes later, she was breathing harshly. Normally, at the peak of fitness, she could have run for about an hour at the same even pace, but the pain in her leg plus lack of food and water were quickly taking their toll, and she found her pace slowing, no matter how hard she tried to keep it up.

Ten minutes later, she knew that she had to rest, otherwise she would never be able to complete the rest of her journey. She stopped and tried to slow her breathing. Glancing quickly over her shoulder, she could see nothing except the desolate landscape in her immediate vicinity. Lifting her face shield, she strained her ears to see if she could hear the truck engine, but all was silent except for the faint sound of trickling water somewhere close by.

Moving off slowly, Jessie prayed that she could find a

place to hide. She noticed that rocks and boulders littered her surroundings and the ground was ascending slightly. Keeping mental fingers crossed, she continued on until a small boulder-strewn hill loomed out of the gloom.

She stopped at its foot, peering up to see how high it was. It was barely three to four meters in height, the gradient relatively gentle, with enough hand and footholds to make it a relatively safe climb. With her injured leg, though, she was a little unsure if she could make it.

She had no alternative but to try. Her trail would end here and she could safely search for a hiding place. First, she needed to obliterate her tracks. Bending down, she grabbed a fist-size rock and moved back for at least five meters. Crouching, she began to use the rock to scrub out her footprints, moving slowly back toward the slope until she reached it. She had done her best to get rid of any evidence that she had ever been there.

Next, she started to walk northeast along the base of the slope, emphasizing her boot prints in the mud and sand. She walked for about five minutes, hoping that the rocky slope would not peter out into the flatness of desert before she was ready for it to.

Gradually, the hill started to descend in height until it was nothing more than low boulders. There she discovered tire tracks in the mud where the truck had obviously swerved on meeting the hill. Jessie stepped onto the deep marks, sinking her weight into the wet ground. She hoped that if the insurgents returned on the hunt, they would see her tracks along the base of the hill, come to the conclusion that she had not been able to climb it and follow her trail until it stopped in their own tire tracks. If they were stupid enough to fall for it, it could throw them off her scent. She knew that it was a pathetic plan—a child could have probably come up with it—but it was all she had.

Jessie turned and, instead of retracing her steps, she began to climb over the rocks and boulders that made up the lower slope of the hill. As the height increased, she found it hard going. The rocks and sandstone were wet and slippery, their edges almost as sharp as razor blades. She lost count of how many times she slipped and, when grabbing for a handhold, tore the skin from her fingers in the process.

She persevered, her injured leg screaming in protest, her lungs hurting from lack of oxygen as she pushed herself to her limit. When she was almost out of energy and strength, she reached the top. Quickly surveying her position, she began to climb around to the lee of the hill, hoping to find a crevice in the rocks or an overhang where she could conceal herself.

Jessie felt a strong sense of relief as she sighted a small opening that was about a meter and a half wide, just big enough for her body. It recessed back into the sandstone for about two meters, so there was plenty of room for her to stretch out her legs. Two enormous boulders loomed on either side…a perfect place of concealment.

Dropping to her knees, Jessie crawled into the space, wedging herself as far back as she could before wriggling into a seated position and resting her head back against the rock behind her.

She tried to relax, but tension thrummed throughout her body. She was exhausted. She needed to eat and drink something but, for the moment, she sat with her eyes closed, trying to slow her breathing and ease the throbbing ache in her leg.

She was almost dozing when she thought she heard a rock tumble down the hill from close by. She had whipped up her weapon, holding it at shoulder level, pointing outward, a trembling finger hovering over the trigger, before she realized she had done so. She held her breath and listened carefully but could hear nothing more. Somebody even moving as stealthily as they were able could not have failed to make a noise.

It must have been my imagination. Calm down, girl.

Laying her weapon back across her lap, Jessie released the quick release pins on her pack and dragged it from behind her, a difficult feat in the confined space. When it was on her lap, she undid its Velcro fastenings as quietly as she could and drew out a bottle of water. Trying not to drink too much too quickly, she took small mouthfuls, relishing the warm fluid as it slid down her throat, feeling like silk.

Knowing that she needed to conserve her rations, particularly the water, she put the bottle away and drew out a couple of MRE bags, wrinkling her nose at the choices she found herself with—beef stew or spaghetti with meat sauce. Opting for the beef stew, she put the other MRE back then opened up the chosen bag.

Flattening her pack, she emptied the contents onto its surface. Identifying each item in turn, she discovered that there was the beef stew, a packet of rice, crackers, M&Ms, a small drink of some sort and a spoon.

Feeling famished and needing food to replenish her energy, Jessie tore open the bag of beef stew, opened the rice and poured it in to make a mix then began to eat. At first, the food tasted like cold, congealed fat, but this soon dissolved into tolerance of the bland food as the first mouthful increased her hunger, and she ate it as quickly as she could. After finishing the main meal, she stowed the empty packet into her pack, then went on to eat the crackers and M&Ms.

Feeling a little more relaxed with her hunger satiated for the moment, Jessie checked her weapon, then, lowering her face shield, she brought her comms online. She grimaced at the harsh static erupting inside her helmet. Her comms were still down. She checked her route and saw with resignation that she still had ten clicks to go before she reached FOB Bostick.

Raising her face shield, she checked her watch. She would give herself fifteen minutes of downtime before starting off again.

She winced as she moved her right leg. Her boot had grown excruciatingly tight and she knew that her ankle and calf had swollen alarmingly. She could not remove her boot to check the damage. If she did, she would probably not be able to get it back on again and she would be in a whole world of hurt.

Enough with the dramatics already.

Pushing herself back into the recess, Jessie leaned her head back and closed her eyes. The rain still fell on her but, partially shielded by the rock face for the first time in what felt like hours, she felt almost comfortable. The silence surrounding her was total. It felt like she was the only woman left in the world. It left her feeling desolate and deeply alone. She yearned to hear a human voice, preferably speaking English.

I want Nick.

An image of him popped into her mind, and her stomach twisted with wanting. She could picture his dark eyes, his slow smile and finally almost feel the warmth of his kisses. She pictured their lovemaking, the way his hands had touched her body, how she had hungered for him, the exquisite sensations that had coursed through her body as he entered her.

Come and get me, Nick. Please. I miss you so much, and I'm scared.

She felt tears start building in her eyes but she refused to cry. To do so would undermine her determination to get herself out of the mess that she found herself in. She opened her eyes and shivered.

I need to get moving. Time is a-wasting.

As hard and uncomfortable as her hiding place was, she didn't want to move. For a fleeting second, she wondered about staying where she was. If the Taliban came back along her route, they probably wouldn't be able to find her. On the other hand, if they suspected that she was hiding, they wouldn't let the chance of a hostage slip by and, being female, she would be like a gift from Paradise for them.

Jessie stirred. Sighing, she repacked her pack and shrugged it onto her back. Grasping her weapon, she shuffled forward on her backside until her legs protruded from the recess. Groaning with discomfort, she grabbed onto the side of a boulder, preparing to haul herself to her feet and stopped.

She could hear something. It was in the distance, faint but distinct...the sound of heavy gunfire, a lot of gunfire. Her heart rate increased. She couldn't pinpoint the direction from which it came but it was sporadic with lengthy pauses between prolonged bouts.

Jessie's breath caught in her throat. *That sounds like one hell of a firefight. I need to get moving, fast.*

Lowering her face shield, the need to get to safety foremost in her mind, Jessie moved out from her hiding place. Maintaining her location to the leeward side of the rocks, she started a hasty descent, occasionally slipping on the surfaces of wet rocks and sandstone. At one point she fell heavily, and before she could stop herself, she slid into a shallow crevice between two boulders. She held back a moan of pain as the skin shredded from the palm of her hand and she banged her injured ankle, the knock conjuring up piercing pain that coruscated up to her groin. She bit her lip savagely in an effort to keep quiet.

Near to tears, Jessie managed to scramble back onto her feet and completed her climb down to the base of the hill, a bright flare of pain swamping her leg. She could not stop to rest and began a hobbling run, her pace slow and awkward.

Keeping an eye on the map etched onto her face shield, she focused on getting back onto her route and once the green dot merged with the green line, she increased her pace. However, although the MRE and drink had increased her energy a little, she found herself quickly flagging.

Run. Run!

Resounding like a litany through her head, the word kept time with each single struggling pace. She eventually found herself repeating it out loud, as though to hear it would enable her to keep going. With every pounding footfall on the uneven terrain, the pain in her ankle increased until she could barely run.

Every few minutes, she turned to look back over her shoulder but could see nothing in the misty gloom. Her fear amplified as the rain began to taper off until it was nothing more than a drizzle. Her profile would be clearly visible against the undulating desert if the weather cleared.

Jessie checked time and distance to her objective. It was 1500 hours with eight clicks to go. Her spirits sank. If the Taliban were hunting her down, she would not make it to FOB Bostick.

I am not going to let them get me. I'll kill them first before they lay their fucking hands on me.

Chapter Twenty-One

Jessie's concentration dwindled to putting one heavy foot in front of the other. She tried to push the throbbing pain in her leg and the aching of her body to the back of her mind, to keep the oxygen flowing evenly in and out of her burning lungs.

With cold fear, she noticed that the rain had almost stopped, the air beginning to clear. She was fully aware that it was only a matter of time before they discovered her, but her determination to get to the FOB before it grew dark never flagged, although she prayed that night would fall quickly to hide her.

She glanced over her shoulder once more and saw something that caused her to moan with fear, stumble then fall to the ground. She began to crawl away from the faint gleam of headlights coming directly toward her through the gloom.

Fuck! Fuck! Fuck! They're coming.

Jessie struggled to get to her feet but her body refused to obey her brain's commands. She fell again, this time onto her side. She lay shivering, a primitive urge to just curl into a protective ball and stay there, surging through her.

Sheer determination and guts gave her a mental boost and, grunting and groaning, she managed to clamber to her feet. With one last glance behind her to confirm the vehicle was still in pursuit, she once again began to run, hobbling badly on a leg that was becoming virtually useless.

Almost at her limit of endurance, all thoughts of keeping her breathing and pace rhythmic long gone, she pushed herself harder and faster. As she strained her hearing to assess if the engine noise was getting closer, Jessie saw another small outcropping of sandstone ahead of her. It jutted up from the desert, barely tall or wide enough to hide a human being, but it was the only place of concealment that was available.

Jessie headed toward it. If she could reach it and hide, the vehicle might pass her by. She would have no time to conceal her tracks, so more than likely her pursuers would see them. At least she had fought to the end, no matter the outcome.

The small hill drew closer and she ran until she reached its foot. Turning to her right, she limped quickly along its base until she reached the end, turned, then began to climb up the butte.

Although small, it was steep and she found herself grabbing for handholds, boots slipping on the slick gravel surface beneath them. At one point, she reached for the edge of a rock, missed, clutched at the air, and almost fell backward. It was only when she dropped her weapon and managed to throw herself forward, landing hard between two boulders, that she was able to save herself.

She lay winded, bruised ribs now adding their chorus of pain to her other injuries before she once more hauled herself to her feet, found her weapon and finished her climb.

Before searching for someplace to hide, she crouched, looking back the way she had come. The headlights were glaringly bright, the shape of the vehicle ill-defined behind them. She was so tired that she was unable to tell whether it was hostile or friendly. It was still coming for her, and she could now hear the snarl of an engine, even though it was muffled and indistinct. She was not about to wait around to find out if she was in danger or safe.

Realizing that she was making a target of herself by staying on top of the hillock, Jessie moved quickly around to the leeward side, casting frantically around for a place of refuge. She discovered it in the form of a small crevice. It was barely big enough to conceal the whole of her body, but she had no choice.

Falling to her knees, she quickly turned, took off her pack and scooted backward into the recess, flinching as sharp stones dug into her bruised body. She had to tilt herself so that her weight rested uncomfortably on her right hip and buttock, the only way she could fit into the confined space. She thrust her pack to rest at her feet, then, locking and loading her weapon, brought her knees up and rested the barrel on them, aiming it outward so that if anyone appeared in her sights, she would have a good aim.

Jessie waited, trying to quiet her harsh breathing, hoping and praying that they would not find her.

The minutes seemed to pass as slowly as though time had stood still. At first, all she could hear was the blood pounding in her ears, obliterating all other noises. As her pulse and heart rate slowed, she heard what she had most dreaded to hear…the sound of a vehicle approaching her location…fast.

Don't let them find me. Please. Don't let them find me.

She waited, panic growing, the engine noise drawing ever closer. It sounded as though it was a heavy, powerful vehicle but she was not about to expose herself to whoever was out there just to take a look. She judged that the vehicle was almost upon her when she heard the hiss of brakes and it suddenly stopped, the engine dying to a low rumble.

She felt her body grow rigid.

They've seen my tracks. They know where I am.

She bit her lip, scrunching up her eyes, trying to block out the terrifying thought that she was about to die. She listened carefully but could hear nothing except the throbbing growl of an idling engine.

I can't sit here waiting for them to find me. I'm a sitting duck. If they find me here, I have no escape route.

Scared beyond reason and without thinking, Jessie scooted out from the crevice, grabbed her pack and ran. There was no thought in her mind except escape. Oblivious to pain and exhaustion, she almost leapt down the slope of the hillock, landing on her bad leg at its base, almost sinking to her knees. Stumbling and trying to regain her balance for a few paces, she was up and running.

As she sprinted away from the protection of the mound, she heard a shout. The noise of it registered, the language did not, and she ran for her life, pack clenched in one hand, weapon in the other.

She heard another shout then the sound of running footsteps behind her. A terror the likes of which she had never felt before took control of her and by some miracle, she found a reserve of strength that she hadn't known she possessed and was able to increase her pace.

Then she went flying. Somehow, her foot had found a slight dip in the sand and her ankle, damaged, weakened and over-stressed, buckled. Her forward motion combined with fatigue caused her to tumble flat onto her face. She hit the ground hard, her weapon and pack skidding away out of reach and out of sight. Winded and spent, she lay motionless, struggling to breathe. She was done…out of strength and resolve and about to die.

Nick. I love you. I'm so sorry.

In the next second, something heavy landed on her legs and body, pinning her to the wet sand.

Jessie fought. With what little strength that remained she managed to roll onto her back. A primal instinct for survival came to the fore and she screamed out her hate and determination.

She pummeled and punched her attacker, pounding against the arms that were trying to pin her to the ground. She jerked her body backward and forward, turning it this way and that, trying to topple her assailant to the side but whoever it was clung like a limpet. The person was strong but she fought like a wildcat, her fists connecting with arms and the sides of a ribcage.

"Get off me, you bastard," she yelled her voice hoarse. "You fucking piece of shit. I'll kill you."

Her fist connected with the side of a helmet and for a

moment she was startled. The Taliban did not wear helmets.

Her own instantly vibrated with what felt like a punch and her head rocked sideways. With her ears ringing, strength and fight left her and she lost any advantage she might have had.

The person on top of her pinned her wrists to the ground, straddling her.

She felt whomever it was bend forward, and a firm, controlled voice spoke close to her face, "Jessie! Jessie, calm down. It's me."

Jessie tensed. She heard her name and recognized the voice but stayed silent, not believing that it could be him.

"Jessie, it's me, Nick. Can you hear me?"

She was still not able to get her body to relax. The idea that it was Nick who had found her felt like a dream.

She coughed and cleared her throat. "Nick?" she whispered.

"Yes, it's me. Jesus Christ. I'm going to release you now. No more fighting me."

He released her wrists and, sliding off her body, dragged her into his arms.

"Nick?" Jessie asked again. She closed her eyes and sagged against him. She could feel the roughness of his combat jacket under her cold hands and the strength of his arms holding her. "Is it really you? I thought...I was going to die. I thought you were the enemy after me."

"It's me," Nick answered. "Fuck, Jessie. I thought I'd lost you."

His arms tightened around her and she moaned, "I hurt."

"I know, darling. You're safe now."

Even though he held her in his arms, Nick could not believe that he had found her. When he had located her ident, the chase across the desert to get to her before the enemy did had almost driven him mad with frustration and impatience.

When he had caught sight of her running, all he had

wanted to do was shout out her name, stop her fear and headlong flight and let her know that she was safe. He would never let her go again, even if it meant disclosing the fact of their relationship and getting her out of Afghanistan.

Nick activated his comms. Attempting to make his voice sound as casual as possible, he said, "Dingle, I have her. Tell the medic. I'm bringing her in."

"Thank fuck, LT," was Dingle's return transmission. "Copy your last. The medic is already on standby."

Nick turned back to Jessie. "Sweetheart," he said, "can you walk?"

Jessie did not respond. Alarmed, Nick shook her gently. "Jessie. Talk to me."

He felt the woman stir in his arms. She moaned and raised her head to stare at him. He winced as he saw her face clearly for the first time – the swollen cheek and closed eye with livid bruising around it, the bloodstains against the pallor of her skin and dry, cracked lips. He ached inside at what she must have been through, the terror and trauma of first the helicopter crash, then her attempt at survival alone in the desert.

"Come on, Jessie. On your feet," he said firmly, shaking her again. "We need to get out of here."

Releasing her reluctantly from his arms, he rose to his feet, slung his weapon over his shoulder, and, bending forward, grabbed her beneath the arms. She was a dead weight to lift and he staggered slightly but managed to get her upright, where she slumped against him.

"Cover us," he ordered into his comms. Putting an arm about her waist, he took a pace forward and was alarmed when she cried out in pain.

"What?" he asked.

"I've hurt my leg," Jessie answered, her voice weak. "I think it's busted or something."

"Crap!" Nick exclaimed. "JR, I need someone over here on the double. Mac's hurt."

"Copy that, LT," responded JR's voice.

Through the rapidly descending dusk, a figure appeared and Dingle went to Jessie's other side and put a supporting arm about her waist.

Between them, the men managed to lift her feet from the ground and, at a rapid pace, move her to the M-ATV some ten meters from their position. The Charlie Recon Section medic was waiting at the open door and all three men managed to help her into the vehicle where she lay down on a stretcher that had been already prepared for her.

Jessie felt as if her nightmare were almost over. When she had initially heard Nick's voice, she had thought that her imagination was playing a cruel trick. If she had believed that she was safe and it had turned out that it was just part of the ongoing nightmare, she would have given up, past caring. It wasn't until he had taken her in his arms and spoken to her again that she realized her ordeal was over.

She lay on a stretcher and for the first time in what seemed like forever, felt at peace. However, the M-ATV was stationary in the middle of the desert, darkness was falling rapidly, and they did not have enough firepower to hold off a group of insurgents.

Jessie became aware of the medic, who she only knew as Paul, kneeling beside her. She felt his hands quickly and competently carry out a quick body assessment, feeling her arms and legs for any sign of major injury. She winced when his hands pressed on tender areas of her body and almost cried out as he manipulated her right ankle.

"You might have broken that," he admitted. "I won't take off your boot. We'll leave that for the CTH to do. Could do more harm than good."

He carefully removed her helmet and checked her eye.

"You've a right shiner there. You might have fractured your cheekbone or eye socket. Do you have any other major injuries?"

Jessie cleared her throat. "No," she answered, shivering violently and trying in vain to stop her teeth from chattering.

"I'm so cold."

The medic took her pulse, then she felt something intrusive inserted into her ear. After a moment, the medic withdrew it, checked the result, and said, "Your body temperature is way too low. We need to get you warmed up."

Jessie felt a number of combat casualty blankets laid on top of her, then heard the crackle of foil sheeting.

"I need to hook you up to some juice," the medic announced. "Let's see if your veins will cooperate."

He forced up the sleeve of her combat jacket, then the tapping of a finger against the soft skin in the crook of her arm. Paul kept this up for a short time, then moved on to her wrist, then the back of her hand. He checked her other arm then shook his head.

"Your veins are non-existent. You'll have to get warm, then we'll check again. If it still doesn't work, we'll need to try an intraosseous infusion. Not very comfortable, but we might need to go that route to get fluids in you."

Jessie nodded. Being a medic, she was well aware that she needed fluids, more importantly, hydration. She knew what an intraosseous infusion was and she was determined to avoid having a needle punched through her bone into the soft marrow so that she could receive hydration and lactate ringers that way for shock.

She was beginning to feel slightly warmer, her extremities starting to tingle and burn. She still had the shakes, but they had decreased in intensity and her teeth had stopped chattering. Paul continuously checked her pulse, temperature and various veins in her arms and wrists, looking for access.

At last, he announced triumphantly, "Good. We have a vein. Sharp scratch, Jessie, then you can sleep. Shouldn't do you any harm to snooze and get some rest."

Jessie winced as she did indeed feel a scratch, then the discomfort of having a cannula slide into the crook of her arm. Knowing the procedure, she felt the needle taped to her skin and a tube connected to the hub. She saw a clear bag of fluid placed on her chest, knowing that it was some kind of hydration fluid.

"Cleared to go, medic?" she heard Nick's voice ask.

"Copy that," Paul replied. "She's stable and will probably sleep now."

"Let's get out of here, Shrek," Nick ordered.

Jessie heard the engine roar, then she felt a jolt as they moved off. She was much warmer now and was beginning to feel drowsy. All she wanted to do was sleep. Nick had found her, and she was safe.

Slowly her eyes closed and she drifted off, her mind comfortably blank.

Chapter Twenty-Two

Surrounded by misty twilight with visibility only a few meters, Jessie ran for her life. Boots pounding the sand, arms pumping at her sides, her lungs burned from lack of oxygen and her breath hissed harshly through gritted teeth.

There was no place of safety in her immediate vicinity and panic gripped her, knotting the muscles in her stomach. She tried to increase her pace but had no energy left, the strength draining from her body at an alarming rate.

She could hear heavy footfalls behind her, getting closer, and she realized that her pursuer was gradually gaining on her. Fear consumed her. She was not only military but also a woman and if they caught her, they would kill her. Before doing so however, she was positive that they would do unspeakable things to her. She would kill herself first before allowing that to happen.

She stumbled and almost fell. Whimpering, she managed to remain on her feet, hearing harsh breathing from the person in pursuit, knowing that they were almost upon her. An image flashed into her mind of a hand stretching out to grab her shoulder – almost in slow motion – a smile of triumph on the unseen face…

No!

Jessie awoke with a start. She was trembling, heart racing, and for a moment she lay still, wondering where she was. Little by little, her vision cleared and she discovered that she was lying in a hospital bed bathed in a dim electric light that was almost comforting.

She was no longer cold, and the pain in her right leg had died to a dull ache. She discovered that she could partially open her right eye, although the vision there was still blurred and there was a twinge of pain when she blinked. The relief that she still retained her sight was enormous.

I'm in hospital. I'm safe.

She tried to sit up in bed but something tugged sharply at the crook of her elbow, restricting movement. Glancing down, she saw a butterfly cannula inserted under the skin of her arm, with double tubes running from its hub up to two clear bags of fluid hanging from a stand. Studying the bags, she identified fluid resuscitation for circulatory shock in one and antibiotics in the other.

A heart rate monitor blipped quietly to her right, its green tracing coming from a finger sensor monitor attached to the index finger of her hand. Craning her neck awkwardly, she was able to read the data, noting with relief that her blood pressure, pulse and respiration appeared within normal parameters.

Jessie's eyes filled with burning tears of relief. Swallowing the lump in her throat and blinking them back, she lifted her head and looked around. She was alone in a hospital ward in the combat trauma hospital — CTH — Camp Bastion.

Resting her head on the pillow, she went back over what she could recollect of her rescue. She remembered her dash across the desert and the all-consuming fear she had felt on thinking that it was the Taliban who were chasing her. She recalled tripping and falling, someone pinning her to the ground then fighting for her life until she realized that it was Nick who had found her.

Memories after that became hazy with warm images of Nick holding her in his arms then becoming aware of being inside the M-ATV and the medic examining her. After that, she remembered nothing — either lapsing into unconsciousness or falling into an exhausted sleep — until a few minutes ago when she had woken up in the CTH.

"Hey, Jessie, welcome back to the land of the living."

Startled at the sound of the voice, Jessie jumped. Turning her head toward the door of the ward, she saw Dingle standing watching her with his arms folded a smile on his face.

Pleased to see him, Jessie smiled. "Hey, you. Come on in, or are you going to stand there all day propping the doorway up?"

Dingle straightened and came to stand beside her bed. "You look…good," he announced after he had gazed down at her for some seconds.

"Yeah, right, and you're a very bad liar, Dingle," Jessie replied wryly. "Don't stand on ceremony. Pull up that chair and sit down." She gestured to the single seat by her locker.

Dingle obeyed and seated himself. "So, how are you?" he asked, his tone light-hearted.

"I feel like I've been run over by a very big truck. What's your next silly question?"

"You want me to be honest? You look like you have," Dingle said, a slight teasing note in his voice. Stretching out a hand, he traced a finger along the back of hers.

Jessie glanced down at the action, then back at his face, seeing a warm expression there. It was the look of a man who was in the throes of an attraction.

Oh, no, Dingle. Please don't like me too much. I don't want you to get hurt.

Gently, she moved her hand so that his dropped to the bed. Dingle withdrew it, as if he sensed her rejection.

After a short, embarrassed silence, he said, "You had us shitting in our combats, girl. LT has been acting like a madman. You must be flavor of the month."

"Lieutenant Ryan has?" Jessie asked, trying not to allow any emotion to show on her face at the mention of Nick's name.

"They were going to postpone the search and rescue because of the weather," Dingle said. "I thought LT was going to blow Major Hayward's brains all over the walls of his pristine tent, trying to persuade him to expedite matters."

"Really?" Jessie cleared her throat. "Can you tell me what happened? I can only remember bits and pieces. How did you find me?"

"Do you think you're up to talking about it?" Dingle asked. "The doctors in this place seem to think you need to rest and not to get upset."

"I'm fine," Jessie answered impatiently. "My leg and eye are hurt, not my brain. Please, just tell me."

"Well, a Watchkeeper caught the distress signal from the Wildcat's transponder, relayed it to Command, who in turn sent it to the operations center at the FOB. We had the coordinates and location soon after the helicopter went down but, as I said, the bloody weather was playing havoc with the equipment. Eventually, LT got Major Hayward to let us go out and do a recce. What's left of Charlie Recon and some of our section stayed behind to stand security at the FOB and me, LT, Shrek, JR and the medic from Charlie Recon volunteered to go out to the crash site.

"HUDs picked up contact with multiple targets a couple of clicks out, so we had to hide the M-ATV and tab the rest of the way. It was one shitty forced foot march, I can tell you that, but LT was like a man out of his head. He wouldn't rest and he kicked our butts to get there.

"We finally made contact with about eight *mujis* and kicked seven shades of shit out of them. LT found the poor bastards killed in the crash and your signal. You also left very clear tracks, Jessie dear. Once we'd ordered up a medevac to pick up the KIA, we retrieved the M-ATV and came after you. After we searched your first hiding place, we moved on and found your tracks again. The rest is history."

Jessie winced as she tried to make herself more comfortable in bed. "Thanks for getting me out of there," she said quietly. "I really thought I was going to die. I had no idea who was coming after me. You could have been Taliban, for all I knew. They drove past me, heading toward where the helicopter went down, and I knew it was only a matter of time before they found that someone was still alive and hunted me down."

"Well, it turns out that your comms were down, but as we got closer to you, we picked up your ident on our HUDs. There was no way of letting you know that it was us on your trail. You had a pretty rough time. But, look on the bright side. You made it."

"Yeah, I did, didn't I? I wouldn't want to repeat it though." Jessie hesitated. "Where's the lieutenant?" she asked at last.

"We've all been relocated back to Camp Bastion, including Charlie Recon, poor sods. They've lost a third of their men, including their commanding officer. Apparently, there were no other sections that could be reassigned to the FOB, so it's been handed temporarily over to the Afghan Army while a crash investigation takes place," Dingle replied. "We all had to give evidence to Major Hayward, tell him what little we know. He wants to speak to you, as well, when you're feeling better, ask a few questions about your side of things."

"That's okay. I'm up for that," Jessie said. She really didn't want to rehash the events of the crash, have to give descriptions of what she had seen and done and her dash across the desert. In all honesty, she wanted to forget about it and move on.

Dingle stood up. "Well, girl, I'd best be off. I have to tell the lads that you're still alive. It's good to have you back, Mac. For a minute there…"

Seeing the warm look in his eyes again, Jessie smiled. "It's good to be back. Thanks for coming to see me."

"You're welcome, Mac. Get in touch when they release you, and I'll come and get you. We have new quarters… No, don't look like that. You won't be sharing with us louts, although *I* don't mind if you do. You're lucky enough to have been given a tent all to yourself. Talk about spoiled."

Jessie nodded. While the only person she wanted to lean on at that moment was Nick, she was grateful that Dingle had opted to take her under his wing. After the last few days, his sense of humor and teasing was something that she desperately needed to keep her mind off the nightmarish visions that she saw frequently in her quiet moments.

She watched as he got up from the chair and headed for the door. He stopped and turned before he stepped out and she saw him wink at her and smile. "Don't cause any trouble, now. Be a good girl."

"Would I?" Jessie retaliated, forcing a smile. She suddenly felt very tired and a little tearful.

As Dingle left, she settled back in the bed and closed her eyes.

Where is Nick? Why hasn't he been here?

Perhaps he had come in when she had been asleep and she had missed him, or he might be busy. The knowledge that he had been frantic when he learned that the helicopter had gone down filled her with warmth, but she was a little disappointed that it had been Dingle who had visited her and not Nick.

If Dingle told the other guys that she was back in the land of the living, perhaps Nick would come in and visit her, and, with that thought in mind, she tried to relax and eventually drifted off into a light sleep.

* * * *

Jessie sat on the hospital bed waiting for Dingle to come collect her. The doctors had discharged her with an order to remain on light duties for a week and a prescription for painkillers to help with any discomfort she might suffer from the torn tendon in her ankle. She was also now the proud owner of a very ungainly Sam splint, a bulky, metal-framed cast bound in thick foam and wrapped in a thick outer layer of elasticized bandage. This now comfortably supported her injured limb and, ugly and likely inconvenient though it might be, she was happy that the pain from her injury had diminished almost completely.

She should have been feeling a great deal happier now that she was on the mend. She had not suffered any major injury in the helicopter crash or during her flight across the desert, and she *was* looking forward to getting out of hospital. A ball of uneasiness and doubt, however, had lodged in the pit of her stomach.

Nick had not been to visit her once during the forty-eight hours that she had been incapacitated. Shrek, JR, Mungo and Dingle had come to see her often, each visit with their usual comedic actions, attempting to keep her spirits up, diverting her thoughts from anything to do with the trauma that she had suffered.

Major Hayward had also called on her to ask questions and take a statement concerning the crash. Her memory of it was still clear in her mind, and she was able to answer his questions clearly and concisely. It disturbed her, though, when she grew tearful and her voice shook when she described finding and assessing the dead members of Charlie Recon and, although the Major had been gentle and sympathetic, after he had left, she felt miserable and depressed, longing for Nick to be with her and comfort her.

Numerous times, she had wanted to ask her section mates where he was, however she knew that the inquiry would raise a few eyebrows and might initiate some teasing. She had managed to convince herself that Nick was probably busy with strategy meetings, the crash investigation and other duties. He would possibly contact her once he knew she was out of the hospital, and now that they were at the base, there would be more of an opportunity for them to be together. This filled her with excitement.

Something still niggled at her conscience. Putting their relationship aside, Nick was her commanding officer, and she would have thought that he would have come to see her as a member of Bravo Recon, just to check to see if she was okay. He hadn't and this worried her.

Jessie heard a voice coming from the corridor outside the ward and Dingle appeared, a wide grin on his face.

"Is there anyone here who wants to leave?" he asked.

Dismissing her somber thoughts, Jessie laughed. "Me. Me," she answered.

Dingle bowed. "Your escort is ready and waiting, madam, right down to your Rolls-Royce, so you don't have to walk."

"Ah, you are so sweet, Dingle," Jessie said, smiling again as an expression of disgust crossed his face.

"Sweet? Christ, Mac. Don't let on to the lads that you called me that. I'll never live it down." He walked across to her and gave her a hug. "It's good to see you up and around. Let's get going. Can you walk?"

"Yeah, I can...well, sort of. I can't bear weight on my bad leg. You'll have to help me and we'll have to go slow."

"Slow and easy it is."

Taking Dingle's arm, Jessie slid off the edge of the bed, putting her full weight on her good leg before gingerly setting her injured one to the floor. It throbbed slightly, but she was able to stand on it as long as she held on to Dingle's arm.

They walked slowly out of the ward — Dingle adjusting his pace to hers — and proceeded down the long corridor leading to double front doors. Before leaving the building, Jessie propped herself against a wall and Dingle went into the Weapons Room to pick up their weapons. She then took his arm once more and he helped her outside to the gravel and sand forecourt that acted as a parking area and turning point for field ambulances and vehicles.

Dingle had parked a sand-colored 4x4 Land Rover directly beneath a canopied area where, prior to transferring into the CTH, casualties were unloaded, and he assisted her to it. After he had opened the door for her, Jessie climbed awkwardly in and settled into the hard seat. She winced at the slight pain in her leg caused by the enforced exercise, then sighed. Dingle hurried around to the driver's seat and climbed in. Before he started the engine, he turned to her.

"Have you heard about the lieutenant?" he asked.

Chapter Twenty-Three

Looking at him, Jessie saw a strange expression on his face, one that she couldn't understand, but she felt an icy lump form in her stomach. She frowned and shrugged, feeling a jolt of unreasonable panic.

Oh, God! What's happened to him? Has he been hurt?

When she answered, her voice sounded a little strange to her ears, "What about the lieutenant?" She struggled to keep her tone casual but full of curiosity. "Is he okay?"

Dingle shrugged and turned to glance out through the vehicle windshield, "Well, it was a bit of a shock, like. None of us had any idea...but then again, why would we? He's hardly likely to tell us grunts about his personal life, is he?"

"For fuck's sake, Dingle. Spit it out, why don't you?" Jessie tried to keep the note of desperation out of her voice. She clenched her hands in her lap, nails digging into the palms. She stared at Dingle, wanting to hear what he had to say but reluctant for him to divulge what he knew.

"Jesus. Bloody women and their demands," Dingle said turning back to face her. "Our LT has been promoted to Captain. Not so unusual, I suppose. But the thing that sent our crap spinning was that he's gone home on leave to old Blighty to get married."

Jessie blinked, unsure that she had heard him correctly. "What?"

Her heart plunged from the safe haven of her chest to her stomach. Her head spun dizzily and she couldn't draw air into lungs that felt crushed. A sharp pain formed in the pit of her stomach, and she found that she was shaking her head in denial.

She coughed, trying to clear the constriction in her throat, "Married?" she echoed. Her voice sounded weak to her ears and she prayed that Dingle would not notice. "Yeah, okay. Is this some kind of a stupid joke?"

She saw Dingle staring at her rather intently, as though he was trying to gauge her reaction to his news. "Nope, it's no joke. He's gone to get married," he answered. "After we relocated back here, he spent a few days in briefings with Major Hayward, then disappeared without even a cheerio. He kept that close to his chest. A bit bad-mannered but that's an officer for you."

Dingle turned to start the engine and Jessie sank back in her seat. She wanted to scream. She was stunned and shocked, her mind numbed by the news. Questions turned over and over in her mind.

Nick married? But he loves me. He said he did. He proved it. He showed me that he did. How can he have gotten married? What the fuck?

The numbness receded as quickly as it had appeared and she felt a multitude of powerful feelings assault her — anger, a deep and fathomless hurt that was like a physical pain and absolute devastation.

He fucking lied to me. He was stringing me along, trying to get into my pants, and I let him. He must never have loved me. I should have known.

She wanted to cry and howl, like a child. The hurt she felt consumed her, pierced her body like a thousand skewering knives.

She became aware that Dingle had been speaking to her, shouting above the noise of the engine.

Struggling to control her emotions, she turned to him. "What?" she asked in a daze.

He had taken his eyes off the road and was watching her with concern. "I asked if you were all right? You look like you've seen a ghost."

"I'm tired and sore," Jessie lied. Her tone must have sounded sincere because Dingle turned his gaze back to the dusty road.

Jessie shut her eyes, feeling physically sick. Her anger had dissipated leaving behind a cold emptiness and a sense of loss so deep that it felt like it came from a bottomless pit.

Dear God. What will I do without him? When he comes back – if he comes back – he'll be married. How will I cope, knowing that he has a wife? Seeing him every day, having to talk to him. I'll have to request a transfer out of here. No. I can't think about that now. It's too much. Nick Ryan, you are an utter bastard!

Jessie withdrew into herself. She didn't want to talk, her thoughts lacerated and crippling, her mind drowning in an abyss of hurt. She felt as though she were suffocating. She hoped Dingle would interpret her silence as a normal reaction to the events she had gone through over the past few days and think that she might be tired, and he would hopefully leave her alone.

About five minutes later, she felt the vehicle make a left-hand turn and she opened her eyes. Dingle had turned into a small gravel area with long, sand-colored tents lining one side. He pulled up and turned to her, smiling.

"Home sweet home," he announced, turning the key to the off position. There was silence except for the ticking of the warm engine.

To Jessie, the muted pinging was the loneliest sound she had ever heard.

"Thanks," she announced quietly. "I appreciate you picking me up and giving me a lift, Dingle." Her voice trembled and she cleared her throat.

"No problem, Mac. Come on. Let's get you squared away and you can rest for a couple of hours. There's a new temporary commanding officer due in later on today to cover for LT…sorry, the Captain, while he's away." He climbed out of the Land Rover and came around to her door.

His words confirmed without a doubt that Nick was now beyond her reach and belonged to someone else. Having played her as if she was a musical instrument, he had left, leaving her heart exposed and her feelings raw.

Struggling to gather her wits about her, Jessie struggled from the vehicle and leaned against Dingle, who put his arm about her waist, holding her so that she did not have to put her full weight on her injured leg.

"This small one is all your own," he announced, gesturing to a small square tent, situated alongside a long narrow one. "You have your own shower, so you don't have to share with us minging lot. We have our own cooking facilities, so you'll still have to put up with my cooking. I've told the lads to leave you alone. I'm sure you don't want them climbing all over you for the first couple of hours."

He helped Jessie cross the gravel, moving slowly and carefully, keeping pace with her. Pulling aside the flap, he urged her in ahead of him and he followed in behind.

Jessie noticed that her buddies had brought back all of her equipment and clothes from the FOB, unpacking and stashing it away, and they had made up her bed. Their thoughtfulness brought tears to her eyes and she had to blink them rapidly away. All she wanted to do was curl up on the bed and cry.

She turned to the soldier standing beside her. "Thanks for doing all this for me, you and the guys," she said, sniffing. She moved into Dingle's arms, needing to be comforted and soothed, even if it was for a brief period of time and by the wrong man.

Dingle's arms went quickly around her waist and he hugged her tightly. "Hey, you're shivering."

"Yeah, I'm shattered," Jessie answered, her voice shaky but muffled by his T-shirt. "I need to get some rest." Stepping back, she wiped her eyes.

"You do that, Mac. You look like shit," Dingle said, reaching out and squeezing her shoulder.

Jessie somehow managed to smile. "Wow, thanks for that," she said.

Dingle winked at her, and she watched as he turned and left the tent.

As the tent flap dropped into place, silence fell. She stood immobile, never more alone than she was at that point.

Nick…

Wondering if she would ever feel normal again, Jessie studied her surroundings but found them of little interest. Sitting down on the bed, she lay back, throwing an arm up to cover her eyes. She felt so tired and her leg throbbed in its SAM splint.

Nick. How could you do this to me?

And then… I love you so much. What am I going to do?

Jessie turned onto her side, facing away from the entrance and shut her eyes. Hot tears burned behind her eyelids and, although she tried to suppress them, they trickled down her cheeks, then came in a flood. The ache in her heart and the loss that she felt was too much to bear. Burying her face in the pillow, she cried as if her heart would break, the sobs shaking her body violently.

I love you. I love you so much. Why, Nick? Why?

She cried for a long time, until there were no tears left and her eyes were sore and swollen. Her shoulders hitched with dry, gentle sobs as she lay exhausted, her mind blissfully blank.

Gradually, her tired mind gave in and she drifted off into a restless doze, later to slip into deeper sleep.

* * * *

Jessie lay staring up at the dim ceiling of her tent, her mind comfortably blank. Darkness had fallen and someone had come in and lit a chemlamp, placing it at the back of her accommodation so it wouldn't disturb her. The dim rays had chased the shadows away from the area surrounding her cot and the light was almost soothing. If she could keep from thinking disturbing thoughts, then she could almost feel relaxed.

As it was, the memory of Dingle's startling declaration

that Nick had taken leave to go home and be married popped into her mind and Jessie uttered a small moan of hurt.

He knew all along. Our night in my tent and the other meetings were all a complete farce. He lied to me and played me for a fool.

She sat up abruptly and bowed her head.

The worst of it is, he told me that he didn't play games and that he loved me. If he did, he would never have gotten married. He would have broken it off.

Jessie put the palms of her hands on either side of her head and squeezed. She wanted to push the painful thoughts away, try to forget about the betrayal. She needed to think clearly about her next step, how she was going to continue on with her deployment and come to terms with the fact that she had fallen in love with a man who was beyond her reach.

Loud laughter from outside her tent interrupted her thoughts and she raised her head. She couldn't stay where she was. She needed to get up and go outside, see the other members of her section, try to get herself together, find some hidden courage to deal with what Nick had done to her.

Jessie didn't want to. She wanted to stay hidden, not have to speak to anyone, lick her wounds and try to find strength to deal with the situation.

She swung her legs over the side of her cot and stood up. She winced slightly as she put weight on her injured leg but found that at least the pain had decreased markedly, and when she took a pace forward, she found that she could walk on it without assistance.

She hobbled over to where her clothes and personal items had been stacked, found a brush, then quickly ran it through her hair. Her efforts were half-hearted but she didn't want to leave herself looking as bad as she felt.

Once she had tidied herself as best she could without the aid of a mirror, she limped over to the tent flap, then stopped.

I can't do this. They'll know something's wrong. I've never been able to hide my true feelings or lie. It's too much.

Jessie turned to go back to her cot, then stopped for a second time. She had never been a coward, always facing up to personal problems and dealing with them. The situation she found herself in now was one of those times, and she needed to step up to the plate.

Before she could change her mind again, she moved back to the flap and swept it aside. Looking outside, she could see Bravo Recon gathered around a small fire that threw gold-red shimmering light onto the surrounding area. She could hear murmured conversation and occasionally a laugh coming from the men. It looked a peaceful scene, considering their location, and she was about to step out to join them when a voice said, "So, lads. Have you been keeping out of trouble while I've been away?"

Recognizing the voice, Jessie froze, sudden panic knotting her stomach. She felt her heart begin to race and the world suddenly started to revolve around her. Clutching a handful of canvas to stop herself from falling in a heap to the ground, she closed her eyes.

He's back. Fuck! Jesus.

She backed into the tent, letting the flap fall, wanting to run away and hide and not have to face the inevitable.

I can't do this. I can't talk to him. I'll just make a fool of myself.

Jessie limped quickly to her cot and turned in a circle, as though an answer to her panic and pain would be visible on the walls of her accommodation. Her breathing was rapid and she began to feel physically sick.

She tensed again as she heard footfalls crunching on the gravel, heading toward the tent and before whoever it was could enter, she hobbled round to the opposite side of her cot. If it was Nick, then putting a solid object between her and him might lend her some strength and courage to face the oncoming confrontation.

As though transfixed, she stared at the entrance, waiting, trying to control her breathing and slow her thundering heartbeat.

A few seconds later, there was the slap of a hand against the outside canvas, and there he was.

Chapter Twenty-Four

As he stepped inside, Jessie felt her emotions fracture and tear apart at the sight of him. He was smiling and looked happy. The wayward lock of hair that had started off the whole of their abortive relationship had fallen onto his forehead, the rest of his hair looked windblown and unruly and there was dark stubble tracing a shadow across his chin and jaws.

She felt her legs go weak and the urge to go to him—despite the fact that he belonged to another woman—throw herself into his arms and cry out her longing for him was beyond anything she had ever felt. As it was, she gritted her teeth and stayed silent.

She saw his smile falter and a frown crease his forehead. "Jessie?"

Jessie looked down at the rumpled sleeping bag on her cot as though she had discovered something of great interest there. "What do you want?"

"What do you mean, what do I want?" Nick's voice sounded confused, his tone turning a little chilly.

Oh, he's good. So convincing.

Jessie stared at the wall of her tent, anywhere and everywhere except at him. If she looked into those dark eyes staring so intently at her, she would be lost.

"Like I said," she said at last, her tone trembling slightly. "What are you doing here?"

Nick stepped deeper into the tent. "I don't know what's going on here, Jessie, but for what it's worth, I came to see you."

Jessie felt a surge of anger. "Well, that's kind of you,

Captain, but as you can see, I'm fine. Oh, I forgot. Perhaps I should congratulate you on your promotion alongside the other...congratulations for your other news?"

Nick was silent, studying her as though he had no idea what she was talking about.

Jessie let the silence go on.

If the situation wasn't so shitty, the expression on his face would be almost comical.

"What's with the attitude?" Nick asked at least.

Jessie let the simmering flames of her anger gain strength, the hurt she was feeling fanning them into bright sparks of fury.

"My attitude? You have the cheek to bring my attitude into this."

Nick folded his arms, the smile completely gone from his face now, the expression on his handsome face one of anger.

"What's going on?" he asked, his voice low, his tone icy. He took a step toward her.

Jessie held up a hand. "Stop right there," she ordered. "Don't come near me."

Nick stopped. "I don't have a clue what shit has hit the fan while I've been gone, Jessie, but I suggest you try telling me what the *fuck* is going on because you've lost me."

Jessie allowed herself to utter a small sarcastic chuckle. "You still want to pretend that you have no idea what this about?" she asked. "Really? Okay, let me remind you. You led me on, Nick Ryan. You played me for a fucking fool, told me you loved me, wanted to get into my pants then when I was no longer on the scene for a few days – through no fault of my own, I might add – you *fuck off* and get married."

Jessie hesitated as she saw Nick straighten up, a look of stunned surprise wiping the angry expression from his face. "You then have the bare-faced cheek to come in here acting the innocent, asking what's wrong with me?" Jessie went on, her temper now almost reaching boiling point, the pain she was feeling at his presence and the lies that he had told her urging her to hurt him as he had hurt her.

"Married?" Nick asked. "Where the fuck did you get that idea from?"

Jessie wondered at the barely controlled anger that she heard in his voice.

"A little bird told me," she snapped. "Oh, please, you're not going to tell me that it's some kind of a joke."

"Jessie, listen to me. I'm not married. I don't know whose sick idea this was, but it's not true."

Jessie stared at him then shook her head. "Tell that to the birds," she answered at last. "Dingle would never…"

She stopped, aware of a sinking feeling in the pit of her stomach. She had just unintentionally divulged whom it was who had told her and, by the look on Nick's face, she had dropped her section mate in a whole heap of shit.

"Dingle," Nick repeated, his tone now sounding deadly calm. "I am now going to have a little chat with him and find out what the fuck is going on here."

Jessie watched as he turned and made his way to the entrance. Before exiting, he turned.

"You know something, Jessie? You might have had the decency to speak to me first before you jumped to conclusions. Trust in a relationship is a big thing with me, and you just blew it to fucking hell."

With his last words, Nick threw aside the tent flap and stormed out, leaving Jessie suddenly breathless with fear and doubt.

He sounded so sincere and hurt. Is he telling the truth? If he is, then why the hell did Dingle lie?

She slumped down on her cot, trying to bring coherence to her suddenly chaotic thoughts.

If Nick is telling the truth, I've really messed things up. He's right. I should have spoken to him first. Me and my pride and big mouth.

She suddenly heard Nick's loud and angry voice from outside her tent.

"Dingle, get your arse in my tent. Now!"

Jessie cringed at the fury she heard in his voice. She had no sympathy for what was about to happen to Dingle. If Nick had spoken the truth, whatever motive was behind Dingle's lie, he deserved what was coming to him. In addition, she deserved to lose the man she loved. Through her own insecurity and lack of trust, she had jeopardized the love between them and if he never wanted to speak to her again, she had to fully accept that.

She felt sick at heart, knowing what she had done. She should have sensed that there was something wrong with what Dingle had told her. The simple fact of the matter was that while on deployment, Nick would never have gone home to get married.

Some personnel on tour were allowed rest and recuperation — R&R — if they were lucky enough. If an emergency occurred with a member of their family, they could get compassionate leave but even that for only a few days. But getting married?

Jessie could have kicked herself. Now that she had allowed herself to think about it analytically, she realized that the content of Dingle's lie or windup had been completely implausible.

She stiffened as she heard a muffled angry voice and recognized Nick releasing a whole weight of sorrow on Dingle's shoulders. She couldn't make out any specific words but detected by the inflections and nuances in the tirade that Nick was letting rip at the hapless young soldier. She wondered what the outcome would be, and although Dingle had managed to destroy the fledgling beginnings of hers and Nick's love for each other, she felt a small amount of sympathy.

Tense and unhappy, she stayed motionless on her cot listening to the ongoing argument until silence fell. Within the space of a few minutes, there was a slap on the tent and Dingle came in.

Jessie rose to her feet and waited silently. She saw the expression of embarrassment on his face and the way he shifted his feet about told of his nervousness.

"I've come to say I'm sorry," he announced abruptly.

Jessie hesitated then moved toward him. Stopping a few feet in front of him, she asked softly, "What's going on, Dingle?"

Dingle focused on a point just above her head and seemed reluctant to speak. At last, he shrugged. "I saw you and the Captain together after we got back from Khavak," he explained. "I overheard you talking and what he said to you. It pissed me off. I was stupid enough to think that we could…have something going between *us* and when I heard…what I did, I saw red. I was jealous, angry, the whole fucking works and when the Captain had to leave suddenly because his dad had a stroke, I took a chance that if I made up some story about him getting married, it might give me a chance. I regretted it as soon as I'd told you. It was a futile and pathetic thing to do, and I'm so sorry, Jessie."

Jessie continued to stare at the young soldier. She didn't know whether to scream in anger at him or hug and forgive him.

"That was a nasty, childish thing to do, Dingle," she said at last. "Do you know what you've done?"

Dingle nodded. "I know now," he replied. "The Captain has given it to me with both barrels, and he is one pissed off and angry officer. I'll be lucky to get through the rest of my deployment without him blowing my balls off."

"I think you're exaggerating," Jessie said.

"You didn't see his face," Dingle responded. "I think if he could have ripped off my arm and rammed it down my throat sideways, he would have done."

"Well, you do kinda deserve it," Jessie said, paused, then went on, "and I'm sorry you did it for the reasons you did. But I never led you on, Dingle. I gave you no reason to expect anything other than friendship from me. If I did give you any wrong messages, then I'*m* sorry."

"You've nothing to be sorry for, Mac. It was all me and I could fucking kick myself. Can we still be friends?"

Jessie hesitated. "Yeah, I guess so. But you're gonna have a lot of butt kissing to do to make it up to me."

Dingle smiled slightly. "I hope you and the Captain can iron things out between you," he said. "If it makes you feel better, the lads know nothing about you and him or what I've done, and it'll stay that way."

"Thanks, Dingle."

Jessie waited until the soldier had left her tent before going back to sit down on her cot once more.

What a mess.

While she knew that Dingle had been the instigator of it all, and she felt a simmering anger for what he had done and wished she could kick his balls into touch, she knew that she was the only one to blame for the wedge that she had driven between herself and Nick. She should have trusted and believed in him. She knew that he was a man of truth and honor, and if he had told her that he loved her, then he had meant it. She wondered if she could mend the rift between them.

Will he give me the chance to apologize? Does he still love me enough to forgive me?

Jessie lay back on the cot. She needed to work out some way of salvaging what she could of their relationship, if there was anything left to salvage. She had a feeling that it was going to be an uphill struggle. Nick was a proud man, and she thought he could be stubborn as well. It was not in her nature to beg, but she would if she could make him see that it had all been a terrible mistake and after all, they did love each other. That should stand for something.

* * * *

Jessie lay wide-awake on her cot, restless and unable to sleep. It was 0300 hours and there were only a few hours left before her alarm went off and she would have to get up to face another day — without Nick in it.

She had an almost unbearable urge to make things right

between them, not only from a personal point of view — which, of course, was of primary importance to her — but so that they could proceed to be able to work together for the rest of their deployment.

As it was, she needed to talk to him to try to apologize, make him see that it was a terrible misunderstanding on her part and hope that he would give her another chance.

Jessie sat up then got off the cot. Before nerves could kick in, she headed out of the tent and stopped outside. With the exception of the low hum of generators, the subdued roar of aircraft engines and *whup whup* of helicopter rotor blades from the airfield, the base was silent.

A faint glow came from the smoldering embers of the fire but apart from the crumbling movement of ash, nobody other than herself appeared to be awake. She glanced at the long accommodation tent beside hers and saw with relief that it was in darkness. The dim light of a chemlamp came from a smaller tent alongside that one and she knew that Nick was awake.

Walking slowly and as quietly as she could, Jessie began to make her way toward Nick's tent. Now and again, her boots made a faint crunch on the gravel and she stopped, heart in her mouth, before moving on.

Reaching the smaller tent, she hesitated, raised her hand to slap the side, then thought better of it. It might wake someone up and she didn't want to make things worse than they already were. Instead, she gently lifted the flap slightly and pushed her way in.

The instant she had stepped inside, a voice said from the back, "What are you doing here?"

Peering through the dimness, Jessie saw Nick lying fully clothed on his cot, staring toward where she was standing. Perturbed at his non-committal welcome — not that she had expected warm welcoming arms at her appearance — she stammered, "C-can I come in?"

"Looks like you're in, doesn't it?"

Swallowing, feeling sick with nerves, Jessie went quietly

toward him, finally reaching his bed. The light inside the tent made it difficult for her to see the expression on his face, but she did ascertain that he wasn't even looking at her.

"I came to talk to you," she began.

"So, talk."

Jessie winced inwardly at his tone of voice, which was short and abrupt. She glanced around for a chair so that she could take the weight off her bad leg but seeing none, glanced down at the cot, and finally balanced on the edge. As her hip touched his thigh, he moved his legs quickly to the side, ostensibly to give her more room or perhaps so he didn't have to touch her.

The silence between them became lengthy and began to fill with tension. At last, Jessie couldn't bear it any longer. Taking her courage in hand, she said, "Nick, I came to say I'm sorry. Dingle came to see me and told me what he had done. I misjudged you, and it was wrong of me."

Nick remained silent and Jessie began to think that it was too late, that she had burned her bridges and there was no going back.

"You know something, Jessie." Nick suddenly spoke, a note of anger and hurt in his voice. "I have *never* told any other woman in my entire life that I love them, except for my mother, of course. I've spent my career in the army avoiding entanglements and relationships because someone always ends up getting hurt. That was, until I met you. You knocked everything that I ever believed in out of the ballpark. The fact that I allowed myself to fall in love with you, then you didn't trust me when it came to it, has just reinforced everything I ever believed in about relationships."

Nick finally turned to look at her. "There's no place for lack of trust in a relationship," he continued with some finality. "You believed someone else before you discussed it with me. If I had been able to visit you in hospital, I would have told you that my father had had a stroke and that I had to leave, but with the crash..."

Jessie knew that it was over between them and the pain in her heart was beyond belief. Her eyes filled with tears and she bit her lip, the brief hurt causing her thoughts to divert from the fact that she was going to break down in front of him. She needed to get out of his tent before she made a fool of herself.

She quickly stood up and took a pace backward. "I'm so sorry," she murmured in a choked voice. She half-turned to leave but stopped when Nick suddenly sat up and reached for the waistband of her combats. He tugged her toward him and placed both of his hands on her hips, arresting any movement away from him that she might have made.

Once she was close to him, he stood up, his arms went about her waist, then he pulled her almost roughly toward him. Shaking her very gently, he continued, "I can't begin to tell you how much I love you, Jessie. I am not lying, or making it up or talking crap just to get inside your *pants,* as you so delicately put it.

"What Dingle did was the action of a fucking dickhead, but I feel sorry for the poor bastard, particularly as it would appear that he's besotted with you, the same as I am. I can't hold you accountable for your actions either. Alone here and being told out of the blue that I was off getting... *married* must have thrown you for a loop, and I can't begin to know how you must have felt."

Nick stopped speaking, looking down at her as she gazed at him.

Feeling his arms holding her firmly and his body against hers Jessie felt like she was in a wonderful dream, one that she never wanted to wake up from.

"I should have trusted you," she said in a low voice. "I should have realized that Dingle's story didn't add up and waited for you to come back. But I love you so much —"

Nick interrupted her. "The only woman I want to marry and spend the rest of my life with, is you."

Jessie's heart missed a beat at his words. "Really?" she

asked, smiling.

"You'd better believe it, Jessie McAllister," and then he had lowered his head and brought his mouth against hers in a firm, hot kiss.

Realizing that she had never lost her man to begin with and that with his last words he had melded their love together for as long as they lived, Jessie returned the kiss with every fiber of her being.

Even though their immediate future held war, adversity and trauma, there was the here and now. Jessie knew that Nick loved her as she loved him, but in war, there were no guarantees. They were together, as much as their present situation would allow them to be, and they would share their love not only in this moment, but for all the moments they had — forever.

For the Love of a Marine

Excerpt

Chapter One

A blood-soaked combat boot, reclining on its side, lay tossed carelessly in a corner of the operating theater among torn and shredded webbing. Bandages and gauze soaked with crimson coiled in clumps on the floor, mixed in with remnants of charred and torn camouflage uniform. Personal effects, pitiful, tragic reminders of those who had been medevacked to the combat trauma hospital—CTH—lay scattered on a metal trolley, waiting to be identified and returned to those who had survived—or returned home with those who hadn't.

Although the CTH was temperature controlled throughout, within Theater One it was hot and humid, the air thick with the coppery smell of blood and an all pervading stench of feces and urine. Dark blood had trickled then dripped from each operating table to pool in splatters on a dark green, rubberized floor, with smudged crimson footprints leading to and from the accumulating puddles where surgical teams and medical technicians had unknowingly trodden through them. Stainless steel instruments clinked mutedly against each other while in the background was the continuous whirr of an air conditioner, the periodic hissing of recycled air flowing in and out of the theater and the soft repetitive clunk from a clock on the wall.

CTH personnel clad in full-face plastic visors used to prevent blood spatter, white mesh face masks underneath, smears of blood adorning green surgical gowns or scrubs and gloves, crowded around the two occupied operating tables. Despite the blood-soaked surroundings and an atmosphere filled with palpable tension, there was no evidence of panic and no anxious overtones overriding smooth, professional voices as the two surgical teams bent all their efforts to saving the lives of the two unconscious young soldiers. Intense expressions of concentration were etched on many faces and requests for assistance and instruments were uttered in quiet, clear monotones. Both the blood and gore was ignored as though it did not exist.

Anyone looking into the busy room would have wondered at the almost emotionless and dispassionate air of the people working there, as though each one possessed an invisible mental shield that prevented them from becoming emotionally involved with their patients, something that each had subconsciously cultivated over the months of their deployment to protect themselves from the daily scenes of carnage and death, harsh realities of a combat zone. The shield was a necessity, a psychological barrier subconsciously erected to prevent burnout and breakdowns caused by unrelenting exposure to the cruel and unavoidable pressures of working in a combat hospital.

Corporal Katie Walker, twenty-six years of age, was a senior combat trauma medic—CTM—attached to the CTH. She was in her seventh year with the British Royal Army

Medical Corp — RAMC — and on her first deployment to Afghanistan, assigned to Surgical Team One alongside another CTM. She had been in-country since March 2014 and had completed four months of a six-month tour.

During the early weeks of her deployment, Katie had experienced her own personal battles with trauma and stress. There had been many times when she had wondered if she would ever find the strength to complete her tour. Nightmares of explosions and maimed bodies had awakened her from sleep night after night, and on one occasion after a particularly lengthy duty, she had taken flight in tears to hide in the female locker room, saddened by the sight of so many brutally wounded and mentally shattered men and women being brought into the CTH. There had been other occasions when she had been on the brink of making a formal request for redeployment back to the United Kingdom, despite the adverse ramifications to her career that this might have brought about. The unpleasant experiences that she had been exposed to had caused her to reconsider how the human species treated one another.

As the long months had passed, however, like everyone deployed to Afghanistan, she had learned how to emotionally protect herself, had unknowingly developed the self-same protective shield as her colleagues — an ability to distance herself from adverse emotions and feelings. It wasn't that she was emotionally cold or numb to the brutal daily truths of the combat world she inhabited. She was a human being with a great deal of compassion and sympathy for those she treated and tried to save, but her detachment was for her own protection, an emotionless armor that helped to harden her mind against the overwhelming pressures that she had to face.

That particular day had been an emotional one for them all. Three British soldiers out on foot patrol in a remote area of the Afghanistan desert had been injured in an improvised explosive device — IED — incident. One of the soldiers had stepped on a hidden mine lying undetected by a mine detector. The explosives, covered by a pile of razor-sharp stones and rocks, blending in with the surrounding terrain, had detonated, the resultant blast throwing shrapnel-like debris through the air, catching the soldier who had trodden on the mine and two others at ground zero. All three had sustained severe injuries and a combat trauma team—CTT—flown out by a Chinook combat trauma flight—CTF—had stabilized the casualties in the field before extracting and medevacking them back to the CTH at Camp Churchill, located in the British sector of Base Independence.

Three trauma teams, waiting outside the CTH, had immediately assessed the casualties then, while surgeons from three surgical teams scrubbed for the surgeries, the gravely injured soldiers had been swiftly taken to the trauma rooms, where the trauma teams standing by had immediately brought heavy bleeding under control, given full body assessments and checked vital signs then, following X-rays, all three were connected up to IV solutions and blood products to replace blood loss and stave off the onset of shock. A decision was made to prep the casualties for immediate surgery and rush them through to the operating theaters.

Three operating tables within Theaters One and Two were now in use. Each surgical team carrying out the surgeries consisted of surgeons who were specialists in their various fields, anesthetists, two surgical nurses and two CTMs. All the medical personnel excelled at what they did, each selected for deployment to the Afghanistan war theater specifically for their specialist skills and for their ability to be able to work under intense levels of pressure.

The surgeries that had been going on for most of the day were almost over, the casualties having come through their ordeals safely. If they remained stable and there were no complications over the next forty-eight hours, they would continue their recovery and rehabilitation back in the UK.

The tension in Theater One slowly began to dissipate and each surgical team began to relax. Conversation around the operating tables lightened in tone and there were a few subdued chuckles as someone made an obscure joke about a subject totally unrelated to the present situation.

Katie checked the IV line attached to her own patient again, tracing the fragile tubing leading from the triple branched cannula in the back of the young soldier's hand up toward a collection of bags containing blood, plasma and saline fluid, ensuring that the life-sustaining products dripping downward were doing so at the correct speed and as freely as they should. She then placed two steady but sensitive fingertips on the casualty's carotid artery and, with a sense of satisfaction, felt the strong throb of a pulse, confirming that the young British soldier continued to remain stable.

Nodding to the attending anesthetist that all remained well, Katie paused, taking a brief moment to gaze down at her patient. A hasty pre-op wash had removed much of the blood and dirt from the young man's face and body, and now that she had a few minutes' respite, she noticed with a deep sense of sadness that he was much younger than she had at first thought, probably in his early twenties, with shorn, dark hair. Stubble covered his chin and jaw line as though he had not shaved in some time, and his skin was pale, almost translucent, making him look as vulnerable as a child, a telltale sign of the trauma that had assaulted his body. He had obviously been out in the field for some time, as he appeared not to have washed in days and a strong smell exuded from his still body. Body odors from soldiers brought in from the field were a normal occurrence for the medical staff. The fetid smells barely stirred or offended their senses.

The young soldier's injury from the IED explosion that day had resulted in the complete destruction of his lower left leg. Even though the golden hour for medevacking him back from the field to the CTH then assessment followed by surgery, was not breached, the leg had been too damaged and had been amputated just above the knee.

So young. The sad thought often intruded into Katie's weary mind of late. *What will he do now?* His Army career had been abruptly and cruelly terminated, the lifestyle to which he had been accustomed had changed irrevocably. He could go on to lead a relatively normal life—most amputees did, and adapted and coped well. With counseling and rehabilitation, the young man would resume his life, but the harsh reality was that it had changed forever. There would be no going back to reclaim what he had once had and moving forward would be the ultimate test for him.

A sudden movement caught Katie's attention, disturbing her thoughts about the patient. Leading surgeon Major Josh Macintyre of Surgical Team One had stepped back from the operating table. Stripping off his bloody surgical gloves, he raised his plastic visor and pulled down his face mask. Rubbing his eyes tiredly, he once again inspected the heavily bandaged stump of the soldier's amputated limb before commenting wearily in a broad but lilting Scottish accent, "Well, that's it, ladies and gentleman. That's all we can do for the poor wee laddie. As long as infection does'na set in and he remains stable, he'll do. Thank you all for your assistance."

Major Macintyre turned away from the operating table, his body posture stooping now as though all the adrenaline and energy that he had drawn on to save his patient's life had drained away. He walked toward the door of the theater, feet shuffling in their protective bootees, and left, Katie knowing full well that he would make his way unerringly down the long corridor to the R&R—rest and recuperation-room—at its far end.

Lance Corporal Henry Barrow, Katie's CTM colleague on Surgical Team One, left the theater unbidden, unknowingly leaving a trail of bloody footprints behind him. He returned moments later pushing a gurney that he aligned lengthwise against the operating table. The five remaining members of the surgical team positioned themselves to each side of the patient and, with Katie carefully handling the IV stand, lifted the young soldier gently onto the gurney.

With the lance corporal pushing and Katie wheeling the IV stand and keeping an observant eye on her patient for any downward turn in his condition, they left the theater, turned left down the long corridor and, moving at a steady pace, guided the gurney with its precious passenger some meters until they arrived at the critical care unit—CCU— beyond the wards on the right. Lance Corporal Barrow and Katie wheeled the patient into the brightly lit CCU where four trauma nurses awaited their arrival. Working in well-honed synchronization, the two CTMs transferred the still-sleeping soldier to a pristine white hospital bed, ensuring that the sheets and blanket were tucked securely about his motionless body.

More books from
Totally Bound Publishing

War, trauma, destruction, death. Personal conflict and a love under threat from adversity and fate. Can they survive? Can their love?

War puts courage and love to the test.

Time is short and the risks are high but victory is priceless.

Book one in the Interludes series.

Sometimes past demons need to be faced before one can embrace what the future offers, and who better to slay them than a Marine?

About the Author

Sharon Kimbra Walsh

Sharon spent eight and a half years in the Women's Royal Air Force. Originally based in London, after she met her husband, Sharon relocated to Scotland to settle in Edinburgh. Already loving the country after having been stationed there during her time in the military, Sharon has never looked back. She lives with her husband and rescue West Highland Terrier, Snowie, (who thinks that she is a Rottweiler in disguise).

In 2014 Sharon started to have visions of writing a contemporary military romance. The ideas started to pile up and there was nothing for it but to get them down on her laptop, regardless of time and place.

Sharon Kimbra Walsh loves to hear from readers. You can find contact information, website details and an author profile page at https://www.totallybound.com/